NADINE IN THE TENDERLOIN

JO CARPIGNANO

Published by Sand Hill Review Press www.sandhillreviewpress.com,
1 Baldwin Ave, #304, San Mateo, CA 94401 (415) 297-3571

Library of Congress Control Number: 2018951945
ISBN: 978-1-937818-91-3 Case Laminate
ISBN: 978-1-937818-90-6 Paperback
ISBN: 978-1-937818-92-0 Ebook

Art Direction by Tory Hartmann, Sand Hill Review Press
Graphics by Backspace Ink.

Publisher's Cataloging-in-Publication data

Names: Carpignano, Jo, author.
Title: Nadine in the Tenderloin / Jo Carpignano.
Description: San Mateo, CA: Sand Hill Review Press, 2021. | Summary: A gifted child lives with her mother and three half-siblings in a poor district of San Francisco.
Identifiers: LCCN: 2018951945 | ISBN: 978-1-937818-91-3 (hardcover) | 978-1-937818-90-6 (paperback) | 978-1-937818-92-0 (ebook)
Subjects: LCSH Child abuse--Juvenile fiction. | Family--Juvenile fiction. | Tenderloin (San Francisco, Calif.)--Juvenile fiction. | San Francisco (Calif.)--History--20th century--Juvenile fiction. | Poverty--Juvenile fiction. | City and town life--Juvenile fiction. | CYAC Child abuse--Fiction. | Family-- Fiction. | Tenderloin (San Francisco, Calif.)-- Fiction. | San Francisco (Calif.)--History--20th century-- Fiction | Poverty-- Fiction. | City and town life-- Fiction. | BISAC JUVENILE FICTION / Social Themes / Physical & Emotional Abuse | JUVENILE FICTION / Historical / United States / 20th Century
Classification: LCC PZ7.1.C37 Na 2021 | DDC 813.6--dc23

This book is dedicated to those who serve children with special needs in our public schools. Teachers, counselors, psychologists, administrators, and social workers who recognize that each child is an individual with specific strengths and weaknesses, and who make extra time and effort to assist.

NADINE
IN THE TENDERLOIN

JO CARPIGNANO

1. Nadine in the Tenderloin

DOWNTOWN SAN FRANCISCO was a relatively quiet place in the seventies. The political and social turmoil of the sixties and early seventies had died down. The beat generation had just about worn itself out, and hippies had either grown up or given up. Most of those who had given up were being identified as "street people," sleeping on sidewalks and lining up for free meals wherever they could be had. "Working the system," became a way of life, and at eleven and a half, that was all I knew.

We lived on Larkin Street, a few blocks north of Market, in a two room apartment in a third floor walkup. The place was a pig sty. Ma didn't think picking up dirty diapers was worth the bother, since another would follow within a short time. They just stacked up on the floor in the corner.

Ma was a single parent with four kids. We were on welfare, and Charlie found us the cheapest apartment in the city. There was a small hotplate, refrigerator, and table with four chairs in the biggest room; a bed, cot and dresser in another. Us three older kids slept on the floor in a little room between the bathroom and Ma's bedroom. We all shared the small bathroom that had an old tub in one corner, and a sink and toilet in back of the door. At thirty-two, Ma already had too many kids, and another on the way. I was the oldest, so it was my job to look out for my two younger brothers. Three-year-old Emily hadn't learned to talk yet. She was a bit slow getting started with things and Ma was growing impatient, as her belly got bigger by the day. Even though the rooms were big enough, there were too many of us for that confined space. *(I like the word "confined." I think it sounds better than "cramped.")*

"The more the merrier," Charlie would say when he made his weekly visits. We heard that it was his routine comment with the others too. He would bring in the groceries, and collect Ma's welfare check. Sometimes he stuck around for a few hours, and he and Ma would lock the door to the bedroom. We kids would ignore the noise, and turn up the TV, and that was OK with me. Ma was not happy for long, though. She came out of the bedroom a tousled mess, stringy yellow hair hanging, grumpy and mean the rest of the day.

But even when Charlie was not around, she was grumpy and mean. As soon as I could get my two little brothers dressed, I was always eager to get out the door. There was a hot breakfast waiting for us at school, and that was OK with me too.

Weekends were not so easy, other food would just about run out, and oatmeal was the usual fare for everyone. It was oatmeal three times a day on Saturday and sometimes on Sunday too—if Charlie didn't show up. One Sunday morning I got snippy with Ma, telling her I was getting tired of eating oatmeal all the time, and she didn't like that at all.

"You Goddamn brat, what do you mean you don't LIKE oatmeal," she bellowed. "How'd you like it if there weren't no oatmeal? Huh? How'd you like that!"

I sat in silence with my chin on my chest. My brothers stopped eating, alert to what might happen next.

"You know what? YOU don't get to eat no oatmeal today, missy, that's what! If you don't like oatmeal, you stand over there by the door, and you can watch US eat the oatmeal."

Stupid me, I froze and refused to move away from the table. That really made her mad. Standing up, she reached out and slapped me across the face.

"You do what I say, when I say!" she growled clenching her teeth and pushing me off my chair. "You stand against the wall by that door, just like I said, you hear?"

I crawled to the wall, my cheek burning, and tears starting. I stood by the door as I'd been told. Ma sat down at the table where the other kids started eating their oatmeal, silent and watchful. I could tell that Ma was still fuming, as she stumbled returning to her chair. It had been the wrong time for me to complain. *She's been drinking again,* I thought. I'd forgotten that Charlie had brought a bottle with the last delivery.

I stood and waited, hoping my silence would keep Ma from another outburst. Instead, she smiled. It was not a happy smile.

"So, you're tired of eating oatmeal? Well then, let's see if *this* is betta' fo ya!"

Carefully she scooped a spoonful of oatmeal from the bowl and turning, flung it at me from across the room. Her aim was perfect, and the oatmeal hit my shoulder.

"Is that betta' now? If you don't wanna eat it, you can wear it, OK?" Another spoonful landed on my forehead, and a third on my chest. I cried while my brothers looked on, fascinated by the oatmeal assault.

Just then the door swung open pushing me to the side, and Charlie walked in. Never before was I so pleased to see Charlie arrive. "What the hell is going on here?" he exclaimed, with a puzzled frown.

"The brat got tired of *eating* oatmeal," Ma said, "so she's gonn'a wear it instead." With that, she flicked another spoonful at me.

"Well Goddamn woman, you gonna turn her into a oatmeal statue, you keep this up," he said, starting to laugh. Ma quit throwing the oatmeal, and began laughing too. My two brothers laughed along with them. Everyone was laughing except for me. I was still crying.

"Well, you stupid kid, don't just stand there. Go get cleaned up!" Ma yelled.

"Hold up the'a honey, let me he'p get that mess off a' ya," Charlie offered.

I finally found my voice, "No! I can do it by myself! No Charlie, I don't need help, thanks anyways." I turned quickly into the bathroom, before Charlie could say anything more. Shutting the door behind me, I gave in to my tearful humiliation.

Charlie must have felt sorry for me that Sunday, 'cause he was awful' nice to me the rest of the morning. He thanked me for helping him bring some of the groceries up from his car, and started talking to me about how sorry he was that Ma got so mad at me. "Ya knows da baby due soon, and yo'a ma, she's jus' about wore out with takin' care o' Emily. Don't know wha's wrong with tha' lli'l one, she don' seem so quick as your brothers was at three yea's. You jes' gotta he'p your ma the bes' you can, 'til the baby gets bo'n."

I wasn't sure what Charlie thought I could do any more than I was already doing with taking care of Tom and Jimmy. And I was not looking forward to another baby either.

"What if things get worse after the baby comes, what then?" I asked.

"Why Honey, we get da social work'a out hea', and find somebody to he'p out. 'Sides, the welfe'a check, it be big'a an' we can do some thin'ese to make it mo'a easy fo' yo' ma," he said, smiling.

Charlie's blue eyes twinkled as the grin on his face got wider.

So that's why Charlie was so eager for the baby to arrive, I thought. The welfare check would get bigger!

In the meantime, I was to continue taking care of my two brothers who attended the same school as I did. Jimmy was not so bad, he was in second grade now, and doing OK keeping up with the other kids in his class. He liked his teacher, and got along with everybody. Tom was another story. His fifth grade teacher was always telling me how he was fighting with other kids—all the time.

"Tom just doesn't seem to be able to get along with others. He insists on being first all the time, even when they play games. And that's not how we do things, you know," Mrs. Brown complained.

"Sorry Mrs. Brown, I'll talk to him about taking turns," I apologized.

Then, using a much more serious tone, Mrs. Brown said, "I really don't think that's your job, Nadine. This is not the first time you've tried to help. Your mother needs to be dealing with this problem. Do you think you could ask her to come to school for a conference sometime soon?"

I took a deep breath and tried to think of something that would explain why Ma could never make it to a school conference. If she got a report about Tom being so bad that the teacher had to see her about it in person, Ma would get out that long wooden spoon, and make him all black and blue again.

"Well, you know, my mother is going to have a baby soon, and I don't think she could walk all that way."

John Muir Elementary School was a good six or eight blocks from where we lived, so I wasn't really telling a lie. Ma could never walk that far now.

"Well, couldn't she take a bus or get a ride from someone?" Mrs. Brown suggested.

"No ma'm, there's no money for bus fare, and Ma don't have any friends with cars. Let me tell her about Tom, then she will talk to him about being good, 'specially on the playground."

I hoped this would satisfy Mrs. Brown, and that she would let me take care of it again. But Mrs. Brown was not to be satisfied by the assurances of an eleven-year-old.

"I think I'll talk to her on the phone, then," she said.

"But we don't have a phone," I answered quickly. "And I'm sure that when I tell her how serious the problem is, Ma will find a way to get Tom straightened out."

"Oh, you don't have a phone?"

Mrs. Brown seemed to be running out of options, and I was hoping that she would settle for my latest suggestion. But no, not Mrs. Brown. She was determined to make that parent contact, and though I'd been able to deflect her other attempt, she found another possibility. *(I'd just learned the word "deflect" in a book I read, and liked to practice using it.)*

"Well then, I think I'd better consult with our principal, Miss Griswald, and see if we can think of another way," she said, pursing her lips and shaking her head as she walked away. After talking to Tom's teacher about his problem behavior, I thought Mrs. Brown would probably find more important things to think about. I had scolded Tom thoroughly, and warned him that I would have to tell Ma if he got in a fight again. Since we had no phone, I knew there was no way for the school to reach Ma, unless they sent a letter. But, it was my job to bring in the mail, so I'd know if they tried that. I could always say that the letter got lost, if I had to. So I stopped worrying about Tom's problem.

Early morning the following week, the boys were getting dressed for school, and Ma was in the bathroom with Emily. As usual, I cleared the breakfast dishes from the table, sliding a good portion of my oatmeal into the sink. I wondered how long it would take for the drainpipes to get clogged. Oatmeal is pretty sticky, so I was pretty sure that someday they would. I forgot about that problem too as I speculated about what kind of breakfast might be waiting for us at school.

As I was collecting my homework from the table, I noticed Ma's purse sitting on the chair. She usually kept it in the bedroom in the bottom drawer of her dresser. She had mentioned being short on cigarettes, and probably planned to go shopping as soon as Tom, Jimmy and I were gone. So the purse was there ready for her to grab as soon as we were out the door and she got Emily cleaned up.

I don't know what made me do it, but I did know how to be quick, so I gave it a try, not even thinking about what might happen if I got caught. The coin purse was waiting just inside the first section of the handbag, so I opened the clip, grabbed a coin, and slipped it into my pocket. The coin purse went back in the bag, and everything looked the same.

"'Bye Ma!" I said, as I herded the two boys out the door and down the stairs. We were on the sidewalk in no time, and hustling towards school and a decent breakfast.

"I saw what you did," Tom said softly, looking straight ahead.

"What did she do?" asked Jimmy, curious, but oblivious as usual to what was going on around him. Sometimes I thought he was trying not to know, and that was OK with me.

"She took money out 'a Ma's pocketbook," Tom said, with a sly grin.

"Wow, are you goanna get in trouble when Ma finds out," Jimmy added, looking worried.

"And how's she goanna find out?" I asked, smugly.

"Well, I bet she knows how much money she had in that little purse. And if she don't remember, I'm gonna tell her," Tom threatened, raising his eyebrows.

"Now why would you wanna do that?" I asked. "You think Ma's gonna do you a favor for tellin' on me?"

"Maybe not. But you boss us around all the time, and I think maybe it would be fun to see what happens when Ma knows you's stealin' from her purse."

"Naw! Come on Tommy. Don' tell. You don' hafta tell," Jimmy said, worry in his voice again.

This was getting really serious, and I thought I'd better do something pretty quick or we'd *all* be in trouble.

"Well, let's see how much I got, and then figure what we can do with it," I said, reaching into my pocket. "Hey, look here, a whole dime. What do you think we can buy with a dime, you guys? Got any ideas?"

"Ain't nothin' much we can get with that," Tom offered hesitantly. But now he was using *we* instead of *you*, so I was making progress in the right direction. I'd known Tom as a baby, and it had always been easier to get him interested in cooperating—if there was something in it for him.

"How about on our way home from school we stop at the corner store and see if we can find something we all like, then we can share," I said. And so the conspiracy was formed. *(I really like the word 'conspiracy.')*

After school, we stopped at the store as planned and, after looking around, agreed to buy a pack of gum, We happily chewed on Wrigley's Spearmint all the way home. At the front door to our own apartment we found a clean spot on the molding to park our gum, ready to pick up the following morning. I put mine the highest 'cause I was the tallest, Jimmy's was at the bottom, 'cause he was the shortest, and Tom's was planted firmly between the two. It gave us all something to look forward to, I thought.

When we walked in the door to our apartment, I could see that Ma had her new pack of Lucky Strikes, and was puffing away. She didn't say a word about missing money from her purse.

Tom kept his silence, Jimmy was the good boy he always was, and I got away with taking something I wanted—even if I did have to share.

It had been easy getting that dime for gum. Taking a chance in stealing it from my mother's purse was dangerous, but I enjoyed the excitement. Getting away with it had made me feel powerful, and I liked that feeling. For once, I had been in control of something in a different way than taking care of my brothers. Besides, I'd enjoyed my deception. *('Deception' is such a neat word.)*

I wanted to try it again, but I had something to work out, in keeping the boys from knowing. Jimmy would be no problem, but Tom was the sneaky one. I could just see him standing there with his hands on his hips, flipping his hair to the side and saying "Well?" He wouldn't hesitate to make the most of squealing—unless I shared with him of course. But if the boys were not around, and there was another opportunity? Hmm . . . Maybe?

2. The Nickel

SEVERAL WEEKS LATER, Ma left her pocketbook on the kitchen chair again, while the boys were still getting dressed in the bedroom. Once more, as I collected my homework from the table, I took a chance, and quickly lifted a nickel out of the coin purse. Immediately it went into my coat pocket, then I waited over by the door for the boys to finish dressing. They were arguing about a T-shirt they both wanted to wear that day.

"You wore it yesterday," Jimmy complained.

"No way. You got your hands on it first yesterday. Now it's my turn."

The red and yellow shirt was an "almost new" from the Salvation Army store, and Ma had bragged about what a bargain she got when she bought it. Both boys being nearly the same build, Ma usually got a size that would fit both Tom and Jimmy so they could share on alternating days. I guessed that they were having trouble deciding whose turn it was, or the other shirts they shared were really grungy. I supposed it was time for me to run a load of laundry, But more important than thinking about laundry, I had to get us out of there before Ma got out of the bathroom.

"Hurry up you guys, we're goanna be late for school!" I shouted.

Just then, Ma came out of the bathroom with Emily, cigarette hanging out of the corner of her mouth, one eye closed against the hot smoke curling up the side of her face.

There was a knock on the door, the sound of a key turning in the lock, and Charlie was there with his big grin.

"Y'all ready ta go babe?" he asked, winking at me as he barged in.

Ma came across the room in rush, jerking Emily by the hand, "OK Charlie, soon as my kids are off to school, we can get ou'ta here. I can't stand bein' cooped up in this place no more."

"Take it easy gal. There ain't no reason ta hurry. Got a real good parkin' space on the street, right in front."

"Tom! Jimmy! Get out here, and off to school with ya'!"

The boys heard the command in Ma's voice, and came out of the other room. Tom wore the red and yellow T-shirt, Jimmy the dirty one.

"Jus' you let me grab my purse," Ma said as she crossed the room.

She seemed anxious to leave in a hurry. With everyone in such a rush, I felt sure that my theft would go unnoticed. But I was wrong.

Ma picked up her pocketbook, opened it, and went straight to the coin purse. Then, running her finger along the inside, she turned to the three of us kids standing near the door.

"Well, looky here, boys and girls, my only nickel is gone from the change purse," she said, with a grin. Her expression and the tightly controlled rage in her voice, told me I was in serious trouble.

"Well, who's got it! WHERE IS IT?" she bellowed.

Charlie, standing in the doorway with an amused expression, remained silent as he watched the drama unfold. *I'll bet he knows just how it feels to get caught stealing something,* I thought.

"Not me," I said quickly with as much conviction as I could muster.

"Me either," Tom chimed in.

"I didn't take nothin'," Jimmy said, firmly.

"So nobody took nuthin' huh?" Ma said with growing fury behind the question. "OK le's jus start with coat pockets. Inside out, ALL of them, and be quick about it."

Terrified at this point, I was convinced of being caught, and cringed at the array of possible punishments. I reached into my pockets and felt the nickel in my right hand. Should I just take it out and hand it over with my confession, say I was sorry, and ask for mercy?

The coin landed between my middle and index fingers, and seemed to settle there comfortably. I took a deep breath. Without separating the two fingers clamped on the coin, I used my thumb to grasp the bottom of the coat pocket and pulled it inside out.

Pulling out my left pocket, I stood there arms spread apart, sure that Ma would see the coin's metal edge between my fingers. But miracle of miracles, while thoroughly checking other pockets in my shirt and slacks, she never looked at my hands. Then she moved on to inspect the boys' pockets, probably thinking that Tom was the guilty one. He was usually in trouble for something.

Since she found only dirty tissues and old lint in the pockets inspected, Ma gave up. I tucked my pockets back into my coat and dropped the nickel in as I did so, thankful that there were no holes in that pocket. That memorable morning three of us raced to get to school before the bell rang, and Ma went off with Charlie and Emily, grumbling about her missing coin. "I was *sure* I still had a nickel in that coin purse," she growled as they walked toward Charlie's car.

I did not share my *ill-gotten gain* with my two young brothers this time, but also decided that I probably would not try to steal coins from Ma ever again. I was convinced that she had discovered the missing dime a couple of weeks ago, and, in her devious way, had set a trap for whoever had taken it. Tom had been right about Ma, she really did know exactly how much money was in that coin purse.

It had been two weeks since Tom's teacher had talked to me about his behavior in school, and I had watched for mail from school every day since then. I decided it was time to forget all about it. Two weeks later, Ma got mad at me over that.

"What the hell did you say 'bout Tommy that the school had to send someone to see me this mornin'?"

"I didn't say anything about Tommy, Ma, what happened?"

"You must'a said somthin'. That counselor person said there was a *discussion*. She said you and his teacher talked about Tommy in the schoolyard."

I could tell Ma was really mad by the way she frowned, and pushed her lips together. I saw her jaw clench tight, and her eyebrows come down over her eyes. I knew I better have a good answer—and fast.

"Oh yeah, that was Mrs. Brown. She was the one complaining about Tom fighting with the other kids in his class. I told her I would take care of it, and I did. I talked to Tommy. Really gave it to him about stopping the fights. He promised he would stop. That's all," I explained.

"Well, I guess that wasn't good enough missy. That school counselor was here this morning askin' all kinds o' questions. She was fillin' out a paper, writin' things down, and makin' a big fuss. She saw I was pregnant, then wanted to ask Emily some questions, and even asked about which doctor I saw. Dammit, I don't want those nosy pests comin' 'round here. Ain't none a' their business what goes on with this family."

"Well gee Ma, what d'you want me to do?" I asked, putting the problem back on her to figure out.

Ma glared, clenched her teeth and for a minute it looked like she might hit me, but she didn't. I think she wanted to, but probably figured she was gonna need me to do something.

"I dun'no what I wan' ya' to do yet. I'm gonna ask Charlie about it 'cause the counselor said somethin' about Tenderloin Family Service, and maybe there's something in that for us. Jus' wait 'til I get a chance to talk to Charlie, THEN I'll tell you what to do."

I wasn't too happy with that, it always got messy when Charlie got involved, and he was already coming around here too often. Always trying to "cheer things up" he would say. That usually meant bringing a bottle with him, so him and Ma could get drunk again.

I wasn't too far off in my thinking about Charlie bein' up to something. He had a big surprise for us the next evening. He said that Friday night was a good time for a party, and invited some people from the apartments on our floor. He found out that not all of them could come at the last minute, but there was Jim and Alice, Peter, Jane, and Marina who said they would definitely come. That was only seven instead of the twelve Charlie invited so he was a bit disappointed.

"Tha's okay," he said smiling broadly, "Jus' make mo'a food and drink for da res' of us."

Charlie had arranged that all the kids would stay in Marina's apartment across the hall, so the grown-ups were close by, but could have some fun by themselves.

Marina was a nice lady. She had a job on Van Ness Avenue in a coffee shop during the day, and had saved her money to buy herself a big TV set. Sometimes she would let me and the boys watch some shows on the weekends. The TV set we had was an old black and white, with a tiny little screen, and something always going wrong with the sound.

Charlie didn't like Marina much, but invited her so she would let all the kids stay in her room while their parents were at the party. Marina was not one to go out much, so she was glad to let the kids watch TV in exchange for a party night. She said we could sleep there too, if it got real late. Since it was Friday night, none of us had to get up for school the next day. Marina put cushions and mats on the floor, for when we got sleepy. It was all nicely planned. Anyways, Ma had been really grumpy all week with her time coming up, and a party might put her in a good mood. And that was OK with me.

Charlie made several trips up our three flights of stairs on Friday afternoon, bringing in beer, chips and cheese from the Safeway store. He even got Ma to fix a tray of crackers and cheese for us kids—guess that was going to be our dinner. Marina asked us to bring toys and games so we could do something else if we got tired of TV.

Charlie put me in charge of the kids, "Nadine, honey, you's a big gal now, so you take care o' things in there? You take care o' the li'l kids, OK? Tha's my good gal. I know ya do a good job."

He was in a hurry, and sounded like there was something special about that night. I speculated about why his party was really important to him. Was he trying to make Ma feel better about things? Was it because she told him about the school visit and the Tenderloin Family Services? He was excited about something—that was for sure. Charlie had never done this party with other folks before, and I wondered what had happened to make him act so happy. Did he win a bet on the horses, or get lucky in a crap game maybe? Curious as I was, I didn't ask. It was none of my business anyhow, and the less I knew about Charlie, the better. It's not that he was mean or anything, and he seldom got mad, but sometimes those icy blue eyes would stare out from under a chock of reddish brown hair. Anyway, lately, I never felt easy when he was around. On his last trip up the stairs, Charlie brought in a record player and an arm full of long play records. I guess he wanted dancing to be a part of this party too.

He grinned at me again, and said proudly, "Lat'a on I could order some popcorn shrimp from that place aroun' tha co'nah. Ev'a have that, Nadine? Oh it's good. Just like I'm home in Louis'ana to eat that stuff. Perfect when ever'budy get hongry."

Wow! Charlie really was in a good mood, if he was buying food.

The party started a little after seven. The kids collected in Marina's living room, and sat on the floor in a circle around the snack tray. We each got a can of coke, and Marina warned us not to spill anything on her clean floor. She turned to the cartoons channel on the TV set before joining the party across the hall. I could see that she was a little bit worried, leaving six kids alone with food and cokes on the floor, and nothin' to do but watch TV and play with toys. She always kept her place so neat and clean.

"All right now, you kids behave yourselves or you'll have to go to your own place and sit all alone. Nadine, if you need anything, or if there's any trouble," Marina said, "you just walk across the hall and get me, okay?"

"Yes ma'm," I said, politely.

We were happy as clams, as Charlie would have said. Seated on the floor, stuffing ourselves with chips, crackers and cheese, and glued to the funny stories of Popeye and Mickey Mouse on TV. There was a short argument from Tom about which program to watch first, but when I threatened to go for Marina, he backed down. I had to make sure he knew I was in charge, or he would make trouble all night.

Hearing the party starting with lots of joking, laughing and loud music, we were content to be on our own, without grownups around. We watched TV cartoons for a couple of hours, then I began to change channels looking for Jack Benny and I Love Lucy. Although the younger kids were not enthusiastic, I insisted on watching these favorites of mine. Tired of watching TV, we played jacks and card games. One of the kids even brought a checkerboard. But after playing for a while, then arguing for a bit, they all got sleepy. Around nine-thirty, one by one, the younger kids began to fall asleep. I stayed awake the longest, but finally fell asleep myself, listening to the muffled music and laughter coming from the party.

I don't know how long it was before I woke up. I heard heavy steps on the stairway, and loud voices from our room across the hall. The music and laughing had stopped. I supposed that someone had turned off the record player. I didn't know what time it was, or how long I had slept. Had I been awakened in the middle of a dream? Waking up in a strange room had confused me, I guess. But when I heard a door open, the shouting got louder.

Had the party got too loud? Was it the police clomping up the stairway? Who was shouting and doing all that yelling? I had to find out what was happening. I got up from my mat on the floor, and started toward the door, when Marina and SueAnn burst in and shut the door behind them. SueAnn looked at me and started to cry.

"What happened?" I demanded, knowing that something had gone wrong across the hall.

"It was a girl," SueAnn said between sobs, "You lost a little sister."

"What do you mean I lost . . .? Are you drunk?" I demanded.

"No Nadine, your mother just lost the baby," Marina said, her lower lip quivering.

I thought that she was about to cry again, but I didn't care about her just now, I was too shocked. My mouth dropped open, and then I rushed toward the door, wanting to see for myself what was going on in that other room.

"No! You can't go in there!" Marina shouted, her back leaning firmly against the door. "They're taking your mother to the hospital. You Tom and Jimmy are staying here with me tonight."

She took a deep breath, then spoke crisply, "You other kids, get your things together, and get ready to leave. Your folks will be here in a minute to take you home."

Sue Ellen took her two kids by the hand and left first. All the other children were awake now, but were still so sleepy they didn't ask any questions. While mumbling complaints about being "woke up too early," they gathered sweaters and coats, put on shoes, and collected their toys.

3. The Baby

IT WAS SEVERAL DAYS LATER when I finally got the story straight about what happened that night. Ma had just come home from the hospital, and looking like she'd been run over by a truck. She was sitting at the table shivering, with a cup of hot coffee. I just got home from school, and though I was a bit worried about asking questions, I really wanted to know what had happened to her and the baby.

"Are you feeling okay, Ma? Are you cold? You want I should get your blanket? What happened to the baby? Why'd you go to the hospital anyway?"

From the clenched teeth and grim expression on her face, I could tell that Ma wasn't too happy with my questions.

"That shore is a heap o' questions comin' outa' your big mouth, girl. Why don' you jus' shut up, an' bring me some shugaa' ta take the bitter out'a this damn coffee."

I started to cry, as I turned away to fetch the sugar bowl from the counter top.

"I just wanted to know what happened to you and the baby," I blubbered stubbornly. I think my blubbering made Ma reconsider.

"Well, tain't no big deal. Everybody makin' a big fuss over nothin'—just a miscarriage that's all. Happens all the time and that's it," she said with resignation. *(I learned that resignation meant "giving-up" in a story Marina read us yesterday, and I could tell Ma was giving up right now.)*

I waited to know what Ma would say next, 'cause I didn't have resignation for what she said so far. I didn't say anything, just waited.

"Got a little complicated at the hospital, though. They said there won't be no more babies. Charlie's mad as hell."

"But how did it happen, Ma?" I insisted. I wanted to know more details.

"I tole' ya' all you need to know!" she snapped. "Now leave me be, I'm tired and gonn'a take a nap. You look after Emily."

I didn't believe that Ma had told me much, and I really wanted to know everything. So, since the boys were out on the sidewalk playing ball, I took Emily by the hand and went across the hall to Marina's apartment. I knocked on the door, knowing that she was probably home from work by this time.

"Hi Nadine, what can I do for you, honey?" she said, warmly.

"I want to know what happened when Ma lost the baby," I said right away. I saw no reason to wait around, or hold back. Marina had been there, and she could tell me what had happened.

I liked Marina. She was always nice to all the kids. She and I had an easy way of talking to each other. She asked us to come in and sit down, poured us two glasses of milk, and pulled three cookies out of her blue and white cookie jar. Me and Emily sat at the table happily, dunking our cookies in the milk.

"What did your ma tell ya' about it honey?"

"Well, she told me about the miscarriage, and said there were complications at the hospital, then she got too tired to talk anymore, so she's takin' a nap," I said, careful not to give up too much.

"I guess it's all right, then, for me to tell ya' what I know."

Marina stopped talking for a minute to take a sip of her milk and a bite of her cookie.

"Well, that party was going pretty good for a while. Your ma was dancing and drinking—having a good time. Then she got a belly cramp, and went to the bathroom for a BM. She sat on the toilet and pushed, and the baby came out. And that's about all. Then Alice screamed, and we didn't know what to do but call for an ambulance.

"You mean the baby went in the toilet?" I asked.

"You could put it that way I guess, but it wasn't like it was alive or anything."

"How d'you know that?" I said, wanting more details.

"Well, it looked funny, you know, not like a real baby. It's eyes were closed, and the skin all wrinkled, and it wasn't moving or anything."

"But if it was in the toilet, maybe it drowned," I insisted.

"Now Nadine, don't you think like that. It was like your ma said, it was a miscarriage, that's all."

"But if she was drunk, how could she know that?"

"I was there, and so was Alice and Sue Ellen and Joanne. Besides, I didn't drink so much, not to know what was going on."

"Was it really a baby girl?" I asked, unwilling to let that picture of a baby slip away.

"Yes, it was another girl. Now that's enough Nadine. I already told you too much. No more questions, okay?"

"But what did they do with the baby?" I insisted.

"They took it away with your ma in the ambulance. And I don't know any more than that. I didn't go with her."

"Ma said there was complications at the hospital. What does *complications* mean, Marina?"

"That means that something went wrong inside, after the baby came out, and your ma won't have any more babies . . . Stop with the questions now, Nadine. I really don't know any more, and I already said too much."

I could see that Marina was getting mad. She was not going to say any more after that. I think she wanted to forget the whole thing, and get on with her own life. My questions were making her remember and I guess she didn't like that.

So as much as I could put it together, that was the whole story. Ma was drunk, she had a bellyache, and the baby was dead. (Before or after it went in the toilet, I would never know.) Then, after she got in the hospital, things went wrong, and there would be no more babies, and that made Charlie mad. And I was still working on figuring that out, though I began to suspect it had something to do with not getting extra money in the welfare check.

Sure enough, Charlie came around the next day, and from then on, I began to listen very carefully to conversations between him and Ma.

"I can' do no mo'a Helen. They's jus' not enuf money from the welfah checks. We gotta live lean fo' 'while, 'til I get anotha' job. "

"That's bullshit Charlie, you got checks comin' outa' your ears. The deal is you gotta feed us bett'a. Kids gettin' skinny and Emily still ain't talkin' but two wo'ds. Sucks her thumb and looks scared all the time. 'Sides, I can't stay home all day, need bus money, gotta take us to the doctor sometime. Shoes and clothes for school? Who's gonna' pay for that? Where do the money go Charlie? You still shootin' dice with the guys?"

"Now Helen, you stop your worry'n 'bout me, you got a meetin' on Tuesday with the people at Family Se'vice. Maybe there's somethin' they can do. I'll give ya' a lif' to the meetin' an' you can tell 'em what you need. You tell 'em It's all for the kids. You know whatta say. An' I'll keep goin' afta' that job on the school bus. Now you stop fussin' with me, you know I don' let yo' down. You jes' stop worryin', ya' heah?"

Charlie's voice told me all I needed to know. He was broke again, spending all that welfare money on his bad habits, instead'a taken care of his "stable."

Yeah, I knew all about that. Kids talk to each other in the Tenderloin, and we don't miss much. Charlie had a half dozen "fillies" turning over checks for the promise of a place off the street, and a regular supply of food. As long as the number of babies increased, Charlie had a good thing going. With the "complications" at the hospital, Ma was not gonn'a be so popular with Charlie any more. It looked like our "bad times" were only gonn'a get worse.

4. November

JUST AS HE PROMISED, Charlie was there early on Tuesday morning to help Ma and Emily get themselves ready for the Family Services appointment. They didn't talk much, and Charlie is not his usual cheerful self. I could tell that he was worried about something. He was growing chin whiskers and his mustache didn't have that usual trimmed look.

Ever since that party a couple of weeks ago, his mood had changed. I wondered if he was disappointed over losing his baby, or if he was thinking about Ma being unable to have any more babies. But whatever Charlie was worried about, I felt pretty sure that he was not going to walk away from us. That meant that I would not need to worry so much about what we'd eat.

I took my time getting Tom and Jimmy dressed, and we left for school at the same time that Ma and Emily went off with Charlie.

"Where are *they* going?" Jimmy asked.

"Charlie is taking them to Family Services where Ma can get some help," I explained

"Maybe they can leave Emily there," Tom said.

Tom had grown irritated with the little sister who never tired of tagging along behind him around the house. For some strange reason, Emily was drawn to Tom, and followed him whenever she could cut loose from Ma. Tom wanted no part of it, tried to avoid Emily, and was always annoyed with her being "a big pest," as he would say.

Emily would go with me easily enough, but only when I took her hand and led her. She was a funny little kid. Cute as a kitten with her blue eyes and wavy blonde hair, but never said anything but her two favorite words: "No," when she didn't want to do something; and "P'ease," when she wanted someone to give her something. Still in diapers at three and a half, it was hard to prevent her from getting smelly. Most of the time, Ma took care of the diapers, but sometimes she told me to change Emily. I didn't mind so much, but the boys made a fuss, and teased Emily.

"Emily is a baby, Emily is a baby," Tom would chant.

Jimmy would chime in too, "Emily wears diapers, Emily wears diapers."

Emily would cry then, and if I were doing the changing, I'd scold the boys for being mean.

They were careful not to go too far when Ma was around, 'cause she would let fly with a swat on their bottom or across the face if she was in a bad mood. She didn't want anyone to upset Emily.

It seemed like that day at school was especially long, with Thanksgiving songs and making decorations for the classroom and hallway, but finally it was time to go home. The boys were ready and waiting when my sixth grade class was dismissed, and we didn't take any side trips, but went straight home.

"Wonder what happened at that place Ma went to this morning," Jimmy pondered. "You think they at home by now?"

"O'course, dummy. They left when we did this morning, I'm sure they's back by now. It was jus' for a interview," Tom sneered.

It was Tom's way to put Jimmy down, but I thought he was worried too.

I felt a little uneasy myself.

Charlie was still there when we arrived. He and Ma were drinking beer and talking. They paid no attention when we walked in the door. They just kept on talking. That didn't stop Charlie from watching while I changed out of my school clothes and into worn jeans. I should have thought to go change in the bathroom, but I wanted to hear what they were saying.

"Well, what the hell, Charlie, we'll jus' do the best we can with what we got," Ma said.

"But Helen, didya tell 'em 'bout Emily, and tha' you had fo'a kids ta feed, an' rent ta pay?"

"O'course I did. You think I'm stupid? I even make up stuff—like kids have no shoes. Make no matter to them. They say not their role ta' do that kind'a help. Welfare do that aprt, they say."

"An' wha'da you say then woman? You tell 'em Welfare not 'nuff?" Charlie insisted. "You tell em 'bout losin' the baby and need'n ta be in da hospital? You say Emily need diapers and them don' come cheap now days?

"Now tha's enuf ' outa you, Chrlie. YOU do tha' interview wid them next time, see if it go better. 'Sides, I need ta go back with all'a the kids nex' time. You gonna come? You know how ta talk bett'a'n me?"

I waited to hear what Charlie was going to say about that invitation.

He hesitated, "Well now, Helen, ya know I can' do tha'. I din' mean ta criticize ya. I jus' need moa time ta git a good payn' job, tha's all."

"I heard THAT story befo'a!" Ma said sharply.

I could tell she was about to lose her temper, and I think Charlie knew it too. He finished his coffee, set the cup in the sink and got ready to leave.

All this time the boys waited wide-eyed, wondering what it all meant.

I thought it was probably a good time for me and the boys to go out for a walk while the weather was still warm enough. It gets cold fast when the fog rolls in, so right after Charlie left, I took them down the stairs and outside. This was not a good time to be around Ma. It would be a mistake to remind her that we were hungry. Being outside, we might beg a snack from the grocer down the street. Mr. Diem sometimes saved broken cookies and set them aside for us kids.

"Come on you guys, let's go see Mr. Diem, maybe he has something for us today," I said, as we hit the sidewalk.

Although it was November, the early afternoon sun was still warm. I was comfortable being outdoors and it was a relief from the worries going on inside. With Thanksgiving coming up next week, it would be winter soon, and being outdoors wouldn't be pleasant much longer.

5. A New Friend

FOR THANKSGIVING we had Thursday and Friday added to the weekend, and that gave us four days away from school. It was not really much fun to be separated from the best part of my life, since I was pretty much confined to our apartment during those four days. *(I use that new word, 'confined,' whenever I can.)*

On Friday though, I did spend some time visiting Marina, and that was better than OK as far as I was concerned. Ma said that if I wanted to go visiting, I had to take Emily with me. I guess she was looking for some time to herself. I was happy to leave the quarreling boys with unhappy Ma, so I took Emily by the hand. Maybe when we got back the boys would be too tired to argue, and Ma would have had time to relax with her favorite pastime --- Lucky Lager beer with Lucky Strike cigarettes ---how LUCKY can it get?

I knew that Marina was at home, 'cause I'd heard her door open and close a couple of hours before. I knew that she was on the early shift this week, and that was perfectly fine with me on this Friday after Thanksgiving.

On special holidays Marina always went out to dinner with some of her lady friends and I wanted to know what other people did for holidays. As usual Marina had a welcoming smile when she opened the door and invited us in.

"Hi Nadine, I'm glad you came today. There's someone here I'd like you to meet."

Sitting at the kitchen table was a man I had never seen before, but I supposed that it was Marina's boyfriend. He was all dressed up, as if he might be going out somewhere.

"Nadine, I want you to meet my friend, Ted. He works at the coffee shop with me, and he just told me he's been promoted to manager. We'll be going out to celebrate his promotion in a little while."

"Hi Ted," I said. Emily stepped behind me trying to hide from a man she had never seen before.

Marina continued, "And Ted, this is Nadine and her sister Emily. They live across the hall and sometimes come to visit me."

"Hello Nadine and Emily, I'm pleased to meet you. Marina had told me that she had friends living across the hall from her. She and I work together at the diner, and she promised to help me celebrate my promotion."

"We're having a cup of coffee before leaving," Marina explained. "Wouldn't you like to join us with your usual milk and cookies?"

I wasn't sure that Emily would be willing to stay around with a strange man there, but I took a chance and said, "Yes, thank you. That would be very nice.

I was making an effort to show Ted that I knew how to be polite. Emily took her time separating from me, but did sit in the chair farthest away from this man she had never seen.

While Marina poured milk in glasses and laid cookies on two napkins, Ted turned to me, "Well Nadine, I've just been telling Marina about how boring it was having to eat my Thanksgiving dinner at work. How was *your* 'Turkey Day?" Ted asked.

"We had a really good Thanksgiving," I said, with enthusiasm. "The best food we had in a long time. Ma took us over to Glide Memorial, and they gave each of us a whole tray of food. There was turkey with stuffing and cranberry sauce, lots of mashed potatoes and gravy, and pumpkin pie for dessert. It was ta-rri-fic!"

"Sounds like you really liked it. Did your mom have a good time too?" Marina asked.

"Sure did. Ma even went back in line for more pie. Tom made a pig of himself as usual, but Jimmy was happy with what they served for kids. Emily was so excited by the crowd, the noise, and all the decorations, she hardly had time to look at the food. But Ma made her eat, so she got her share of the good stuff."

"I guess it was nice for all of you to have a happy Thanksgiving together after all the trouble you've had," Marina said. "Maybe things will get better now—for you, your mom, and Charlie."

"Well, maybe," I said hesitating. "But Charlie doesn't have a job yet."

"Did he join you for the Thanksgiving dinner?" Marina asked.

"Nope. Charlie didn't show up at all. Ma didn't say anything, so I don't think she expected him."

Thinking it was time to find out what Marina and her friends did, I asked, "So where did *you* go on Thanksgiving?"

I was curious about what it must be like to be at a nice restaurant and eat a fancy holiday dinner.

"Oh, we decided to go to Fisherman's Wharf for the fresh crab," Marina said. "I hadn't had a good seafood dinner for a long time, and since none of the other ladies were excited about turkey, we agreed to do something different. It was lovely. We started with clam chowder, then had a shrimp cocktail. The crab season just started, so the steamed crab we ordered was perfect. Three of my friends had theirs with a special seafood sauce that had lemon and garlic, two others decided on mayo, but I had mine with melted butter. It was delectable!"

(I needed to look up "delectable" so I can use it too, I thought. But I'd have to wait until Monday to get to the school library.)

Then, I thought I could learn the word now, and not have to use the library.

"Uh . . . Marina? . can you tell me . . .? What does that word "delectable" mean?"

I was taking a chance that Marina and Ted might think I was stupid, but I was feeling lucky today.

"Oh sure, Honey, it's just the same as "delicious." It means tasting very, very yummy," she said with a warm smile.

Guess they didn't think I was "stupid" after all.

"Thanks . . . I . . . kind'a like new words . . . I make a list for the ones I don't know . . . then look them up in at school," I explained, still unsure of Ted and Marina's opinion.

"That's a wonderful way to learn new words, Nadine. Glad I added a new word to your list. . .

Ted interrupted, "My high school English teacher used to say that making a list like that was the best way to increase your vocabulary." Then he looked a little doubtful. "You *are* familiar with the word *vocabulary* aren't you?"

"Oh yes," I said, with a confident smile.

I really liked Marina, and was starting to like Ted too. I'm glad Marina lived just across the hall. I always felt better after talking to her.

Emily was just finishing her second cookie, and I thought we better get back across the hall, before she had another "accident."

"I think we need to go now. 'Bye Marina and Goodbye Ted, nice to meet you," I said, starting to wonder if Marina and Ted might get together and someday move away from here.

"Say 'bye' to Ted and Marina, Emily, and 'thanks' for the cookies too," I prompted, while knowing it was a waste of time trying to get Emily to say anything.

Emily smiled at Marina, which was as close as she would come to a "thank you," but she ignored Ted completely.

"The word 'bye' and 'thanks' are not in Emily's vocabulary yet," I explained smugly, proud of having used the word 'vocabulary' correctly. I giggled.

Marina laughed too, "Very nice use of the word *vocabulary*, Nadine. And you are welcome to come again ladies," she said, as she followed us to the door.

I left Marina's regretfully, feeling that I was leaving a comfortable blanket of warmth behind.

I wanted to hold on to the good feeling a little longer, so after Marina shut her door, I bent down to Emily and whispered, "Shall we go outside for a little walk, Emily?"

Emily looked up at me with a question in her big blue eyes, then as we headed toward the stairs, she smiled. It was going to be OK with Emily if we took a little walk.

6. Bob

FOLLOWING THE SECURITY OFFICER seemed like it was taking forever to go through the library to his office. The officer was a big man, and he was taking long steps, and I had to hurry to keep up. Along the way, I kept telling him how sorry I was about falling asleep, and how I could go straight home now, and would never fall asleep in the library again. But it made no difference. He just kept walking.

I thought about turning around and making a dash for the door. I wanted to avoid being asked for my name, and address, and all that stuff that would make worse trouble. I turned my head to see how far away the doors were, but a firm voice spoke a warning.

"Now, I know you're probably pretty quick, You kids can really run fast, but all those doors are locked up tight," he said. "If I were you, I would put that thought right out of your mind."

How did he know what I was thinking? Did other kids try to stay here before? I was curious, but not about to ask. Besides I would never admit that I wanted to escape. Now, knowing that the doors were all locked, I gave up the idea of getting away. I decided it would be better just to go along.

"Well, here we are. You can sit over on that chair across from my desk," he said. Pointing to a brown chair with a worn cushion, he seated himself on the other side of the desk. He had a black leather chair with a back that tilted. He faced me from one side of the desk; I was on the other. Just like being in the principal's office, I thought

"Would you like a drink of water?" he asked after we were settled.

"No thank you," I said, deciding I would be polite, but say as little as possible. Maybe I could find a way to get this nice man to let me go home.

"My name is Bob. What might your name be?" he asked politely.

I sighed deeply, "Nadine," I said, reluctantly.

"Nadine is your first name?"

I nodded.

"What is your last name, Nadine?"

I hesitated. "Jones," I lied.

"Oh, it's Jones, is it? Well Nadine Jones, how old are you?"

I tried to think fast—if I said I was older, would it mean I could get out of here faster? If I said I was younger, maybe he would feel sorry, and just take me home.

"I'm eight years old," I said, hoping I'd chosen in the right direction.

"Only eight? Well I'm surprised that your mother would let someone so young go to the library alone," Bob commented.

Dammit. I'd got the wrong age. If I'd said I was older, like fifteen, maybe he'd have let me go with a warning. He was watching my face now, and must have known I was thinking up another lie.

"More like twelve?" Bob asked with a smile.

"Almost," I admitted, shamefaced.

I saw Bob scribble some notes on a form on his desk. But there were still a lot of blank spaces on that sheet of paper.

"All right now, we have a Nadine Jones who is twelve years old, and where does Nadine live?"

"She lives on Larkin Street," I answered, leaving out the exact address on purpose . . . But that didn't help a bit.

"And where on Larkin Street does she live?"

This back and forth went on for some time, and Bob got all the information he needed to fill in all the spaces on that paper. He was a very persistent man, and very patient. Never once got mad when I tried to lie, only asked the question in a different way. I could tell that he had probably done this many times before. He was just doing his best to finish the job. He wanted to get it right.

When all the lines on the form were filled, Bob made a copy on the copy machine, then picked up the phone and dialed.

"Hi Phil, this is Bob. Found a young lady here after hours," he said. "No, she's not upset. Twelve. Lives on Larkin Street. Not far from here. Okay, we'll wait here in the office."

"What . . . who were you talking to?" I asked, feeling something drop in my stomach. All of a sudden, I didn't feel so cocky any more.

"That was a friend of mine. His name is Phil and he's a police officer. I think you'll like him. He gets along fine with the kids on Larkin Street."

I think Bob's voice was supposed to be reassuring, *(That means to make someone feel at ease.)* but I began to feel my head get light. Now there would really be hell to pay! When Ma finds out about my getting mixed up with the police, I'll wish I had stayed around to take that beating for walking off with Emily. Already regretting that I had run away, my breath began coming in short starts, and for the first time I felt really scared. I started to cry. Bob handed me a tissue, then sat down again. He smiled, and looked me straight in the face so that his eyes looked right into mine.

"Nadine, a young girl should not be sleeping in the corner of a library on a rainy night. She should be home with her family having a good hot meal, then sleeping in a nice warm bed. Now, if that can't happen for some reason, we need to find out why."

Bob said all this in such a nice voice, and I had a strange feeling hearing somebody talk to me in a caring way, that I cried all over again. Bob put the box of tissues close by on the desk. Then I heard a buzzer ring, and Bob went off to open the door for Officer Phil. I sat and waited. I knew that I would not be able to escape from this really big trouble that was coming my way.

7. Officer Phil

OFFICER PHIL was not as big a man as Bob, but he was a bit taller. He looked nice in his uniform, and smiled as he came in. Maybe, if I was lucky, he would just walk me home.

"Well now, what do we have here?" he asked as he came through the door. The blue uniform made me feel uneasy. I kept quiet because I was not sure what to say.

"Bob says you were taking a nap in the history section?"

"Yes," I said.

I was not going to say any more than I had to. Officer Phil might be very nice, or he could be very mean, I couldn't tell yet. Smiles don't really mean very much. Charlie smiled all the time, so did the school principal. I waited.

"Suppose you tell me . . . why you forgot to go home when the library closed," Officer Phil said slowly.

"I fell asleep," I said.

"Well . . . the library is not really a very good place to sleep. Don't you have a place to sleep at home?" he asked.

"Yes," I said.

"And why are you not sleeping there?" he asked.

"I fell asleep here . . . and Bob found me," I said.

"I don't think you're going to get any real answers here," Bob interjected. "Best to take her on home, and find out what is going on there."

"Nothing is going on there!" I said without thinking. "Just let me go home, and everything will be just fine."

"Me thinks she doth protest too much," Officer Phil said, smiling at Bob.

What a funny way to talk, I thought. But since I had already said too much, I decided not to ask any questions.

"Come along young lady, let's get you home."

Officer Phil turned sideways, lifted his hand and crooked his finger letting me know that I should follow him.

"I'll call to let you know how this all turns out. And thanks for the call," he said to Bob.

I followed the officer to the back door, where he stopped and held out his hand to take mine. I frowned and held back a bit, but did comply. *(Comply means to do what is expected.)*

"Sorry," Officer Phil said. "I know you are a bit old to be holding my hand, but I don't want you to consider the idea of running away. I'm too tired to be chasing a kid through these streets at night."

"I'm NOT going to run away," I said. "I wouldn't know where to run. Anyways, it's dark, and it's raining."

Officer Phil looked at me, and tilted his head, "Is that a real promise? Cause if it is, I'll let go of your hand. Then I can open my umbrella and we won't get so wet."

"Yeah, it's a promise," I said, reluctantly.

I had run out of ideas, and it was time for me to face Ma. She would really be mad now, but taking a beating from her was better than being chased and arrested by a policeman.

He didn't ask any questions on our short walk home, and that was fine with me.

Up three flights of stairs to our apartment, then Officer Phil knocked on the door with his stick. It was really loud, and the door swung open right away. Ma was speechless, and her frown melted as her jaw dropped when she saw the police officer. but she pushed her stringy yellow hair out of her eyes and got herself together real quick.

After taking a deep breath, and giving Officer Phil a crooked smile, she looked at me and said, "Well, there you are Nadine. We were really worried about you. Where have you been all this time?"

"Well Ma'm, we found her asleep in the library, and decided it would be better for her to sleep at home. May I come in for a minute while she gets herself to bed?" he asked while sliding his foot inside the door.

"Uh, I'm afraid things are in a terrible mess just now," Ma said, shaking her head side to side. "Can you come back tomorrow? "

I prayed that Officer Phil would not leave. If he came back tomorrow, I might be dead by that time.

"Oh, I don't mind a mess. You should see how my kids throw things around at my house. We have three, and there's no keeping things in order.

And how many children do you have ma'm?" he asked, with a friendly grin while stepping into the room.

He was not going to leave, and Ma had to back away when Officer Phil took a step in.

"Ah . . . well," she sputtered. "I got four now, and . . . and . . . we was about to have another . . . but, but I had a miscarriage you know . . . so . . . so there ain't gonna be no more comin'." Ma spoke in a rush, like she was trying to hurry things along while trying to convince him that everything was under control.

Officer Phil was taking his time to look around, "So you live in here with four youngsters?" he asked, politely.

But I could see that he was checking out the diapers in the corner, the dirty dishes on the table, and the two boys standing at the bedroom door half asleep and half naked .

"Where do you sleep, Nadine?" he asked, turning to me.

"In there." I pointed to where the boys were standing.

"It's a big room," Ma said quickly, trying to smooth her hair, as if she really cared about her appearance.

"And the little one?" asked Officer Phil, nodding at Emily.

"She's in tha' oth'a room with me," Ma said. I had never noticed how unkempt Ma looked. It made me ashamed to show a stranger our apartment.

"Seems a bit crowded," said the officer. He was quiet for a minute, and I thought he might ask if there was a man around to help out.

"We been on welfe-a a long time," Ma answered, after a minute to think up something to say. "An' we going to see Family Services in a couple a days. Maybe get a bigga place."

I could tell that Ma was trying as hard as she could to say something that would get rid of this policeman. I think she worried that he might start investigating. *(That means looking into everything.)* That would not be a good thing. So Ma was making up reasons to get him to think that we would all be just fine, and he didn't need to worry about it.

"Do you have any idea why your daughter was in the library so late at night?" the officer asked.

"No, got no idee. She jus' went out tha door, while I wuz changin' the baby, an never tole' us where she was goin'."

Officer Phil looked at me, "You want to tell us why you left in such a hurry?" he asked.

"Just wanted to read a book at the library," I said. "Then I fell asleep, that's all."

I shrugged my shoulders, and hoped everybody would be happy with my answer. I wanted Ma to be glad that I didn't tell the whole truth, and I wanted Officer Phil to go away right now when everything was calm, and Ma was being careful.

8. Family Services

OFFICER PHIL took another look around our combined living room, dining room, kitchen—then smiled at me. I could see why he and Bob were friends. They both had that slow way of taking time to check things out, before deciding what to do.

Pressing his lips together and nodding his head at Ma he said, "Well, I guess it's time for me to go now. Nadine is back home with her family, and it was my pleasure to help her get her here safely."

After a short pause, as if he was thinking about something to say, he went on. "I'll be on patrol in this neighborhood starting next week . . . So, if there's any need for my help, just ask, and I'll see what I can do. Okay?" He looked right at Ma and with raised eyebrows, and nodded at her as he went toward the door.

I watched Officer Phil leaving, and said, "Thank you," just loud enough for him and Ma to hear.

Then, he closed the door, and was gone. I could hear his footsteps going down the stairs, and was surprised that I felt sorry to see him leave. It wasn't just because his being here protected me from Ma, but more because he seemed to understand. He had looked around, and could see that everything was a big mess, but didn't look surprised or disgusted. Except for Charlie, most other people who came in here turned up their noses, and left as soon as they could.

Now came time for me to "face the music" as Charlie would say when something nasty was coming his way.

Ma closed the door, locked it for the night, then turned to me with hands on her hips, "Well missy, you shu'a screwed up good this time."

The boys standing in the bedroom doorway were wide eyed, waiting for the "axe to fall," which is something else Charlie would say.

Emily, clutching Ma's dress, started to whimper.

Instead of going for the long wooden spoon hanging on the wall, Ma smiled at me. It was just like the smile she had just before she started throwing oatmeal. I stood there and waited, telling myself that I would not cry, no matter what.

"Seems you got ideas about runnin' away from us," she said, slowly. "Well, tha's what ya wann'a do, why don't you start runnin'? What you waitin' fo'a?"

I didn't know what to do. She had locked the door, so she knew I couldn't run away again. I didn't know what she wanted. Did she want me to run around the room? That didn't make any sense.

"Oh, dear me, Nadine can't think of nowhere to run," Ma sneered.

I waited, so scared my teeth began to hurt, and no matter what I'd decided, I started to cry, "I'm sorry Ma, I'm really sorry."

"What is it you're sorry for you little shit? You jus' tell me what you's sorry for."

I blubbered and stammered my way through a list of all the things I thought she might want to hear. "I'm sorry—for—for taking Emily outside for a walk. I'm sorry—for running away. I'm sorry for—for falling asleep in the library. I'm sorry for—letting a policeman take—take me home."

"Well," Ma said. "I'm glad ta hear you's sorry for all them things, but you forgot the mos' important' thing to be sorry 'bout."

I waited, knowing I must have done something terrible that I'd forgotten.

"You forgot ta be sorry you was born," Ma said, angrily. She took a step toward me, and slapped me hard across the face with her right hand, then turned a bit and slapped me with her left. It really hurt, and I went crying into the bedroom, pushing Tom and Jimmy aside.

"And don' you think tha's tha end of it. You think about wha's comin' nex'," Ma said bitterly. "You jes' sleep on it, if ya can sleep a'tall."

I didn't bother taking off my street clothes, just kicked off my shoes, and pulled the covers up over my head. I thought about what Ma said—about what would be in store for me tomorrow. But after a time, I did fall sleep.

In spite of her threat, Ma did not come after me with the wooden spoon the following morning. Maybe it was because Charlie was there and they were having a long talk. I heard bits of what they said, but knew better than to come out of the bedroom.

"Now see hea Helen, you keep on hittin' Nadine, tha' cop hear 'bout it, he be back to make trouble . . . School be askin' questions too if she got marks on her."

Ma said something that sounded like "where it don't show." But I couldn't hear all of it.

"Naw Helen, not'a good idea. 'Sides, you gotta think 'bout how she gonna be helpin', when you take 'em kids ta the Famly Servces meetin'. You wan' they see her all beat up? Maybe she gonna tell 'em you hit yoa kids. What they's gonna do then? . . . An' 'sumpin' else Helen . . . Nadine a big girl now, not a li'l kid no more. She be tha only one ta hep' ya' wid da young 'uns."

I listened, confused about why Charlie was sticking up for me. Was he thinking that I might help to get more money from welfare? Was he telling Ma about different ways I could help, so he wouldn't need to? I couldn't figure it out. Charlie never did anything for anybody, unless he had something to get from it.

Ma didn't follow up on her threats, but glared at me all weekend. I knew that she must be thinking about what she would like to do, and I was careful about keeping out of her way.

The swelling on my face had gone down by the time Monday morning came around. My teacher said something about my having blue circles under my eyes, but that was all. I told Ms. Brown that I would not be in school the following day because of an appointment. She nodded, and made a note in her record book so it would show that my not being there was an excused absence.

Ms. Brown took this opportunity to tell our sixth grade class how important it was to come to school every day. She said that every teacher was required to keep a record of how many children actually came to class each day. These records were called registers, and are part of California state law.

"This is how each city in the state receives money to provide education for the children."

By the time she answered all the questions we asked, it was more than fifteen minutes later that Ms. Brown finished explaining.

"So, now you know why it is very costly for our schools when a student is absent without good reason."

I thought it was a complicated way to pay for our schools.

After school on Monday, we all took turns taking a bath. Ma told me to take my bath first, because I was the cleanest. Jimmy went next, in the same bath water. By the time Tom was finished the water was not only cold, but really dark. He complained, and I didn't blame him.

Ma said that before we got home from school, she and Emily had taken their baths together. We three kids were lucky that Ma filled the bathtub with fresh water after that. As each of us got out of the bath and dried off, Ma took out her scissors and cut our hair to make us look even cleaner. The boys smiled proudly, but Emily cried at having her hair cut short. Ma handed me the scissors and said I should do my own haircut. And that was OK with me.

For dinner, Charlie brought in some Kentucky Fried, and we had a good meal while talking about what kind of questions might be asked at the meeting. We spent a lot of time on what answers we should give the next morning. It was like a rehearsal for a show, and as long as Charlie was there playing the person who did the interview, it was kind'a fun.

Charlie started with Tom, "Well son, y'all get to school on time ev'ra day?"

"Yes sir!" Tom answered firmly, as if as if he were reading his answer from a play. He started raising his hand to salute, then looking at Ma, put his hand down. I could tell from the smile on his face that Tom was enjoying himself.

"And you young man, what kind'a grades you get on yo'a report card?" Charlie said, turning to Jimmy.

"Well, I think my grades is pretty good," Jimmy was prompted to say.

"Okay now, you's gotta tell me wha'cha don' got, tha'cha really need ta have. We gonn'a start wid you Helen."

Ma pursed her lips and started at the top of her list. "We need ta have more money."

"An wha'cha need money for, ma'm," Charlie said, winking at us kids.

"We need money for ta buy good food an' some clothes for the kids, and pampers for Emily. We need money for the bus—so we could go shopping—and to the docta, and—and for curtains, and a good TV set tha's workin'. We need money to get a bigger place—for kids to have they own rooms. We needs money for everythin'."

"Well ma'm, sounds like you need lot-a money," Charlie said, smiling at how well the practice was going.

"Then Helen, they gonna ask how much you get in yo'a welfare check—and they figah out how much more ya need. Okay?"

Ma nodded and seemed pleased. Maybe 'cause Charlie had found nothing to add or correct to what she said. I think they must have talked about this before sitting down with us kids.

Charlie turned to me. "Now Nadine, what you gonna say about what a young lady need?"

I hesitated. "Well, most everything that Ma said I guess."

"Yeah, well how 'bout somethin' you might need jus' for youse'f ?"

I thought about going to middle school next year and being the only one with scruffy clothes, "Maybe clothes for school, and some new shoes?" Thinking about going to a new school, I got a better idea, "But if I'm in middle school, I might need to buy some books, or pens and pencils, maybe some notebooks?"

"Tha's good thinkin' Nadine, I knew you was smart," Charlie smiled.

Charlie turned again to Tom and Jimmy, "How about you guys? What else you gonna need 'sides new clothes and school stuff?"

"I need a bike, so I won' hafta walk to school," Tom said. "And a baseball glove and bat so I could play baseball with the other kids."

"I need candy and gum," Jimmy piped up.

I guess he thought if this was going to be a wish list, he might as well get his wishes in too.

Everybody laughed, and Jimmy frowned, confused, "Why is that so funny?" he asked.

"Well now, son, we mos'ly want to think o' 'sential things fo-a fam'ly needs ta live on," Charlie explained, running a hand through his thinning hair while his blue eyes seemed to glimmer with excitement. He waited.

"Like bread and water," piped in Tom with a smile.

"We got that," said Jimmy, angrily.

Charlie frowned. "Maybe bettah let yoa ma 'splain what y'all needs ta have," he said.

"Sep' maybe smarty pants?" Ma said. "She always find some good way a talkin' to policemans and folks in the libr'y."

The sneer on her face told me that when she said that, it was not meant to be a compliment.

Charlie ignored the comment, and went on to give more directions. "Now I know you's all wanna look good fo' da interview, but not too much ya he'a?" He shook his head side to side.

Ma looked surprised, "Wadda you mean 'not too much'?" she asked.

"Well, not all gussied up, and high heel shoes, an all that. Make em ta think you is doin' jes' fine, don' need no help."

Ma frowned, then curled her lip, "The kids just have a bath, want I should mak'em go outside an' git dirty again?"

"Naw, that be goin' too far. Clean is okay, jus' don' get all fine an fancy, tha's all."

The argument went back and forth between Ma and Charlie, until I thought they might get into a fight. But Charlie convinced Ma that they both wanted the same thing, and convinced her that he knew best how to get it. So they finally ended it by deciding that it was okay to be clean and neat, but we shouldn't wear anything that might look new or flashy. And that made sense to me.

Charlie made us a cup of hot chocolate before he left, and we were delighted to have this special treat. Guess Charlie wanted everybody to be in a good mood when the people at Family Services talked with us. I was starting to understand Charlie's philosophy. *(I like the word philosophy—it means a way of thinking about life.)* Anyway, Charlie's philosophy seemed to be that you should get as much as you could, and use as many tricks as you had.

9. The Interview

OUR APPOINTMENT was at 9:30 the next morning, and Ma got us up early to be ready for Charlie who was to drive us to the center. Ma had taken extra care with her appearance, combing her hair neatly behind her ears and using powder to take the shine off her nose. Charlie was there promptly at nine o'clock and we were all set to go. Driving Ma to her appointments was part of the deal, but we would walk our way home afterwards.

"Y'all look mighty fine," he said, with a broad grin.

"You sure we is not too fancy?" Ma sneered. I guess she was remembering Charlie's comment last night, about not looking too good for this interview.

Charlie was not driving his usual flashy Caddy, and I wondered if it was in the shop for repairs. Five of us getting into this little Ford was a bit tricky, with Emily on Ma's lap in the front seat, us three kids in the back. Good thing Charlie had no car seat for Emily, or two of us would have to ride on the hood, or maybe the roof of this thing. Anyhow, crowded into the back seat, Jimmy squirmed and Tom complained a lot. He stopped his grumbling, after I snapped at him that I was squashed too, and so was Jimmy.

"Why are you drivin' this little ole Ford?" Ma demanded.

Charlie chuckled, "Like I tole' y'all yeste'day, we can't look like we too well off."

"You think they be lookin' out tha winda, see how a car look?" Ma sneered.

Charlie continued driving the short few blocks to Grove Street, cheerfully, making jokes about us being "snug as sardines." But nobody thought his jokes were funny. We all breathed a sigh of relief climbing out of that small car.

Ma took us through the entrance, into the building, and walked directly to the front desk.

"We got a' appointment here at 9:30," she said.

"Your name please?" the desk clerk asked, without looking up or smiling.

I thought that she might have got up too early this morning, or had a bad night, or something. Hoping that she was not the one that was going to interview us, I tried smiling at her in a friendly way. Didn't make any difference, she still had a sour face and acted grumpy.

"Just wait right over there. Mr. Lewis will be with you in a moment," she said, pointing to the bench along the wall.

We waited almost twenty minutes before Mr. Lewis came. "Good morning Mrs. Williams, my name is Sam Lewis. I'm so sorry that you were kept waiting such a long time. Please come this way," he said with a warm smile. Thank goodness somebody in here can smile, I thought,

Mr. Lewis' office had ten big filing cases, and six chairs. After we were all seated, Mr. Lewis explained that we would each be interviewed by different people.

"That way, we'll be able to move through the process much more quickly—and you won't need to be here so long," he said smiling again, as if he were doing us a favor.

I think he saw the worried look on our faces after he said that. So Mr. Lewis smiled again, and took time to explain that we would "not really be separated."

"The interviewing rooms are right next to each other, and though the social workers will talk with you separately, you will be able to see each other all the time."

I could see that Ma was pressing her lips together, and she started to say something, but Mr. Lewis quickly interrupted, "Of course, you and Emily will stay together, Mrs. Williams," he added, reassuringly.

Everyone seemed to relax after hearing that. I was perfectly relaxed, of course. After all, I had already been 'interviewed'—by Bob at the library, and by Officer Phil too. Having had all that practice, I was not at all worried. Well . . . not very much worried.

The person who interviewed me introduced herself as a "social worker," and that was even better. Social workers had come around the apartment often enough for me to know that they seldom said anything mean. This one told me that her name was Mrs. Becker, Susan Becker.

"You may call me Susan if you wish. Your name is Nadine they tell me? Well, Nadine you and I need to talk. I'll ask some questions, then you will answer them—if you can. But you don't have to answer questions if you're not sure, or don't know how to answer. Sometimes, the things I ask about might be hard to answer. So take your time and answer whatever you can," she said.

I thought Susan Becker was kind'a pretty. And she had a nice smile too. Her words sounded like she really meant what she said. Since I felt comfortable with what she said, I was pretty sure we'd get along fine.

Ma was in the little room across from me, and through the glass, I could see that Emily was beginning to squirm. She was probably tired of sitting on Ma's lap so long—in the car, on the bench, and now in the interview room. Ma's social worker must have said that it was okay for Emily to walk around. Emily was in a hurry to get off Ma's lap, but she didn't do much wandering. Emily was not one to go very far without Ma or me.

My social worker, Susan Becker, was easy to talk to. Her questions were mostly about how I was doing in school, and what I wanted to be when I grew up. She also wanted to know how many friends I had, and what I did in my "free time." I said that I didn't have much free time.

"What would you like to do if you did have some free time Nadine?" Susan Becker asked.

"I du'nno . . . I guess I'd go to the library and read a good book, or go to a movie with a friend, or go to the playground and learn some of those tricks on the exercise bars."

"And why can't you do those things now?" she asked.

I knew what she wanted to know, but I hesitated. I wondered if she would talk to Ma about my answers. I didn't want to be in trouble again.

"Nadine, if this is too hard to answer, it's okay," Susan said.

I clenched my teeth and pursed my lips for a minute longer. I was not sure that I could tell this stranger how Ma made me do so many things, I never had time to do anything but homework.

"That's a kind'a hard question. You told me I didn't have to answer anything that was too hard, right?"

"That's exactly right, Nadine," said Susan. She looked at me with a great big smile, as if I had told her the answer to her question, even though I didn't.

When we got home, everyone was very tired. I could not understand why we should be so tired when all we did at the Center, was sit on a chair and talk.

After a peanut butter sandwich for lunch, we sat at the kitchen table, and Ma wanted to know what everybody told the social workers.

"You first Nadine," she ordered.

I started by saying that I answered questions about my schoolwork, and my report card, and what I wanted to be when I grew up.

"And what di'ja say about your wantin', hunh?" Ma said with a sneer.

Why was she mad at me now? I wondered. What had I done that she couldn't look at me without being angry?

Deciding to answer in the shortest way possible, I said, "I told her I was thinking I might study to be a teacher, or a librarian, or nurse maybe."

"Oh! The little shit's gonna grow up to be a teacher or a nurse? Well missy, you have anotha' think comin'. You is gonna grow up an get a J.O.B., and bring me some money! I take care o' you so far. Now, soon as you finish school, you gonna take care o'me . . . Ya hea'?"

Determined not to cry after this new attack, I closed my mouth tight, not wanting for her to see me cry, and stood up by my chair.

"And where d'you think you's goin'? You gonna run away again? Well missy, you go out'a tha' door an' I'll break ever'a bone in your skinny ass!"

I looked at Ma, and knew that she meant every word. Turning away slowly, and without rushing, or making a sound, I walked into the bathroom, and locked the door.

10. Learning the Facts

SAFELY HIDDEN IN THE BATHROOM, I looked at myself in the mirror. Gritting my teeth, I refused to cry, though it probably would have felt better if I had. Instead I washed my face quick with cold water, and blew my nose. What to do now was the next question.

I felt kind'a sticky between my legs, so sat down on the toilet to wash up a bit. It wasn't yet time for a bath this week, but a quick wash would make me feel better, I hoped. Looking at the wash rag I saw something I'd never seen before. There was blood on it! *How did that happen*? I thought. I'd got away before Ma had a chance to hit me, and I didn't remember scratching myself. This was really scary.

What should I do anyway? I can't tell Ma. It would give her another reason to blame me for something I didn't do. It could be something that would go away. I'd had lots of bloody cuts before and they all stopped bleeding after a while, so I decided to forget about it.

After waiting a bit, I sneaked out of the bathroom, and into the bedroom. I kept all my clothes on just like I did before, and climbed into bed. I slept all night, but got up very early the next morning. The bleeding did not go away; matter of fact, it was getting worse. I folded my panties up tight, and stuffed them in my pocket. I decided it was time to do something.

Ma was still in her bedroom, and I could hear that she was scolding Emily about making such a mess. So I yelled through the door that I was going across the hall to see Marina. Ma grunted something like 'Good riddance.'

Working on the late shift this week, Marina was probably still asleep when I knocked on the door. But the third time I knocked, she talked through the door.

"Who's there?" she asked, sleepily.

"It's me Marina, it's Nadine, I need to talk to you right away!"

"Just a minute Nadine, I have to go to the bathroom—and get my robe. Be right back," she said.

Relieved that she was going to open the door, I waited patiently. It gave me time to speculate about what was happening to me. Did this happen to others? Was this what some of the girls whispered about at school? I hadn't asked any questions about it when I saw them huddled in a corner. I thought it was something they were ashamed of—like dandruff, or a rash, or a new boyfriend.

I was grateful when Marina came to open the door. She looked like she'd just had a bath. The ends of her wavy hair were still wet and her cheeks were pink. She was tying the belt around her blue robe.

"What's wrong, honey? Did you fight with your ma again? Lord, I guess you two will never get along."

She continued talking as she walked into the kitchen to put on the coffee pot. "Your ma has such a fierce temper, I don't know how she gets along with anyone these days. She's even getting worse now, after losing that baby."

It was time for me to interrupt. "No Marina, that was last night. And, Ma did all the fighting—I didn't fight at all."

"Well then what is so urgent Nadine? I thought you said 'right away' for a reason. What's the problem?"

"Yeah, well, *this* is the problem," I said, showing her the blood stained panties that I had in my pocket. "What *is* this? And what do I do to make it stop? . . . I promise, I didn't do *nothin'* to make myself bleed." And even though I had told myself that I would not cry, I started to blubber.

"Oh," was all that Marina said. She put her arm around my shoulders and held me close for a minute or two.

"Well, you're right honey. This *is* a problem. Did you tell your ma?" she asked.

"No! I don't want Ma to know about it. That's why I'm here—I know *you* won't get mad, and I had to find out what to do," I continued while the tears streamed.

Marina was very quiet for a long time, while we stood together. Then she sighed, kept her arm around my shoulder, and led me to a kitchen chair. "Okay Nadine, let's sit down, take a deep breath, and figure this out together You do know that your mother will have to know, sooner or later?"

"Okay, but later is better," I said feeling relieved when she'd said that we could figure this out together.

"First tell me how to make it stop!" I said, as the crying slowed down.

"I guess that's our first problem, honey. It's not going to stop."

"WHY NOT?"

Then came the long discussion about why not, and what for, how often, how long, and what to do about this monthly event. Marina even gave me a belt, and safety pins, and a funny pad she called a 'Kotex'. She showed me how to fold the ends and helped me get it on. I felt so lucky that I had Marina for a friend.

"Listen now Nadine, you understand that this is just temporary. Just for today. Now you have something that's hard for you, but you *have* to tell your mother. She won't get mad at you, 'cause she had the same thing for a long time—until she lost the baby. I'm sure she'll understand."

"Do you have this too?" I asked Marina.

"Yes, Nadine, me too, and all girls around eleven, twelve, or thirteen. That's why I'm sure your ma can't get mad for something like this—something you couldn't stop from happening."

"That never made any difference before," I said.

"Well . . . you want me to go with you? Be there when you tell her? Would that make it easier for you?"

I thought about what Marina was offering. And I knew that Ma would not dare hit me if Marina was there. But after all Marina had done already, I thought I might be able to do this by myself.

Leaving Marina's apartment, I took two steps toward our door, then stopped. I *couldn't* go in there. No way I could face Ma all by myself. I knew what was waiting for me on the other side of that door. There would be yelling and screaming, and I would be crying, and the boys would be standing there watching . . . And I just couldn't face that right now. So I turned around and went back to knock on Marina's door.

She smiled when she opened the door, "Well, young lady, I see you did that job in a great big hurry," she teased.

My lower lip quivered, "I couldn't do it all by myself. I'm sorry." Tears welled up again. This was not going to easy at all.

Marina held the door open, and I went in quick, before she could change her mind.

"No need to cry, Nadine, you can't be brave all the time. Come on in, coffee is almost ready. We can have breakfast together."

It was lovely, having breakfast in a quiet room sipping milk with coffee and sugar, and eating toast and jam. I was so glad that Marina did not like oatmeal.

The radio played soft music and we didn't have much to say until breakfast dishes were washed and stacked in the dish rack. Then Marina turned the radio off, sat at the table with me, and took my hands.

"I know how hard this is for you honey, but you got to live with your ma for a few years yet," she said

"I know. But why does Ma hate me, Marina? I can never do anything right. This is just going to be one more reason to punish me for something. I think I'll need for you to help me a little, if you still want to. Ma won't show how mad she is if you come with me. I don't think she can get so mean if you're there, can she?"

"Probably not," Marina said, hesitating for a minute. Then she seemed to make up her mind about something.

"Nadine, I'm going to take a chance with you. I think you're smart enough to understand something that I probably shouldn't tell you. But I'm going to tell you anyhow—if you can promise not to ever tell anyone. You do know how to keep a promise?"

I was puzzled. Marina was talking about secrets. Kids had secrets, and grown-ups had secrets, but I didn't know much about when grown-ups shared secrets with kids. But, figuring I could promise Marina anything after what she did for me this morning, I thought I could keep a promise.

"It's kind of a long story I have to tell you about your ma, so let's get more coffee," Marina sighed. The warm milk with a little coffee tasted good, and I waited for Marina's story.

"Your ma grew up in a bad neighborhood in a big city called Birmingham. That's in the state of Alabama in the South. Maybe you could look it up on your U.S. map at school? Your ma's dad was kind'a mean, and her ma did house cleaning for a rich lady in the city, and was hardly ever at home. Your ma never had any friends of her own, and had to work in her dad's grocery store every day after school. She was only allowed to talk with people in her family. Well, when she dropped out of school, she worked in her dad's store full time. She was probably a good lookin' gal by the time she was sixteen. Then she met a guy named Danny. Danny delivered fresh fruit to the store, and told Helen how pretty she was. Well, long story short, she fell for him, hard. They found a way to get together, and that's when the tough times started."

Marina waited for me to say something, but I just wanted to hear more. Ma never said anything about Danny, or her family, or when she lived in Birmingham.

"You with me so far, Nadine? Got any questions?"

I shook my head.

"Okay. Well, when her folks found out she was in the family way, that means she was pregnant, they didn't want any more to do with her, and told her to get out of their house. Danny was not going to marry her, and she had nowhere to live. She was completely on her own. You know what's comin' next Nadine?"

"I guess she's gonna have a baby by herself?" I asked. "And was that going to be me?"

"Yep, you got it right. Now, there's Helen, all alone, a baby coming, and her ma and pa that don't want her around. What do you think she can do about that?"

"I don't know, I guess she gotta get welfare?"

"Couldn't get welfare in Alabama then. But Helen's uncle tells her there's great welfare in California, hands her a hundred dollars, and puts her on a train to Los Angeles."

"All by herself?"

"All alone—pretty brave, huh? Next thing is—well, a couple things happen in Los Angeles, then Helen ends up here in San Francisco. Tries to get a job—but all she knows how to do is work in a grocery store, stack soup cans, and put out fruit for display. Besides, she can't work regular hours with a baby to take care of. So Helen gets on welfare just like her uncle said to do, and tries to keep off the streets. At first she has enough to rent a room, feed you, and keep things going, but pretty soon it gets too hard to keep up."

"Is that where Charlie comes in?" I asked.

"That's exactly what happens. Charlie tells Helen that with that welfare check he can keep Helen off the streets, pay the rent, and do the grocery shopping. That's why Charlie became so important to your ma, she really needed him when she was on the street and struggling to take care of you at the same time. She was ready to do anything to feel safe, and Charlie promised to take care of everything. But he also wanted more babies, so that was fine when your brothers and Emily came along. But that's a new problem for Helen—now that there won't be any more babies.

"So . . . I'm not going to go on and on, Nadine. Your ma tells me these things when we get together. When I'm home from work, and you kids are still in school, me and her get together for coffee—but only if Charlie's not around. There's just one more thing I want to say, then we'll need to go see your ma, and tell her about your problem, okay?"

By this time, I was wide eyed with wonder at having learned so much about Ma and Charlie. I was so interested in her story that almost forgot about myself.

"Okay," I agreed.

"Now, you said you wondered why your ma hates you, Nadine? Well, sometimes when bad things happen to people, they feel trapped. It makes them frustrated. And then they get angry 'cause they can't do anything about it. I don't think Helen really hates you, Nadine. I think she gets mad because she remembers all those awful things that happened with her folks. She looks at you and you remind her of how her troubles started. Now, I know that's not fair, and it was not your fault, but can you understand a little better why she gets mad at you?"

After taking a deep breath, I tried to think of how Ma must feel when she looks at me. Maybe she's thinking if it wasn't for me, she would never be in such a mess.

Marina took my hand as we walked across the hall to face Ma together. "Remember your promise, Nadine. Not a word about anything I said. Your ma would *really* be mad if she knew what I told you."

The boys were probably out playing, and it was naptime for Emily, so it was a good time to get this over with.

11. Confrontation

I WAS DETERMINED to keep my conversation with Marina a secret, just as I had promised. When I opened the door to our apartment. Ma looked up, and before seeing Marina, she growled at me.

"Where the hell'eve *you* been?"

Marina came in behind me but spoke before I answered, "Hi Helen, hope it's alright with you that Nadine had breakfast with me this morning."

"Hello Marina, didn' see you there. Sure, you c'n feed that one any time. She eats more than she's worth anyhow."

"Now don't be so hard on Nadine, Helen. She had big news this morning and you weren't up yet, so she came over to tell me about it."

Marina jabbed me with her elbow . . . I didn't know how to start.

"Well girl, speak up, what news ya got?"

"Well, I was bleeding . . . and Marina told me I got my first period."

"Oh yeah, that," Ma said shrugging, "not a big deal ya know, happens t'us all."

Marina came to the rescue again, "You got a spare cup a' coffee Helen?"

"Sure, sure. Go get Marina a cup o' coffee, Nadine . . . Then you'se c'n look in da bottom draw in ma bedroom—I got haf'a half box Kotes lef' thea. You'se can have 'em. I'se not gonna need 'em no more."

And that's all there was to it. Ma didn't throw a fit after all, and we just didn't talk about it anymore. All I needed was that little belt with tags that Marina gave me, and a couple of safety pins. The hardest part of it all were the questions that two curious boys kept asking.

I had Marina to thank for helping me with that difficult transition. *(That means to change from one stage to the next.)* And I'm really glad that I went back to her for help with telling Ma as well.

12. The Tests

WHEN WE HAD LEFT the Tenderloin Family Center, Mr. Lewis told us that we needed to come back, one at a time, for some "individual testing." The tests would be given by someone like a social worker, who was called a psychologist, and this psychologist would get information to help decide what each of us needed. We were told that the tests would be fun, and we would get to draw pictures and work puzzles, along with answering some questions.

In the weeks that followed, it was my job to schedule after school appointments for the boys and for myself. Ma was going to take care of getting Emily to the Center. She wasn't too keen on any of this. But the words "find out what we needed" convinced her to go along. I knew that if there was any possibility of getting something, she was going to make the effort. She set things up so that she would take Emily in after the three of us kids were finished.

I got an appointment for Jimmy first, thinking there might be less fuss from Tom, if I worked it out that way. He would not want to miss out, if Jimmy had all the fun. So after school, I took Jimmy back to the Center for the "further testing."

"Why do I have to go back again?" Jimmy complained. "I already answered all the questions they asked. I don't know any more answers."

"I don't think it will be the same questions, Jimmy. I think it will be more like arithmetic, and spelling questions like you have in school. You don't have to worry, there are other things too, like drawings, and games and stuff."

I didn't really know what kind of questions there would be, but I had to make up something that would make Jimmy feel okay with it. He looked worried, and I knew that he would stop talking if he was really worried, then the tests wouldn't come out right.

I sat on the bench in the waiting room while Jimmy was having his interview. Good thing I brought a good book with me, cause it took a lot longer than I thought.

Jimmy was smiling when he came back to the waiting room, and I asked, "Well, how was it?"

"Some of it was fun, like at the end, I could draw pictures of people and houses and trees and things. I looked at some funny pictures an' told stories 'bout 'em. But some o' the questions was kinda hard, and I couldn't answer all of 'em."

"Sounds like you had a good time though," I said. "What kind of people did you draw?"

"I drew a picture of Charlie, cause he's skinny and has funny hair," Jimmy said smiling. "I couldn't make his red hair though, I could only use a pencil, no crayons."

"Better not tell Charlie you made a picture of his funny hair," I said with a grin, picturing Jimmy's perfect description of Charlie.

"Na'a, I ain't gonna tell Ma neither."

The following day was Tom's turn, and I wondered how he would feel about this testing business.

"Well, Jimmy said it was not too hard, and he had some fun things to do, so I guess it won't be so bad," Tom said, trying to pretend he was not worried.

He came away smiling too. "She said I did real good, and I'm probably smarter than Jimmy too."

"Did she really say that?" I asked, knowing Tom liked to tell stories, especially when it made him sound good.

"Well, she did say I did a good job. I jus' know I's smarter than Jimmy. She didn' have ta tell me."

When it was my turn, I kinda' looked forward to it. But when I got to the Center, my testing was a little different. Mr. Lewis said that the psychologist who was scheduled for me, was sick that day. He asked would I mind it if he did the job.

"I was a psychologist too for a few years," he explained. But then they said the Center needed an administrator, more than another psychologist, so I took the job. I thought I was moving up in the world, but it's not as much fun. So, if it's okay with you, I'll see if I still remember how to do this."

"Sure," I said, wondering what the difference was between psychologist, social worker, and an administrator. *I gotta look that up*, I thought.

So Mr. Lewis gave me blocks, had me follow mazes, do math problems and puzzles. There were so many questions, I thought I would never be finished.

"Nadine, I know how much you like words. Can you tell me what the word *connection* means?"

"Sure," I said, "a connection is when two things come together."

Then he asked me to explain the meaning of *obedience* and *revenge*. After that, I had to remember some sentences that he said, and it was easy to do that. It was fun repeating things like *Tom Brown's dog ran quickly down the road with a big bone in his mouth,* but I was getting tired and began to squirm. Mr. Lewis had a warm smile and always sounded interested in my answers. Now and then he looked at a watch as I answered questions. I wondered if an alarm would ring if I took too long to answer, so I asked about it.

"How much time do I have left 'til the alarm goes off?"

Mr. Lewis laughed. "You don't need to worry about that, Nadine. This watch is just to let me know how long it takes you to finish something. There's no alarm and no time limit, so you can take as long as it takes. Besides, most things on the test are not timed at all. Ignore the watch if you can, or I'll put it away if it bothers you."

I considered asking him to put the darn thing in his pocket or something, but he was so nice about explaining it, I just smiled and said, "That's okay, I just wondered."

"We're almost finished anyhow," Mr. Lewis said, tucking the watch into a little box so I couldn't see it. "I just want you to tell me what you see in these pictures. Can you tell me who's in them and what you think they might be doing or talking about?"

After talking about the photos, and drawing a picture of a person, I was finished with the tests.

Mr. Lewis looked pleased, "You did very well on these tests, Nadine."

"Isn't that what you tell all the kids?" I asked, remembering what Jimmy and Tom had reported.

Mr. Lewis laughed again. "Yes, I guess we do say that a lot, but mostly it's true. If kids are doing the best they can, then they're doing very well, aren't they?"

I nodded. "Yeah, I guess that's true," I said.

"Now that all the kids have had a turn, we will need to have your mom come in with Emily, then we'll have a conference with her about all the testing."

"What are you gonna tell her about my tests?" I said. An uncomfortable feeling started in my stomach.

"Don't you worry. She will get an excellent report on all of your testing."

When I got home, Ma asked a lot of questions about the tests. She asked what the questions were and what we answered. I think she wanted to be ready for what was coming when they did the tests with Emily.

Ma insisted that I go with her when she brought Emily to the Center for her tests. "Charlie ain't intr'sted a'tall 'bout this testin' business. Jes' keep' tellin' me to ask for more money. Don' undastan' what goin' on wid' tha' man these days . . . 'Sides, you been goin' there three time' now. You know what to do, so you comin' wid us."

I could tell that Ma was worried about something to do with Charlie, but I didn't know exactly what. Sounded like she wasn't sure about it either.

"Ain't too far for Emily to walk, with both you an' me helpin,'" Ma said firmly. And that was that—both of us would go for Emily's tests, and I missed another day of school.

Ma got Emily cleaned up good. Put on her best pink t-shirt and pants. They were nice and clean from the last batch of laundry I did on the weekend. Emily really looked cute, and seemed happy to be going out. She walked along with a smile, holding on to Ma, then holding on to me, whenever she got tired of walking by herself.

When we arrived at the Center, Mr. Lewis said that he would do the testing with Emily too, just like he did with me. That made Ma smile for some reason.

"I'm glad it's going to be my turn again. The psychologist is still sick with a bad flu, and won't be back until next week," he said, returning Ma's smile. "I'm not glad she's sick you understand, I'm just glad that I have the opportunity to do more testing."

Mr. Lewis asked Ma if she had any questions, said hello to Emily, then winked at me. I giggled. Emily frowned when Mr. Lewis took her by the hand. I wondered if she might object to taking a stranger's hand. She looked around to make sure Ma and I were both following, then she went along without protesting.

Mr. Lewis talked to Emily while we walked through the office space, "Emily, why don't we go into that big room in the corner," he said. "There are more chairs in there, so everyone can sit."

The big room had lots of drawers, and shelves with all kinds of toys. It had and kid-sized chairs and a round table that was just low enough where Emily could sit comfortably. Me and Ma sat in regular chairs.

"Would you like a cup of coffee, Mrs. Williams?" Mr. Lewis asked.

Ma shook her head, and he looked at me, eyebrows raised, "A glass of water for Nadine?" I shook my head too.

"Now, I'll be working with Emily at this little table. I will ask her to do things and answer questions. I might ask you two to help sometimes, but you can't give her any answers, or show her what to do, okay?"

"She ain't gonna answer much," Ma said, in a low voice.

I didn't say a thing, but was thinking this is going to be very interesting. And it was.

Wide eyed, Emily looked at the toys on the shelves, and pictures on the walls. She let Mr. Lewis seat her at the low table where he handed her a plain plastic doll. Emily looked at the doll, then looked at Mr. Lewis.

"Sure, you can play with the doll, Emily. That's what dolls are for." A warm smile came with the invitation, and Emily slowly examined the toy. She bent the arms and folded the legs, then put the doll down.

"Emily, can you show me your nose?" he asked.

Emily looked at Mr. Lewis, but did not respond.

Mr. Lewis demonstrated, "Here is my nose," he said, touching his nose with his finger.

"Where is your nose? Can you point to your nose?"

Emily looked at Ma, who nodded, "Go ahead, show 'im your nose."

Emily look puzzled, then pinched her nose.

Everyone smiled, sighing in relief, and Mr. Lewis said, "Thank you Emily, that was very good."

Pointing to eyes, mouth and ears followed, with Emily gaining confidence all along. Then Mr. Lewis handed Emily the little doll again.
"Emily, can you show me where the doll's hands are?" Mr. Lewis asked.

Emily looked at Mr. Lewis, then at the doll. She looked at Ma, and looked at me. I nodded my head at her, but didn't say anything. She looked at the doll, picked it up by the arm and found the doll's hand.

"Good, Emily, you found the doll's hand," Mr. Lewis said, smiling. Ma smiled too.

Mr. Lewis then asked Emily to find different parts of the doll. Mostly she got things right, but had trouble with "back" and "front."

After questions about the doll, Mr. Lewis put the doll away and brought out a big picture of a boy in a red jacket, black shorts, white socks and black shoes. It was really a stupid picture. Nobody dresses like that.

"Here is a picture of a little boy, Emily, can you show me the boy's shoes?" he asked. Emily pointed.

"Good for you Emily!" Mr. Lewis said, with a big smile.

I couldn't figure why he was so excited about this, but he seemed very pleased.

"Now, let's find the boy's coat," he said

Emily did, then looked up at Mr. Lewis. It was like she was waiting for the next question, and more praise. I think she was happy with this game.

"Emily, what color is the boy's coat?"

Silence from Emily.

"She doesn't talk yet," Ma reminded him.

Mr. Lewis nodded, took Emily's hands, looked in her eyes and said, "Is the coat blue, Emily?"

Nothing from Emily, but a blank stare. She turned to look at me, but I didn't say anything.

Mr. Lewis turned to Ma and asked, "I know that Emily doesn't talk, but does she use any sign for 'yes' or 'no' when she wants or doesn't want something?"

"She just cry when she don't like something, and smile when she does," Ma said.

"Okay, since she can point to representations, let's try some more pictures to find out what words she understands."

Mr. Lewis took out a book of pictures and opened it to the first page. "Look, Emily here are some pictures for you to look at. There's a picture of a ball, a shoe, a car, and a hat. Can you show me the picture of the ball?"

Emily looked at him, then looked at the pictures and put her hand on the picture of the ball.

Mr. Lewis was pleased at the response, and praised Emily for her correct answer. He then asked Emily to select one of the four pictures shown on the next page. After the first few pages, the pictures got harder for Emily, but she kept on pointing, and looking up at Mr. Lewis for approval. I didn't think she understood what she was pointing to, so when

Mr. Lewis asked Emily to point to the picture of a stove, I raised my hand to get his attention.

"Yes Nadine?"

"Emily can't point to a stove because she never saw a stove before. We just have an electric hotplate."

Mr. Lewis raised his eyebrows. "Oh. I should have thought about that. Well, I think it's time for us to stop here anyhow," he said. "We've kept Emily working long enough."

Mr. Lewis turned to Ma and thanked her for bringing Emily in. He also thanked Emily, then turned to me. "Thank you for pointing out something I failed to consider, Nadine. That was very helpful. Now wait just a minute."

Mr. Lewis went to his desk and brought something over. "Here is a special sticker for Emily. It's a sticker of an elephant. Elephants are very wise and don't say much—even though they know a lot."

Emily walked away with a big smile. Me and Ma walked away happy that the testing was over. I grinned all the way home, proud of myself for helping. I liked Mr. Lewis. At that moment, I decided to be a psychologist too when I grew up.

13. Test Results

IT WAS JUST BEFORE CHRISTMAS vacation when I found out anything about Ma's final interview with Mr. Lewis and the other psychologists at the Family Center. She mentioned that the social worker was there too, but didn't say much, except that she would do all the work to see that things were "followed up."

It was a rainy day, and the two boys were down the hall playing a game with their friend Randy. I was in the bedroom with Emily, looking at pictures in a magazine. She would point to a picture and look at me to name it, and then go on to another picture. I think Emily had learned something new at the Center, and was enjoying the "pointing" game. I think she was pretending to be Mr. Lewis, maybe? Once an a while, I would ask *her* to point instead, and if I'd already named the picture, she would sometimes remember and point. She always looked at me for approval, and smile when I said she was getting it right.

Ma and Charlie were in the kitchen, and I could hear most of what they were talking about. I wanted to hear everything they said, and playing with Emily was not taking much attention.

"You mean they don' say nuthin' 'bout raisin' the welfa' money?" Charlie was asking.

"Now you listen hea' Charlie! They say we gotta think o' the kid's education first. They look at welfare after that get settled.'"

"Yeah, sounds ta me like a run aroun'. What they say about the kids anyway?" Charlie sounded reluctant.

"Which one ya' wanna' hear 'bout first?" Ma asked.

"Don' matta' ta me, jus' start wid' them boys. They got testin' first."

"Okay then, we startin' with Tom. They say he did all the tests fine, and looks like he got some brains. But, they kep talkin' bout "social skills" to worry 'bout. They say he have trouble gettin' along wid' other kids, and . . ."

"Hell, we a'ready know that. Don' need no fancy test ta tell us he got a nasty tempa.'"

"Yeah, *we* know that. But they wan'na give him some counselin' at school. Could he'p him get along bettah, they say. I say *sure*, you go ahead, give him anythin' ta make him settle down. Whippin' ain't done no good."

"Okay, okay, what about Jimmy, den?" Charlie was getting impatient, I could tell. He grumbled something else, but I couldn't hear exactly what he said.

"Well, we ain't got no gen'yus there, ya' know. But he can do betta in testin' with da stuff he do with his hands. And they got a good idea, he maybe need a special class ta help him with readin', writin', and talkin'.

"Special class? Wha' good it gonna do ta have the otha' kids call him stupid?"

I thought it might be time for Charlie to get up and leave. He was not hearing anything he wanted to hear. Test results were all about us kids, not about Ma getting more money from welfare.

"You ain't heard nothin' yet," Ma continued, her voice dropping. "Emily need' to go to a special school. Mr. Lewis said she got some "po-ten-shal" but needs a lotta help ta develop basic skills."

"What da hell ya' sayin?" Charlie erupted, a frown practically split his face in two. "My lil' Emily goin' where?"

"Now you jus' keep your shirt on, Charlie. This here school is special for kids jus' like Emily. Slow in learnin' ta talk, an' still ain't trained on'a potty. She's almos' four years old, Kris'sake, and no sign o' wantin' ta grow up. I can't do no more than I done, an' she need somethin' else pretty quick. And that's jus' how it is mista', like it or not!"

I think Charlie heard Ma's determination. Though he kept grumbling and complaining, I just knew he was not going to make a big fuss. That tone in her voice was firm.

"An' what about the smart one?" Charlie asked.

"Well, another story on her. You sure you wann'a hear about a kid not yer own?" she said.

What was it Ma said? Were they talking about me? Was she saying that I was the only one *not* Charlie's kid? I always knew that each of us was different, but were the other three all Charlie's kids?

"Yeah, tell me, might as well," Charlie said.

"Well, they said maybe she's too smart for regula' class. They say special class for her too, but for *high achievers*. They might even let her skip a grade. I'll be thinking about that—not so sure it's a good idea." Ma said. Then her voice got very quiet, and though I tried, I heard no more of that conversation.

"Maybe with kids bein' gone all day, I can get a job an' bring in some cash." Ma's voice became clear again. She sounded like she was either relieved or pleased to be thinking about doing something outside this place, in the real world.

That night, I fell asleep thinking of all the changes comin' soon. I wondered about Emily's school, and Jimmy's special class, and Tom's counseling. And then there were all those things that I had learned about me!

14. Christmas Vacation

I COULD NOT BELIEVE so much had happened in the short time between Thanksgiving and Christmas vacation. I got my period for the first time, all of us kids had finished our tests at the Family Services Center, and plans were made that would separate us all from each other. It was interesting and exciting, and I was looking forward to all the changes, but a bit scared too.

In the meantime, the two week Christmas vacation from school did not turn out to be so much fun. After learning that Emily would be going to school in the Fall, Ma started to change things around, like she had an itch to get things started. Maybe she was thinking that next Fall, with all of us out of the house between eight in the morning 'till three in the afternoon, she would have time to herself. I wondered if she might be thinking about looking for a job when school started in September. But between now and then she was still stuck with taking care of Emily.

One afternoon a social worker from the Welfare office paid us a visit. The boys had gone off to play with Randy, and I was doing homework, when there was a knock at the door. Ma crushed her cigarette and answered.

"Good afternoon, Mrs. Williams. My name is Sandra, and I'm from the Department of Welfare." She extended her hand, and stated cheerfully, "I've come to evaluate the situation and help with Emily."

"I don't need no help with Emily. We need more money for this whole family," Ma said. I wondered why she sounded so angry, when someone was offering to help.

"Well, I know that Mrs. Williams, and we are paying attention to that too. We intend to look into things here very thoroughly."

Sandra then had some questions for Ma, asking her about "resources", number of children in the family, living space, etc.

"Well now, finding you a larger space is a priority for sure, but bigger welfare check may not be possible. In the meantime, Emily has qualified for special education services, and there are some conditions to be met," Sandra explained.

"Whad'da'ya mean conditions? I thought it was all settled about Emily going to school."

"Well, it *is* all settled, except for one thing. Louise Lombard school cannot enroll children unless they are toilet trained. The teaching staff is not qualified for that type of training, and the Department of Health is very strict about health conditions in public schools."

Sounded like trouble brewing, I thought.

"So, now you're telling me Emily can't go to school like they promised? Jes' like everything else. Promises that don' mean nothin'."

"Not so, Mrs. Williams, we *do* keep promises. It's just that Emily must be able to take care of this one thing, and she needs to learn to do it by herself."

"She ain't gonna learn, I tell ya. I tried everythin' I know and nothin' works," Ma insisted.

"Do you have a potty chair for her to learn on, Mrs. Williams?"

"You think we got extra money for fancy things like that?"

"Well, it's something we need. So next time I come here, I'll bring one, then we can get started. It's only December Mrs. Williams, we'll have time to get Emily ready for school by September. If we work together, I'm sure we can do it."

"Well, you jus do what ya gotta do Ms. Sandra, and good luck to ya," Ma said, a challenge in her voice.

That was how it all began, the transition. *(That means to start making changes.)* It was a long time between now and September, but I could hardly wait. Until then, things would go on as usual . . . or so I thought.

"WE GOTTA HAVE MORE money, mista'," Ma complained when Charlie arrived with groceries on Sunday. "I gotta get things ready for when we move outa this place. I need another bed for the kids, and some cash right now to get a couple of Christmas things for the boys. They been after me ta get a soccer ball, and other stuff for their games. They ain't gonna quit their fussin' 'til I do somethin'."

"Aw now settle down Helen, I c'n get all that all stuff, and prob'ly get a few trinkets for Emily too. We c'n wrap 'em up real nice for Christmas."

Ma was not very happy with his answer. "Dammit Charlie, what happen' wid all the money in them welfae' checks, anyhow?"

That old argument was starting again over Ma's welfare money. And this usually lasted a long time. They went at it back and forth, and back and forth, until I decided I could avoid listening to it if I went for a walk. Ma said it would be okay to take Emily, if we didn't stay out too long.

When Emily and I got back, they were having a quiet cup of coffee, and I assumed *(That means that I guessed.)* that they had settled the problem.

"Come on ova' hea' honey, we gotta talk to you," Charlie said, as I was taking off my jacket.

Tom and Jimmy had come back from Randy's, and were in the bedroom wrestling. Ma yelled at them, "Hey, you two, get in hea'. You boys gonna be in it too."

When all three of us were standing beside the table, Charlie began to explain. "Me an' your ma, we had a great ide' an' we got a plan to git more money for Christmas—so you guys c'n have some new things."

I looked at Ma. She was nodding her head. "Time for you kids ta be helpin' out a bit now that you gettin' older," she said.

I waited, wondering what plans they had made.

"We got a lotta rich people in San Francisco. Rich people in this city, they get out ta shop and go see movies, an' plays, an operas at Christmas time," Charlie said with a sly smile. I could practically see the wheels spinning in his head. "Maybe turn loose some change, for poor li'l kids like you?" He blinked a couple of times and turned his chin to look wistful. But I could see it was all fake. His slimy smile turned my stomach.

I didn't say a word, but glanced at Ma. She was grinning too. *Then, I got it.*

"You want us. . . to go begging. . . for money?" I asked.

"Bes' time o'year, for rich people givin' to the poor folks," Ma said.

And that was the plan they'd decided on. Me and the boys were to dress ragged, and go stand on the corners, or near the big stores. On Opera nights, we were to go where the taxi's let off rich people, so we could get the men to show off to their ladies how generous they could be. When the Orpheum ticket booth opened, we needed to go wait near the box office to catch people when they had hands in their pockets.

"It shouldn' take long for you to bring in enough for me to make a good Christmas dinner. Or we could even buy some toys for Emily, and get new clothes for everybody," Ma agreed.

"Now you Nadine, you stand back a bit, the boys is smaller, people give more money to the li'l kids," Charlie directed.

Charlie and Ma tried to make it all sound like simple fun to beg for money. But I didn't think it was so simple, or much fun, or anything good at all.

15. Another Conspiracy

CHARLIE WAS EAGER to show us where to wait at the best department stores off Market Street. He said that the doorways at Magnin's and City of Paris were perfect places to meet up with rich ladies doing Christmas shopping. Waiting at the corners was okay, but we should not bother with the bus stops. People waiting for a bus were not going to have enough money to give away.

"And in the evenin' there's a gold mine at da Opera House and picture shows are good too," Ma added.

At night Charlie planned the strategies. He knew what time the Opera was playing, showed us where to wait for the taxis, and how to put out our hands. He knew when the shows started at the theaters, and told us the best time to be there, before and after the shows.

"Now Honey, you stand back a bit, let the young uns go first. You be there ta look after 'em, and you keep the money safe," Charlie directed.

And that's how we spent Christmas vacation—learning to beg for money. I knew the way street people begged all the time, so it didn't scare me. Some of them just sat on the sidewalk, put their hat on the ground and waited. But I never thought we would need to do something like this. I was ashamed and angry that we had to be asking for money. I was afraid that some of the kids in my school would see me on the streets, or maybe the teachers we knew would be shopping and recognize us.

I had never liked Charlie, but I began to hate him for making us do this. I think I hated Charlie more during this Christmas vacation than I ever had hated anyone. And it was not a good feeling to be really mad at Ma either.

The days passed quickly enough, with waiting at department store entrances first; then waiting on the corners at Stockton and Geary, then

Powell and Geary; then going to the movie box offices. Once in a while we waited at the Opera House where they had musical shows.

One day we were standing there before a matinee at the Opera House. *(Matinee means middle of the day.)* A nice man took a look at us raggedy kids, and reached in his pocket while turning his head side to side—as though he felt sorry for us. He took out a ten dollar bill and handed it to me.

"You kids get yourselves something to eat," he said. "You look like you could use a good meal."

"Thank you," I said, dropping my chin, and feeling the shame rise up the back of my neck and into my cheeks.

Not right! I said to myself angrily. *This is all wrong! I might as well be walking the streets, asking guys if they wanted to party. Then at least the money would be mine, and I could spend it however I wanted.*

"Come on you two," I said, grabbing Tom and Jimmy by the collar. "You heard what the man said, we can all use a good meal. You heard him, this ten dollars is for us to get something to eat. And that's what we're gonna do."

"You's crazy Nadine. Ma will kill us if we don't bring back all the money we get. She said so, just as we went out the door, don't you remember?" Jimmy said.

"What are you gonna do?" Tom questioned. He was wary of defying Ma, but also seemed interested in what my plan was.

Looking at their worried faces, I tried to convince them that we would be doing the right thing, "The man said we should get something to eat! Compton's is just a block away, and I think it would be a great place for us to do just what he said. Ma doesn't need to know what the man said, or how much he gave us, or what we did with it. Got that? You already know how to keep a secret. Remember when we got chewing gum with that dime from her purse?"

I think that while trying to convince the boys, I was convincing myself at the same time. I looked at them, they looked at me, and they looked at each other. Then we all smiled, turned around, and headed for Market Street.

Passing the windows of Compton's many times, I had drooled when looking at the stacks of pancakes and waffles served on big plates. Butter and syrup were always oozing over those stacks. Some even had bacon and eggs on top.

It didn't take us but two minutes to get there, and it would not be far from home anyhow, so we wouldn't be losing much time. Ma would not expect us for another hour, and we had collected enough so that she should be satisfied with the rest we collected.

In the restaurant, I read the menu to Jimmy. Tom managed on his own, and we made quick decisions. Ten dollars was not much to cover three meals, so I was careful to make sure that if we shared, we might have enough money for all of us to get what we wanted. It was the first time that Jimmy had ever been in a real restaurant, so he was looking all around at things he had never seen before. Tom and I felt more grown up, because we had come here with Marina once. I had never forgotten that day, and neither had Tom.

When my stack of pancakes arrived, I put butter under each one, waited for the butter to melt a little, then poured syrup all over the top. I shared one of my stack with Jimmy, and it was just right with his bacon and eggs. Tom ordered a big waffle, smeared butter over it, then topped it off with strawberry jam. He let Jimmy have a bite to taste, but balked when I asked for a bite.

"There won't be any left if you take some too," he complained. I didn't have the heart to argue with him.

I was thinking of how he and Jimmy had stood out in the cold, hands outstretched for a quarter or a dime, saying "Please lady," and "Could you spare a little for me and my brother?" and "We're really hungry, mister." I smiled watching both of them devour their gooey meals and warm drinks.

When they finished every last morsel, I insisted they use the restroom, and told them to wash up good. "Be sure you wipe the sticky stuff off your mouth, and be ready to act grumpy instead of happy when we get home. Otherwise, Ma will smell the sweet stuff, and start asking questions," I warned. The boys came out of the restroom looking just as raggedy as before, but their hands were washed and mouths rubbed clean.

Ma didn't suspect a thing, and was happy with the money I handed her for the day's collection. The three of us had once more carried out a successful conspiracy. I fell asleep that night pleased with myself, and much less angry and hateful.

16. Charlie Trouble

CHRISTMAS VACATION ended at last, and after counting up all the money we had collected from two weeks of begging, Ma reminded Charlie about his promises, and handed him a wish list she had drawn up for him.

"Okay Helen, okay. Ya know I keeps my promises," he reassured her. And off he went to shop with a little over fifty dollars in quarters, dimes and a few dollar bills. Didn't take him long to come back with a shopping bag full. Sure enough, he had the baseball for Tom and the soccer ball for Jimmy. I got the big spiral notebook I asked for, and Emily had three little stuffed animals that she immediately fell in love with. There was something that looked like a diamond necklace for Ma, and everybody was happy.

I asked for the empty bag, so I could keep my notebooks together, and at the bottom of the bag I found the receipt from Salvation Army. Charlie had spent some of our money for us, but only a little more than half of it. I didn't ask any questions, cause Ma and Charlie would have a big fight, and since everybody was in such a good mood, I let it go. But I couldn't forget about it.

ONE AFTERNOON, about three weeks later, there was a hard knock on the door, like someone was using a stick, instead of knuckles. When Ma answered the door, I heard the surprised "Oh-h-h" in her voice. She let go of the doorknob then, and I saw Officer Phil standing there. But he had already told her something. That's when we learned the bad news about Charlie.

"What are you talkin' about? Whadda ya mean he's in jail?" Ma questioned, after letting go of the door.

Officer Phil, tried to explain, "Yeah, sorry. Charlie got caught selling coke, and one of the guys he sold to was a cop. They had to arrest him for drug trafficking."

After a muffled, “Oh God!” Ma stopped trying to talk. With eyes wide, and both hands folded over mouth and nose, she dropped her head and went quiet. That stringy yellow hair fell all over her face again.

Officer Phil waited for the news to sink in, then went on. “I saw him at the precinct a while ago, and he said that you would be expecting him to bring the groceries on Sunday. So I came to let you know he won’t be coming.”

Ma’s shoulders drooped, and I could see that her energy was draining away at the news. She stepped away from the door, so that Officer Phil could get in. After stepping inside, he closed the door behind him, as if to keep anyone from seeing him, or hearing what he had to say.

“How long he gonna’ be in jail?” Ma groaned. “What are we gonna’ do now? How will we get milk for Emily and other stuff, if Charlie ain’t gonna’ go fer it?”

“Well Ma’m, I suggest you ask some other friend to help, or get a grocery store to deliver? There is a “mom and pop” store not too far from here. I believe they might be able to help,” Officer Phil suggested.

“Charlie don’ like that store. He always go ta Safeway. He say prices is better there, and he could get more things,” Ma said, wringing her hands, and getting more and more squirmy.

“Sorry Ms. Williams, I only came to let you know about Charlie, so you would know he won’t be coming around to help,” Officer Phil said. “I won’t be able to do much about the groceries.”

He looked around the room, saw me and smiled, “Hello Nadine, any more trips to the library lately?”

“No sir, no more trips,” I said, without smiling back.

“Glad to hear that,” he said. Then nodding to Ma, he opened the door, stepped out, and was gone.

Thinking I could make Ma feel less scared, I said, “Don’t worry Ma, I can go shopping for you. Mr. Diem likes us kids.”

Ma took a deep breath, “Shut up! You’re not in charge o’ shoppin’. I take care of things ’round here. When I need he’p from you, I’ll say so.”

I could tell that Ma was really more scared than mad, but it was not a good idea for me to say anything more. I left Ma alone after that, though I wondered how things would get sorted without Charlie. He only came around once a week, but Ma waited for him to bring in groceries, and take care of the bills. I didn’t know who was going to do that now. Cashing the welfare check, and paying the rent were all things that Charlie did. He always knew what day the check came, and was right here when the mail arrived. Now Ma had to find another way to do it all.

Then I began to think it over. Maybe it was a good thing that Charlie would be gone for awhile. Maybe things would get better if Ma got out of here, and did some things for herself. She couldn't use the excuse of being pregnant anymore, so there was no reason for her to stay home all the time. Drinking coffee, smoking cigarettes, watching TV and cleaning up after Emily couldn't be that much fun. If she had some reason to get out more, it might be a good thing for us all.

THREE OF US KIDS were back in school now, looking forward to the end of the school year. I was getting good at avoiding Ma in her bad moods, keeping out of her way, and doing my homework on the bedroom floor instead of in the kitchen. She did start to go out more, especially on afternoons after I got home from school. While I looked after Emily, Ma could do the shopping and get to the bank. But when she got back home, she always found something I'd done wrong.

"What the Hell did you do, puttin' these things in the top drawer?" she shouted one day. She threw Emily's freshly washed, carefully folded shirts at me.

Without thinking I snapped, "Because you said ***not*** to put Emily's clothes in the ***bottom*** drawer." I should have known better, apologized, and kept my mouth shut. Ma's heavy right hand came up quicker than I could duck. It hit that left cheek again, and it really smarted, but I didn't cry. I was getting good at not crying, but I needed to get smarter about not saying what I was thinking.

"Don' you sass me, you little shit. Pick 'em up, and put 'em in the ***middle*** where they b'long."

WASHING THE LAUNDRY, keeping dishes washed, and taking care of Emily after school every day, took a lot of my time. But I kept up with my homework and learned new words almost every day. My list of words was getting so long that I was going to run out of room in my Christmas notebook. I would need to find another one soon.

Sandra, he social worker, came around every week to see how Emily was doing with learning to use the potty. She came one day after Ma had gone out shopping, so I started to help a little. I really wanted Emily to be ready for school, but was afraid she would never learn to do it all by herself. I told Sandra that I didn't think Emily would learn.

"It may take a bit longer for her, but Emily *can* learn to do this," she said with confidence. Her cheerful smile spreading to her dimpled cheeks made me feel like it was going to be possible.

Sandra used the potty chair and a doll to show Emily how. Emily watched the doll being placed on the potty chair, then later watched me on the toilet, and after a bit, began to get the idea. She learned to *sit* on the potty chair "just like the dolly," but it was a lot longer before she learned to *use* it. We all celebrated when she was successful, and Emily smiled when we clapped for her.

17. School Bussing

SPRINGTIME was pretty busy at school, with end of year tests, and trying to get ready for what the teachers were talking about as "preparing to move on." I really didn't realize that graduating was going to be such a big deal, until the whole school began to be called for assemblies in the auditorium. Graduation rehearsals took time, and the vice-principal got impatient with some kids who "refused to take this seriously."

After lunch one day there was a special assembly. Two counselors from junior high and high school came to talk to us about what to expect at the next level of our "journey in education." For us elementary school kids, a big change was about to happen, and this assembly was supposed to help us get prepared. They called it an *orientation* meeting.

The first counselor representative was tall and skinny. She had frizzy yellow hair and spoke in a squeaky voice. "By now I'm sure you all understand that next semester you will no longer be considered "elementary level students." You will experience a number of changes that might be considered strange to you. You will not be in the same class with the same teacher all day, as you do now. And you will not be with all your friends in the same room every day. Instead, you will be assigned to different classes, with different teachers, and may not see any of the friends you have now—in *any* of your classes. This is going to be your first step toward 'educational independence,' and you will need to learn how to adjust to a different system. Your daily schedules will be prepared in advance. These will be ready for you on your first day in the new school."

The skinny one with frizzy hair took a deep breath at this point, and then coughed a bit. She then introduced the other counselor, "Mrs. Schmidt will explain this in more detail," she said, coughing into her tissue.

Mrs. Schmidt was short and fat. She began with greeting us cheerfully. "Good morning future middle school students. Congratulations on completing the first six years of your education. Now, when you come to junior high, you will attend five different classes that meet for one hour each day. You may not meet for the same classes every day, except for the first hour each day, which will be in what is called a 'home room.' This is the only class that will meet each day, at the same time, with the same teacher. Your home room teacher will take attendance, review your grades in each class, and supervise your progress. After the home room class, students will then attend different classes throughout the rest of the day, moving from one classroom to another every hour."

The short, fat counselor stopped to take a drink of water, then continued. "Teachers at this level are all specialists in the subjects they teach. One specializing in our language will teach English, another will teach Science, another Math, and so forth. Your schedule will be determined by the course of study you plan to follow in high school. However, you will be allowed to make some choices, and these are called *electives*."

Mrs. Schmidt went on and on, but I had stopped listening since it sounded like we would just need to go along with whatever was already planned. It didn't sound like "independence" to me. It was only a different way of the school organizing things.

Then I heard some kids in the auditorium groan, others were buzzing with excitement. They must have heard about something different, so I started listening again. The word "bussing" was being passed around.

The counselor continued. "This new system of *school integration* will insure that students from different parts of the city will have the opportunity to become acquainted with those from other neighborhoods. We will then be in compliance with the new federal law that prohibits segregated schools. That means that students who live in different racial or ethnic neighborhoods will be bussed across town to other schools, and vice versa. The purpose is of desegregation is to provide an equal education opportunity to all children."

There was another buzzing sound in the auditorium, while kids talked to each other about the new system of riding busses from one part of the city to another.

Mrs. Schmidt used the microphone to increase the volume of her voice, and said, "I know that sounds like a big challenge for some of you, but it is a necessary adjustment that we can all make."

A tall boy in the second row shouted, "Latinos from the Mission will be all over the place. We goanna haf'ta learn ta talk Spanish?"

Another smart aleck in the same class, yelled, "Nah! We gon'na learn ta talk Chinese—first Cantonese, then Mandarin."

Everybody started laughing, but I was confused. *What was all this fuss about?* I wondered.

"Yeah, an' how about the tough black kids from Hunter's Point? They goanna be put in our new schools too?" another asked.

"Now, let's all calm down here," Mrs. Schmidt said. "Nothing has been decided yet about the distribution. Things will not change in your educational programs, but a more diverse population of ethnic and racial groups will be a good thing for all of us. We can learn about different kinds of music, and new kinds of food, and many other interesting things."

I could see she was getting a bit frantic. Her face turned red, and she began to shift from one foot to another. I could see that she was worried about keeping control of this meeting.

My problem was that I needed to learn some new words. I made a mental list of *compliance*, and *distribution* and *regulations*, and *integration* and *diverse*. Until I understood those words, how could I make up my mind about whether this bussing thing might be a good thing—or not?

18. Transitions

AFTER SCHOOL THAT DAY, I found out that Tom and Jimmy had heard about the change in neighborhood schools too. *Bussing* was the main topic of conversation between us kids that afternoon, but I mostly had a lot of questions. The boys' teachers had explained that the *bussing* would be for elementary level students, as well as for secondary kids. Ma listened, but didn't say anything, and that was not usual for her. I wondered what was going on in her mind about this school bussing. I wanted to know what grown-ups were thinking about their kids going to school all over town in school busses. Maybe I could ask Marina what she thought, even though she didn't have any kids. Besides, I was curious to know about those words I was not understanding very well.

As soon as the boys stopped yammering, I said abruptly, "Ma, I think I'll go over to visit Marina for a bit,"

That got a reaction right away. She yelled, "The HELL you will. You's gonna take care of Emily while I fix supper, that's what YOU gon'na do!"

I didn't say anything more then. I had forgotten that Ma didn't like to be told things that way. Later, while I set out the dishes for supper, I asked again, but more politely. That way she would think of it as her decision.

"Ma, do you think I could I go see Marina after supper—maybe after washing the dishes?"

"I'll think on it," Ma said abruptly, and I heaved a sigh of relief, knowing I would have pretty good chance, if I didn't make her mad again. There were things I needed to remember about how to ask Ma for things I wanted to do. Anyways, I was okay about waiting. That was something I had learned to do a long time ago. The possibility of getting some answers to my questions was worth the wait.

After we ate our boiled potatoes and greens with a little slice of Spam, I washed and dried the dishes in a hurry. Then I asked, politely this time, if I could visit Marina.

"Ya don't stay very long, ya hear?" Ma bellowed while focused on watching some silly TV show. I think it was called *We Love Lucille*, or something like that.

Marina had just finished her dinner when she answered the door, and asked if I wanted to join her for some dessert. I smiled, and said, "Yes Ma'm, I surely would. Thanks a lot."

While we sat at the table nibbling on cookies, I told Marina about the schools planning to bus kids from one place to another next year. I asked her about the words I was stuck on, and she said she would try to explain. I thought those were pretty hard words, but Marina patiently repeated things in a different way when I didn't get it right off. I thought she did a good job of explaining.

"Well Nadine, let's see," she started, resting her chin on her hand. Marina had such pretty curly hair. She said that she'd inherited those curls from her Latino mother. "I read a little bit about this problem in the *Chronicle* this morning. I think that, in this case, the word *compliance* means that the city schools have to obey a federal law against segregated schools. Maybe think of the word 'comply' in *compliance*, as being the same as 'obey'. You know what *obey* means, right?"

"Oh yes, I know what *obey* means," I answered confidently. "So *compliance* just means the schools have to obey the law?"

What's new about that? I thought to myself.

"That's right," Marina continued. "Seems that this law against segregation in schools has not been followed in San Francisco. So, in order to obey this law, San Francisco needs to distribute kids from segregated neighborhoods so schools can be more balanced."

I jumped right in without thinking, "Okay then, how about that word *distribute*? How do you *distribute* kids?" I asked.

Marina didn't mind about how blunt I asked the question, she just explained *distribution* too, then went on to talk about the other words that puzzled me. She explained the words *segregation*, *integration*, *discrimination*, and *diversification*. It all took a lot longer than I thought, so when I went back across the hall, Ma yelled at me again, 'cause I was late. But I didn't care, I just said "sorry" and got ready for bed. Marina had helped me with what I needed to know, and after scribbling the new words and their meanings in my notebook, I went to bed happy.

THE FOLLOWING DAY was Saturday, and while I was doing the laundry in the washroom downstairs, I practiced my new words. *Discrimination* was when there was a group of people who were treated unfairly in some way. So if kids in the Mission and Chinatown and Hunter's Point got less education, it was unfair, and the law was supposed to change that, by *distribution*. And *distribution* meant to mix up those kids with kids in other parts of the city. I think I understood better what bussing was all about, but I was still confused about why those kids got less education than others.

"Get your butt back up here," Ma yelled from the top of the stairs to the laundry room. "What are you doin' down there, washing one thing at a time?"

"No, it's just a big load this week, Ma," I answered quickly, feeling guilty. "I'll be right up."

Back in our room, Ma was still upset. "Can't understan' why it takes so damn long to do such a li'l thing as toss some clothes in a washin' machine! Do ya need ta count how many times it gets tossed around in the water or something?"

"No Ma, I just needed to make sure there was enough soap for the big load, that's all."

"Dammit! Nadine, I need to go to the bank before it close' up. The welfare check come in yeste'day and I couldn't leave Emily alone. Ya know I got'ta do everythin' now Charlie's in jail. Why can't ya' be here when I need ya'?"

"Sorry Ma. I'll take care of Emily now. You go ahead."

Ma was leaving me to take care of Emily more and more these days. I guess she was beginning to set up her own routine now. I was not complaining about that, but taking care of house chores was not my favorite thing to do, and Emily had never been good at playing by herself. She wanted to hang on to me all the time. I wanted to find someone who could tell me more about what my new school would be like. I needed to find out what to expect when school started again in September.

19. Official Plans

IT WAS MID-SUMMER now and finally, Family Services Agency called for an appointment. Yes, we had a phone now. It was one of the first things Ma did in her new life without Charlie. She was now cashing her own welfare checks, shopping for groceries, and taking trips to the thrift shops. She began to take charge of things in a very confident way, I thought. She was keeping track of what she spent, and even started saving a little for things she wanted to buy later, when we moved to a bigger place.

Ma was so busy doing things for the first time that my summer was spent taking care of Emily. We went for long walks around the park beside City Hall, and often to the library. I liked the section where I could read some children's books to her. Emily listened to the stories, but was mostly interested in the pictures, and pointed to those she wanted me to name. Once in a while, she would try to repeat what I said, which I thought was a good thing. When I praised her for the words she tried, she always smiled.

I was also learning how to cook simple things on the hotplate—like boiled potatoes. Once in a while Ma brought home some canned soup. I could cook soup just fine by adding water to each can I opened and heating it. As long as I watched for the pot boiling over, I did okay. I could also use a can opener real well, and could feed myself and the kids if Ma was late getting home for lunch. She told us that she was trying to find a job. Most of the food Ma brought home was in cans, so it was easy for me to fix.

Then came a phone call from Mr. Lewis, telling Ma it was time for a follow-up appointment. Ma said he wanted to see us as soon as possible, because the new school year was about to begin, and he was anxious to make sure everyone was ready to follow the plan. So we all went there together, to find out what we would do in September.

Mr. Lewis met us at the reception desk with a big smile and a hearty greeting.

"Well, Mrs. Williams, I'm glad to see that you have the whole family with you today. Let's find a room with places for everyone to sit and be comfortable. We have quite a lot to discuss."

We all followed him to the big room with the book shelves, the same place where we came with Emily for her testing. The first thing Mr. Lewis did was hand Emily a toy elephant from the shelf. Emily smiled, and hugged the toy. Maybe she remembered what Mr. Lewis had said about elephants being very wise, even though they didn't make much noise? I wondered how much she remembered of that day. Maybe she didn't remember anything but the good feelings she had when she was here.

Mr. Lewis sighed. "Okay, let's start with the plan for Emily. The social worker, Miss Sandra, reported that Emily has had a successful potty training experience, and is ready to start school. Now, Mrs. Williams, you know that Emily will need to ride a bus to school—nothing to do with the bussing for integration. All children who attend Louise Lombard School have always been provided with bus transportation."

Mr. Lewis addressed Ma, "You will be responsible to wait for the bus with Emily every day. The bus will arrive at the curb where you live each morning. The bus driver will have your address and will pick up Emily at the same time every day. The school will let you know about the exact time in about a week, when the schedule for all the children has been established."

Emily smiled. She knew they were talking about her.

Ma interrupted, "We got a phone now, and maybe you could write the number down so they could call me in plenty a' time."

"Oh yes, I have your phone number, and the school has that number as well. The principal will call you for an appointment soon, because a special plan will be made before school starts, to decide what Emily needs to learn. It's called the Individual Education Plan, or IEP for short."

Ma interrupted, "We already knows what Emily need ta learn. She need ta learn how ta talk."

"That's probably *one* of the goals, but there may be others. Now, this IEP meeting will be scheduled at your convenience, Mrs. Williams, and you don't need to worry about transportation. A school van will pick you up and take you home. Emily will not need to be there, but you can take her along if you wish."

Ma seemed to be mulling that over, "Ya mean I gotta go ta the school for this plan you's talking about?"

"That's right, Mrs. Williams. It won't take too long, but you will have a chance to see the school, and help the teachers decide what kind of program would be best for Emily."

Ma frowned, but didn't say anything else.

Mr. Lewis continued, "Next, we'll be talking about you, Jimmy." He turned toward Jimmy and nodded. "Though Jimmy was promoted to third grade, Mrs. Williams, he may need more intensive help with his school work than a regular classroom provides. A special education class might be helpful for him, and he does qualify for placement in that class at John Muir School. He already walks to school with Tom, so both will continue to attend John Muir. Neither of them is scheduled for bussing out of their neighborhood school. Now Jimmy will need an IEP meeting as well, so the principal will call you for that appointment soon."

Ma frowned and shook her head side to side, "Anotha' meetin'?"

Jimmy did not smile. I think he was worried about being teased by his previous classmates, or bullied by others.

Mr. Lewis continued, "Now Tommy is a very smart boy, but is not living up to his potential it seems. The schoolwork does not seem too difficult for him, but he has some problems with behavior. John Muir does not have a counselor on a regular basis, so I was wondering if Tom could come here, to talk with a social worker once or twice a week?"

Tom frowned, but Ma said that would be fine. "He need some talkin' to all right," she said, glowering at her oldest son.

"Now, we get to Nadine," Mr. Lewis said smiling at me. "We are suggesting that Nadine be placed in a class for advanced students. They have an opening at Lowell that would be perfect for her. The school also has a counselor who would work with setting up individual classes for her."

My jaw dropped. "Oh, but Lowell is not a junior high, is it?" I interrupted.

"No, but these special classes include students of several ages. It's an enrichment program that would work out well for you. What do you think Mrs. Williams?"

"Does that mean she'd finish out'a school earlier than if she went to a regula' junior high school?"

"No, she would still be identified as a junior high student, but be able to take some advanced classes. If things go well, she could take high school classes early and later even earn some credits for State College."

"Oh I'm not shu'a 'bout that," Ma interrupted, shaking her head.

"You don't think Nadine will be going to college, Mrs. Williams?"

"Nope. Nadine's smart enough ta go ta work, soon as she graduates high school," Ma said, firmly.

Mr. Lewis raised his eyebrows, and lowered his chin, "Well, maybe we can re-evaluate, after we know how well she does in this advanced class? We don't need to make a decision right now, do we?"

"Sure, eval-yate much as ya like," Ma said, sarcastically.

I knew by the tone of Ma's voice, that she had already made up her mind. But I would think about that later. I was more worried about what would happen to me on the first day of school—at Lowell High!

20. The Big Picture

AS THE SUMMER was coming to an end, I pondered our situation. Everyone in this family would be going in a different direction. It was like starting all over again—like beginning a new life. I told Marina that it was almost like a *fresh start*. I was excited about going to Lowell, and could hardly wait. But at the same time, I was really scared for myself, and also worried, about the rest of the family.

I was told that starting on the day after Labor Day, the school bus would pick me up early every morning, and bring me home late in the afternoon. Lowell High was a long way from Larkin Street, and I wouldn't be back until long after Emily and the boys came home. Could Ma manage to do everything by herself now? Would she be able to keep track of money, make plans with welfare, do all house chores, and look after the three kids?

The middle of August, Louise Lombard School called Ma to tell her what time Emily's planning conference would be. They said that Ma needed to be there by 9:30 on Tuesday morning. The school van would pick her up at 9:00, and she probably would not be back until around noon.

Ma decided she would not bring Emily along. "Marina's workin' on Tuesday mornin', so you gotta take care o' the kids Nadine," she ordered. "I ain't gonna' take Emily along. I got e'nuf ta think 'bout."

"Okay with me Ma," I said, trying to sound confident. "Is it alright if we go to the park by the library?"

"Jes' make shua' you be back hea' in time for they's lunch," Ma warned.

I think that Ma was so worried about the meeting that she couldn't think about anything else. I probably missed my chance to ask for streetcar money. We could have taken the Van Ness bus to Aquatic Park, maybe walk on the sand by the bay. Oh well, I wasn't sure it was such a good idea to take Emily all that way anyhow.

When Tuesday morning came, the boys were ready for our adventure, and Emily seemed in a good mood too.

"Better wear your warm jackets, you guys," I said, as the boys started to go out the door in shirt sleeves. "It's the middle of August for goodness sakes. San Francisco is always freezing in the middle of August."

I couldn't believe they were acting so weird about this walk. They walked this way to school all the time. They dressed like clowns, playing on these streets with their friends. Why was this short walk any different? Maybe, since Ma got dressed up this morning, they thought they should do the same? Maybe talking about going back to school was making them nervous too?

We waited with Ma until the school van picked her up, then took off toward City Hall. Emily was not upset when Ma got on the van and left. It was a good sign. The park was not a long distance from home, and the boys knew the way from our trips to the Opera House during Christmas vacation, so they raced ahead.

"Hey you guys, don't get so far ahead of us. You know Emily can't walk that fast," I yelled when they took off.

"Why do we hav'ta wait for Emily? We know where ta go. Besides, she's a real slow poke."

"You heard Ma! She said we stay together or else!" I warned. "And you *know* what that means."

"Yeah, yeah," Tom answered reluctantly. Jimmy didn't say anything, he just came back to where me and Emily were plodding along. He looked unhappy.

"Well Jimmy, looks like it won't be long before school starts again. Won't be more than a coupla' weeks now," I said.

"Yeah, in a coupla' weeks," Jimmy repeated.

"What do you think about that?" I asked.

"I think it stinks," Jimmy said, frowning.

"Why do you say it stinks?" I asked.

"Cause it won't be the same. Not the same room, not the same teacher, not the same kids."

"True, but it is the same school. And you can still walk there with Tom every day. It's not far from home either ..."

"Well, it still stinks," Jimmy insisted.

"What if you had to ride a bus every day—to a new school for the *bussing*, like some of the other kids in your school? And what if the school was far away from home, way across town, like mine is?"

"You mean it could be even worse?" Jimmy asked without much interest.

"Could be. And how about Emily?" I continued, thinking it might help if he felt sorry for his sister. "She's never been in *any* school, never even *been* on a school bus, never been away from home. Don't you think it might be even worse for her when school starts?" I asked.

"I guess," Jimmy admitted, shrugging his shoulders. I knew I'd made a mistake talking about others' problems. Jimmy didn't feel any better just because Emily had it worse.

We'd arrived at the library by the time that Jimmy and I had ended the conversation, and we found a bench where Emily could sit down.

"How about going into the library?" I suggested. "They have a great collection of books for kids, and I know the kind of books that Emily likes."

I knew full well, that this would not be a popular thing with the boys. But I said it anyhow, hoping for a miracle.

"Nahh, that's a *terrible* idea," Tom stated, with emphasis. *(That means he said it in a very strong way.)* "We gonna' haf'ta read plenty o' books when we go back to school. Why should we start school stuff now? It's all gonna start too soon anyway. I don't want to go to the library."

"Me neither," Jimmy joined in.

I tried to find a better suggestion, but I hadn't been thinking ahead.

Tom took a minute to consider, then said, "How about the playground at John Swett School? We can play on stuff there. Maybe meet some other kids and have some fun?"

"I thought you said you didn't want to start school early," I teased.

"That's different," Jimmy chimed in. "I like the schoolyard better than the library." His opinion was clear.

I decided to try for a compromise. "Well, okay. If me and Emily walk all the way to the playground, then, when we come back this way, can we spend a little time in the library before going home? Otherwise we can just stay here so Emily and I can watch you two chase each other around the square."

It didn't take long for the boys to agree: play first—library after. When Emily had rested a bit, we crossed Van Ness and went on to John Swett playground. On our way there, I kept Tom beside me while Jimmy skipped ahead.

"Are you worried too, about all the changes that will happen when school starts Tom?"

"What changes? Just going back to school, like every other year."

"But everything will be different now; Emily in school all morning, Jimmy in a special class, me at Lowell High. Doesn't sound like every other year to me," I pointed out.

"Oh yeah, all that," he said, absently.

I could see that Tom was not worried about our big changes. If it didn't affect him, he wasn't concerned. In his book, it was *every man for himself.*

21. More planning

WHILE TOM AND JIMMY played happily on the school playground equipment that afternoon, I continued to worry about Emily. My frail little sister was the one I had most doubts about. While she and I watched the boys climb the slide and tumble around the Jungle Jim, I wondered if she would ever learn to play like other kids.

Right now, she seemed interested in watching her brothers play with other boys, but showed no interest in taking part in any of the activities. I decided to try an experiment.

"Emily, let's go watch the kids on the slide," I said.

She looked at me with those big blue eyes that always questioned me. It was hard to know what she might be thinking. However, not finding any strong objection, I decided to see how far she might go. Taking her hand, I led Emily to where three children were waiting to take turns on the baby slide. "Look at that, Emily," I said with enthusiasm. "There are little kids just like you all waiting for a turn. I guess it must be fun to climb up and slide down . . . What do you think, Emily? You think it might be fun?"

Emily looked at me without expression, but she was paying attention to what I said because she looked back at the waiting children, and watched as one of them slid down from the top.

I laughed and clapped my hands. "Good job," I said to the little girl when she landed on her feet.

Emily looked at me and started clapping her hands too. But it was probably only because she saw me clapping.

I thought this might a good sign, though. She seemed to understand something of what I was trying to show her.

When there were no more children in the line. I took Emily over to the stairs, wondering if she might go up, if I helped her. However, there was *nothing doing* when it came to taking that first step. As I stood behind her, gently urging, Emily pushed back against me, and frowned.

"No!" she said firmly.

"Okay Emily. It was just a thought," I said.

We watched as two more children climbed up and slid down. Then I had another idea.

"Emily, would you like to sit on the bottom of the slide?" I asked. Then, having even a better idea, *I* sat on the bottom of the slide. Emily watched, and smiled.

"Come on, you can do it too," I invited, beckoning with my hand.

It was a slow process, but while I sat on the bottom of the slide, Emily sat on my lap. Then Emily sat on the bottom of the slide on her own for a minute or two. When she giggled while sitting on the warm metal, I knew I was on the right track.

By the time Emily allowed me to guide her down the last few feet at the bottom of the slide, it was time for us to get back home for lunch. I didn't want Ma to get back before we did.

WHEN MA ARRIVED HOME, I asked about what had happened at the Louise Lombard meeting. At first she just grunted, "Ain't none o' your business, Missy!"

But after lighting a cigarette, and drinking a can of cold beer from the refrigerator, she began to grumble about the conference.

"Them school people was all fired up about makin' a fancy purse outta' pig's ear. The teacher she say 'Evera' yea' there's kids jus' like Emily come to school. They neva' been out'a da house, neva' been 'round otha' kids. Not ta worry,' she say. 'Afta' few days, all is gonna' be fine.' They mos'ly talk 'bout learnin' ta get along in school 'vironment, an all such nonsense. They sez learnin' ta talk ain't so important, if Emily don' learn *social skills*. What the hell that means?" Ma sounded resentful, and confused.

"Here smart ass!" she said abruptly, shoving some papers at me. "You read this IEP* thing, and *you* tell me what it say, you's so smart!"

I looked at the papers, and knew after starting to read them, that I was not going to be any help at all. I sat and thought about what to do next.

* Individual Education Plan

"You think we could ask Marina to come over?" I asked carefully. "She knows a lot about paperwork. I think she's in charge of keeping track of the register receipts where she works."

"And whad's wrong wid' you!" Ma shouted. "Why can't you do it?"

"I just thought Marina could help us with these papers. I can't understand 'em either, Ma."

"Yeah, well then, you is not so smart after all, huh?"

"Maybe Marina can figure it out. This is pretty complicated," I persisted, ignoring the nasty remarks.

"I'll think on it," Ma said frowning at me with disgust.

I could see that Ma was worried. She didn't know what would happen to Emily in that strange school. It was too far away, and Ma could no longer control everything. I began thinking that she might refuse to put Emily on the bus. I was afraid that Emily might never go to school, unless somebody helped explain things to Ma.

It was not until several days later, when Ma decided to ask Marina for help. She hadn't said anything much during that time. I wondered what was going through her mind.

"These here papers is what the school gave me," Ma said when Marina arrived. "I ask' Nadine to figa' it out, but she's too smart!" Ma said through a sneer.

Marina smiled, "Well, let's see what it says, okay?"

Marina took her time to read the papers, then she reread them again. Finally, she took a deep breath and told us what she thought they meant.

"Well Helen, I can understand why you and Nadine were confused. It's mostly written in education language, and some is even in legal language. I don't think I understand all of it either. But, much as I can tell, it's a kind of summary of all they think about Emily's education. It's everything the psychologist said about how much Emily knows; what the social worker said about how Emily learns new things; and what the teachers said about how they plan to help her progress."

"You mean everything they writ' there was what they say befo'a?" Ma asked.

"I think so. And now it's all in writing, and all in a record that the school keeps. And this copy is for you to keep. It's the plan for what Emily needs to learn, and then see how much she can accomplish during the year."

Ma heaved a sigh of relief, and I did too. Marina smiled. I think she was pleased that she was able to help.

"Thanks Marina. That helped a lot!" I said.

Ma gave me a dirty look, and I decided I better say no more. I could talk to Marina later, if I wanted to.

I think I knew why Ma had been confused. She had met with a teacher, a social worker and a psychologist, all at the same time. They had given her lots of information in that long meeting on Tuesday. Even though she'd heard it all before, it was too much when it came all at once.

22. Not this Time

AFTER SUPPER ON AUGUST 29, I began planning exactly what to wear on my first day of school. Now that Labor Day was looming (*That means it was coming up very soon.*) there was a lot to think about: how to dress, what to take with me, making sure to be on time for the bus. Mr. Lewis was in a hurry the day he told me what time the bus would come, and where to wait for it. But he stopped rushing long enough to warn me that there might be some confusion on the first few days of school.

"Now listen Nadine, about the new busing program for school integration this year . . . There will be a great deal of uncertainty. Both students and teachers are going to be confused . . . Rumors are flying over just about everything. Many kids could be anxious and resentful of the new system. The schools expect that most things will go smoothly, but some parents have raised strong objections to this new system. This may spill over into how kids behave."

He shifted his weight from one foot to the other, "You know what I mean? Being one of the younger students at this school, you will need to be watchful and careful, right? Think you can do that?"

I just nodded my head, agreeing to everything he said, even though I was thinking, *I have enough to worry about. How could I possibly add anything more to my list of things to be careful about?*

I was both nervous and excited at the same time, and wanted to talk to someone about it. I didn't think Ma would be helpful, and I did think of talking to Marina. But it didn't seem fair to keep bothering her with *all* of my problems.

I had just finished washing the dishes, and since I'd been busy thinking about all that, hadn't said much to the boys during dinner.

"Well, what the hell'r you moping around for?" Ma said when she sat down for her coffee and cigarette. She had been glaring at me all afternoon.

“It’s nothing Ma, just thinking about school,” I said quickly, not about to complain to her about anything.

“Well I got somethin’ for ya’ ta start makin’ a sour face about.”

“What’s the matter Ma, are you still worried about Emily?” I asked.

“Nah. Emily’s gonna be jes’ fine. Specially since you gonna be takin’ care o’ her evera’ day when she get home.”

How could Ma forget that I would get home too late for Emily?

“No Ma, I won’t be here. Don’t your remember Mr. Lewis told us that I won’t be back home from school until long *after* Emily gets home?”

“Well now ya see—it just ain’t gonna’ work out that away.” Ma sneered and took another drag on her cigarette.

I knew that tone. A cold chill ran through me ’cause whatever she was going to say next, was not going to be a good thing for me. “What does that mean, Ma?”

“Tha’ mean you is gonna be right *here* when she get home. I got me a job at the grocery store, an’ the first day o’ September, is my firs’ day ta work. I don’ get home until five that day, somebody gotta be here.”

I could hardly breathe. My heart started pounding and I began to feel dizzy. My jaw dropped, and a cold chill ran up my back. I took a deep breath and swallowed.

“No Ma! That’s my first day of school! I *gotta’* be there. I *gotta’* be there for everything. It’s when we get our classes, when we meet teachers, when we get books, when they give out the first homework . . . I *gotta’* be there!”

Ma stood up from her chair, walked over to me, and put her face down to mine. Nose to nose, she said, “You gotta’ be lotta’ things, Missy. But the first thing you gotta’ be is what I tell ya’ ta be . . . and where I tell ya’ ta be. You got that?”

And that hard right hand came up across the left side of my face.

I don’t know what got into me, but in that split second both my hands acted together, all by themselves. It was like I was watching myself do something I would never do if I had time to think about it. Those two hands pushed Ma so hard she sat right back down in her chair.

Then I shouted back at her, “No, not this time! I’m *not* going to be *here*, ’cause I’ll still be *at school. You* have to be here, ’cause you’re Emily’s mother and that’s what mothers do.”

With that I started to cry, and the rest of what I said was a lot of my blubbering about all the reasons I had to be at school on that first day.

Ma sat there with her mouth open. I'd never seen her so surprised about anything before. It guess she was pretty shocked that she had been pushed down in her chair.

Her voice was a bit shaky at first, "Well now, seems you got a bit o' temper there, Missy, but you is gonna git over it real soon."

Here it comes, I thought. *She's gonna beat me silly, and I'll be black and blue on my first day of school.*

But she didn't go for the wooden spoon. Instead she took me by the shoulders and shook me hard. *Doesn't want to leave any marks,* I thought, as I struggled to get away.

"My first day o' work is more importan' than the firs' day o' school. 'Sides, you c'n go to junior high, right nea' hea', and don' gotta' go ta fancy school t'otha' side a' town. You is too smart a'ready. Don' need ta be no bettern' everabody else. I gonna call that high school an' say I change mah mind about lett'n ya' go thea."

"No, Ma! No!" I was trying to think fast. "You can't do that . . It's too late. The bus will be here to pick me up on Monday morning. You can't change the schedule now!" I tried using reason, but it didn't work with her.

"Okay, so it's too late. You jes' stay home on Monday. Tuesday mornin' I call an' tell em' not to come no more. I call the junior high and tell 'em you comin' next day. Then you be home when Emily get here."

The rage returned full force, then I found my voice, "No way! You can't *do* that. Mr. Lewis made all the arrangements. I'm getting on that bus Monday morning."

"I'm gonna' be there wid ya and tell 'em ta go away. I'll say you gotta' stay home."

"Then I'll go on the streetcar, and get there by myself!"

"Ya' doan' know how ta get there from here!"

"Easy! Every bus has a driver. All I need to do is ask the driver. I'll get there just fine."

Where ya gonna git the money? You don' got no money!"

"I'll beg for it. Just like you and Charlie taught us. Remember Christmas vacation?" I saw then, that Ma was confused by my answers, and couldn't think of another way to stop me.

I had managed to answer all her arguments. No matter what she did or said, I was determined to get to my classes at Lowell on the first day. I had made up my mind that this time nothing was going to stop me.

23. Hello Again

IN THE MIDDLE of this heated argument, there was a tap on the door. My first thought was that someone had heard our loud voices, and we would get a complaint. But maybe it was Marina, and there would be someone sensible to step in and make things right.

I heard a key turn in the lock, and in walked Charlie with a big grin. "Wow! I heard you'se guys all the way down the hall. What's a goin' on hea'?"

Ma and I were both shocked into silence. Then I sat down to wait for what would happen next.

"Charlie! Ya' old goat. We thought you was in jail," Ma said. "What happen' to ya? Break out? Bribe a guard?" Ma laughed as she ran over to hug him.

Charlie laughed too. "Nah Helen, no breakin' outa' that place. Jail got too crowded. No mo' room for us good guys. Hadda make room for the real criminals done shootin' or killin'. Let us good guys go early."

"Well, alright then, come on in and have a beer," Ma sounded cheerful. But I could tell by the way she smiled that she was not exactly overjoyed to see Charlie back.

"Where's my boys?" Charlie wanted to know. "And where's my little one. Emily doin' okay these days?"

"Boys is sleepin' already. Emily went down befoa' five tonight," Ma said.

"Well, I gonna' see 'em firs' thing in the mornin' then. Been a long time not ta see ma' kids . . ."

Then Charlie noticed me, "Hey there Nadine! Been awhile girl. Look at ya', all grown since last I saw ya'. You sure lookin' good. How old ya' be now?"

"Hi Charlie. I'm still twelve," I said, hoping I didn't sound too disappointed to see him.

"You git ta bed now Nadine. Charlie and me got a lot o' catchin' up to do," Ma ordered.

I was happy to obey her this time, and went into the bedroom, closed the door and curled up on my mat.

I had trouble getting to sleep that night. I thought about what Charlie's return might mean. What would Ma do? Would she keep her job at the grocery store? Or would she let Charlie take over again?

What would Charlie do? Would he take the welfare checks again, do all the shopping, keep Ma happy with beer and cigarettes? Maybe he would take care of Emily after school? I didn't think so. But, if Ma didn't work, she could be home to care for Emily. I wasn't sure what to wish for.

How about me? What would I do? Well, I'd definitely made up my mind about going to school, that's what I would do. No sense wondering about that.

THAT LABOR DAY WEEKEND was the longest three days of my life. Waiting to find out what was going to happen was not easy, especially when I was so anxious about my special school.

Charlie decided to celebrate with us after visiting his other friends. He bought pizza and ice cream and the boys were delighted to help him with the party.

"Hey, I thought you was never comin' back," Tom laughed while filling cups with Coke. "Glad you got here before school started."

"Yeah, we sure missed ya,'" Jimmy, in charge of paper napkins, chimed in. "We never got no pizza while you was gone."

"Well, I ain't gonna' go nowhere now. I's back ta stay right here wid' you kids and your ma," Charlie assured them with a big smile.

Ma was pretty quiet those last few days of summer. It was hard to know what was on her mind. She said no more about Emily, never mentioned my school plans, and avoided talking to me about anything. And that was okay with me. I wasn't looking for another argument, but had my teeth clenched just in case.

24 Silent prayers

WELL, I HATE TO TELL about what happened next, but maybe I should have expected it . . . Did I mention that Charlie brought in the pizza and ice cream on Labor Day, the day before school started?

"Labor Day's a good day ta celebrate," Charlie had declared, "New 'ventures for evra'budy." And we did have a good time devouring pizza and ice cream, and drinking cokes. Us kids got sent to bed early though, right after we finished eating. I was so excited I didn't think I could fall asleep.

"You'se all gotta git up early in the mornin'. Da firs' day o' school, ya gotta be on time," Ma said firmly. I think she just wanted us out of the way so she and Charlie could get drunk.

Sure enough, after we went to bed, I could hear Charlie and Ma talking. I figured they were making decisions about who was going to do what the next day. The two of them had been drinking a lot of beer with their pizzas, and just opened more. Ma always gets talkative when she drinks too much beer. The only thing I heard as I was going to sleep was Charlie saying something like, "Well then, it's all settled, right Helen?"

In the morning, I was really excited getting ready to meet the bus for Lowell High School, when Charlie appeared from Ma's bedroom. I guess he had stayed all night.

"Good morning ta all a' you stud'nts," he said cheerfully. "Big day comin' up for evra'body. Firs' day o' school's a really big deal."

We all hurried through breakfast. I helped Emily dress in a clean outfit, and the boys got themselves ready in new tee shirts. Tom and Jimmy went off first, excitedly talking about finding old friends and exchanging summer vacation stories.

Ma had decided she would go with Emily on her first day of school, so they both waited for the bus together.

"I thought this was going to be your first day at work?" I asked Ma.

"My first day will be next Monday, not this one," she said, curtly.

Curious about her change of plans, I wanted to know more, but decided not to ask just then. There was too much going on and I didn't want to miss my bus.

My bus was scheduled for fifteen minutes after Emily's bus, and Charlie waited with me, though I didn't know why. I got really nervous when the bus was late, but Charlie said they probably had a lot of new addresses to learn. Finally my big yellow bus came around the corner .

"I'm goin' wid you," Charlie said, firmly.

"What? Why?" I asked, in a panic.

"Gotta find out what kind'a school that is. I seen where Emily's school is, but neva' the school you's goin' to."

"What do you mean? What are you gonna do when you get there?" I asked, my heart pounding.

"Look around, ask me some question', fin' out what's goin' on there." The casual tone Charlie used was fake, I could tell. He was being too calm, too quiet. What was this all about? Why did *he* need to go with me?

"Did Ma tell you to do this?" I demanded.

"Your Ma said because she was goin' wid Emily, she couldn't go wid you. She say we both need ta take care o' our kids better—now they'se all in school—all day. See if they need'n something. Today maybe you's gotta buy somethin'? You maybe need special book'? Some money fo' yo' lunch?"

"I don't need nothing Charlie. I got everything I need right here with me in my backpack. Paper, pens, pencils, lunch, everything. I got ready a long time ago Charlie, everything I need is right here. You *don't* need to come with me. I don't *want* you to come with me!"

"Well now, don' you go fussin' honey. It's all settled with your Ma. She say I go wid ya, and tha's what I do."

I started to think fast, "You can't come on the school bus. It's only for students! They won't let you get on. That bus is just for us kids!"

I was frantic as the bus pulled up, but I couldn't think of anything else to keep Charlie from getting on the bus and spoiling everything.

"Not ta worry. Your ma called and got it all settled. First day o' school, adult cn' 'company kids on a school bus," he said, confidently.

So Charlie and Ma had it all settled. I had not prepared for this. I'd been too busy thinking about what to wear, what to bring, what to say, and how to behave in the new school. I even studied a map at the library, thinking I'd better know how to get there just in case Ma cancelled the bus, like she threatened to do. Failing to pay attention to what they were planning had been a big mistake. But it was too late now. Charlie was getting on the bus right behind me.

"Hi Burt," he said to the bus driver.

"Hello there, Charlie," the driver answered.

How is it that the driver knows Charlie? I wondered.

I saw Charlie shake hands with the driver and pass him something. Then he came to sit beside me.

We sat side by side, me and Charlie, with his commenting now and then about what a nice day it was, how special this would be for me, and what a good driver we had.

"How do you know this bus driver?" I asked.

"Well, ya know Nadine, I been 'quainted with lots a' drivers when I was takin' them tests for school bus drivers. Burt is one of 'em," Charlie explained vaguely.

After that, I sat in silence, not hearing the rest of Charlie's commentary along the way.

An awful feeling started in my jaw, clutched at my chest, and churned into my stomach. All the way up Market Street, and over Twin Peaks I felt like I might throw up my breakfast. Then the terror got worse when we got to Nineteenth Avenue, and closer to the school.

Oh God, what am I gonna do now? Oh God, what's gonna happen next? Oh God, how can I get away from this? Oh, God, Oh God, Oh God!

25. Time to Decide

WHEN WE ARRIVED at Lowell High School, all the kids got off the bus, and I followed, expecting that Charlie would be right behind me. Instead, he had another surprise.

"You go on ahead, honey, I gonna talk ta Burt for a spell, catch up wid ya later on."

I heaved a sigh of relief, but I knew this was not the last I would see of Charlie. Whatever he and Ma had planned, I knew it would not end here. I needed to think of something fast.

If I ran away again, it would only mean more problems for me, and nothing else would change. I had to think of something that would get rid of Charlie, and keep me out of trouble. Getting Charlie out of my life right now was really important. I would never be able to do everything I had to do in this school with him around. I would always be wondering what he and Ma were planning to do.

My mind was racing. What kind of story had I read where a problem that was solved by the main character was able to punish the villain? But this was not a storybook problem, this was a real problem. Anyway, who would I tell the story to, even if I had a story?

Maybe I could make up a story about Charlie being a stalker? Could I tell somebody he was a drug dealer? Should I ask a teacher for help, a counselor, the principal? Who should I appeal to and what would I say?

Make up your mind right now! I commanded myself, *You don't have time to make a big plan, you have to make a fast plan, or it will be too late.*

"Where is the principal's office?" I asked the first grown-up I ran into.

The young woman smiled, "Are you lost dear?"

"No Ma'm, I have a big problem," I said, firmly.

"Mr. Simms, the Vice Principal, is just down the hall, third door on your left. I'm sure he will be able to help," she said. It looked like she was in a hurry to get to a classroom or something.

I liked the way she gave clear directions and didn't beat around the bush with a lot of silly questions.

"Can you tell me your name?" I asked, thinking I might need to find her later.

"Sure, I'm Miss Greenly." She smiled again, and stopped her rush to wherever she was going. "You can tell Mr. Sims that I sent you. He's probably pretty busy today, so saying a teacher sent you might get his attention."

"Thanks a lot," I said, sincerely thankful for a friendly face, and walked down the hallway to the office as Miss Greenly had directed.

"I need to talk to Mr. Simms," I said to the secretary as soon as I walked in.

"And what's this about, young lady?" the secretary asked, crisply. I figured that she must see a lot of kids who walk in needing to talk to Mr. Simms.

"Well, there's a man who followed me to school . . . and Miss Greenly said I should see Mr. Simms about it," I said frowning as if I were really worried. Actually, I *was* really worried, otherwise I wouldn't be in the vice principal's office on my first day in Lowell High School.

The secretary looked at my worried frown and said, "Oh, that does sound serious. Just wait right here and I'll see if Mr. Simms can see you when he's off the phone."

Before I knew it, I was seated across the desk from Mr. Simms.

"And what is your name?" Mr. Simms asked, pleasantly.

"My name is Nadine Williams," I said, a tremor in my voice. And feeling safe for the first time since I got on the bus that morning, I burst into tears.

26. Truth and Consequences

MR. SIMMS SEEMED a bit confused by my tearful outburst, but I went ahead anyhow, afraid that if I stopped now, I would never be able to say anything at all.

"Well . . . see . . . I got on the bus this morning, just like I was supposed to . . . and he followed me. I didn't know he would . . . and I didn't know what to do about it . . . so . . . so . . . didn't do anything," I blubbered.

Mr. Simms handed me a box of tissues, and looked sympathetic, but needed more information. "Okay Nadine, I can see that you're upset, but just slow down now, and take your time. What do you mean he followed you? Was he in a car?"

"No, he was on the bus . . . He got on the bus with me . . . and . . . and sat beside me all the way . . ."

I blew my nose and tried to stop crying.

"What did he say to you? Did he want you to get you off the bus?"

"No! No! . . . He rode all the way with me . . . All the way here . . . to this school!"

"Is he here now? Did he come in with you?" Mr. Simms asked, leaning across his desk.

"No! NO! He didn't come *inside* the school, he stayed on the bus. He was talking to the bus driver."

"To the bus driver?" Mr. Simms sounded like he was confused.

"Why was he talking to the bus driver? Why did the driver let him on the bus?"

"He knows the bus driver . . . and, and . . . gave him something when he got on . . . I don't know what he gave the driver . . . maybe it was money . . . maybe it was drugs . . . it was in an envelope, and I couldn't see what it was . . . I can't *tell* you what it was . . . cause I don't *know* what it was." My blubbering started again.

Mr. Simms shook his head and stood up. I thought for a minute that he was going to say that he didn't believe anything I'd said, that he thought I was telling a story . . . so I started to cry hard again.

Instead, he patted my shoulder and said gently, "Nadine, this is much more serious than I can deal with today. It's the first day of school, and the first day of public school integration in the city. There are lots of people going to need for me to solve their problems. Your problem will take more time, and needs much more attention than I can give it. I will get Security involved with that bus driver. And you will need to get your whole story recorded by a counselor. I'll ask my secretary to take you to the counselor's office. You try to calm down, Nadine . . . and I'll see that we get all of this sorted out. It seems that it will take a little more time, that's all."

Mr. Simms escorted me to the door, and said to his secretary, "Mrs. Conrad, this problem will be better dealt with by our counselor. Nadine is very upset by this incident, and needs to take more time to report all the details for the record."

Mrs. Conrad put her arm across my shoulders, gave me a little package of tissues, and led me down the hall.

There were two other students waiting in the counselor's office, so I questioned Mrs. Conrad, "How can I start my classes if I have to wait here a long time?"

Mrs. Conrad smiled and assured me that it wouldn't be very long, and this would be a good time for me to collect myself, and be well prepared when it was my turn.

So I sat and waited, and blew my nose, and dried my eyes, and pretended to be in charge again. Then I needed to use the bathroom, so I asked one of the waiting girls where the restrooms were.

"I don't know. This is my first day. Why don't you ask somebody else?"

I decided I could find my way to the restroom on my own, and left the grumpy girl in the waiting room. When I got there, I splashed my face with cold water, and it felt good. I made up my mind that I had cried enough, and would not let myself cry any more. Anyhow, crying was only wasting time, and I was missing important things on my first day.

Back in the counselor's office, the two waiting students were gone, and I was the only one left in the waiting room. When the door opened, Miss Greenly stood there and asked me to come in. When I met her in the hallway, I had thought that she was a teacher on her way to a classroom. So

I was both surprised and pleased that she turned out to be the counselor who would hear my story.

"So, we meet again," Miss Greenly said, with a broad smile. Then she tilted her head, "And so soon after our first encounter."

That made me smile, and I felt things would be okay now.

"Mr. Simms secretary said your name was Nadine Williams? You said something about a man following you to school?"

"Yes Ma'am."

"I think we better start at the very beginning, Nadine. Tell me where you live, a little about your family, and where you went to school last year. Take your time so I can get the whole picture, okay?"

So I started with my address on Larkin Street, then said I lived with Ma, my sister Emily, and brothers Jimmy and Tom. I told Sally Greenly about us kids being tested during the summer, about Mr. Lewis and Family Services Center, and the social worker teaching Emily to use the potty. I talked about Ma going to school meetings, then finding a job after Charlie got arrested. I told her that he got released early because of overcrowding in the jails.

Miss Greenly asked a question now and then, but once I got started, I didn't seem to need many questions. I just couldn't stop talking. It felt like turning on a faucet, and letting the water run, while I poured out all the things that had happened. There was one thing I was not sure that I should tell her—about running away from home, and getting caught in the library. So I gave a short version of that story. When I got through I felt empty. It was a good feeling, and I heaved a big sigh of relief.

"Well Nadine, you have had quite a time of it. Now tell me about today, and what happened on that bus ride."

27. The Ball Starts Rolling

"FROM THE BEGINNING PLEASE, Nadine, I want to hear everything about what happened this morning. Don't leave anything out, okay?" the counselor encouraged, smiling.

I took a deep breath and began telling Miss Greenly as much as I could remember of what happened on that bus ride with Charlie.

"I was really upset when Charlie got on the bus. I told him he wasn't supposed to go with me—that I didn't *want* him to. But he knew the driver, and gave him something, and just got on. Charlie never bothered with me before . . . And . . . and when I asked him why, he told me that Ma wanted him to go along in case I might need something, like books or pens, on the first day of school . . ." I stopped, wondering if the counselor thought this sounded like a made up story.

"Go ahead. What happened next?"

Miss Greenly was not smiling or looking bored, just listening carefully. So I sighed again, and went on, hoping that she believed me.

"Well, I told Charlie I already had everything I needed, and he didn't need to come along for any reason."

"And what did he say about that?"

"Treated me like a baby. He said I shouldn't get so excited, and everything was going to be just fine."

"Then what? What did you think when he said that?" Miss Greenly prompted.

"I got really scared, 'cause I thought he was lying. I couldn't understand why Ma would want Charlie to come with me, and was worried about what would happen when we got here at school."

"So he told you that your mother *knew* he was going to be with you?"

I nodded in agreement. "That's what Charlie said."

"And how does your mother know him? Can you tell me a little more about Charlie and your mother?"

Sounded like Miss Greenly was really interested, so I didn't hesitate any more, or worry about if she believed me, "Charlie is Tom and Jimmy and Emily's father. He came to collect the welfare checks, and did the shopping for food and beer and cigarettes . . . but then he went to jail."

"So, do you know why Charlie went to jail?

"Yes, he went to jail because he was selling drugs."

"And Charlie is not *your* father, but father to your brothers and your little sister?"

"Right. I found out that I was born before Ma and Charlie got together. So I don't know who *my* father is, " I explained.

"So did your mother tell you about this?"

"No, Ma never told me anything like that. Marina told me, and I promised not to tell . . . but I guess I just did."

"Okay, now who is Marina?"

I talked for a long time then, telling all about Marina and how she was a good person, and about Charlie's visits every week, about the party when Ma lost the baby, and about me running away . . . and all that stuff.

"Thank you Nadine, I think I understand better now about your life at home. Let's get back to what happened on the bus. You say that Charlie gave the bus driver something when he got on the bus. Do you know what it was, or can you guess what it might be?"

"I don't know. I already told Mr. Simms that I don't know, and I really don't!" I said, angry for not knowing.

"I understand, Nadine. We won't worry about that now. I'll talk to Mr. Sims later on. It's really not your problem anymore. Is there anything else that Charlie did or said to make you feel uncomfortable on that bus ride?"

I stopped to think for a minute, "He just told me not to worry, that he and Ma had it all worked out . . . He said he wanted to take care of me, make sure I had everything I needed to make me happy, and make Ma happy, and weird things like that."

"What was *weird* about that?" Miss Greenly asked.

"It was weird, because I'm most happy when Charlie is not around. I wish that he had stayed in jail. I wish they would keep him there—and never let him out!"

"Why do I get the feeling that you don't like Charlie very much?" Miss Greenly said, smiling. She waited, looked at me for a minute, and tilted her head and raised her eyebrows in a questioning way. Then we both burst out laughing. It felt good to laugh with her.

Miss Greenly stood up then, "We've talked enough for today, Nadine. You've missed your first period class, but I have your schedule here for the rest of the day. I'm going to ask that you try to think about what happens next—right now—right here at school, and try to forget about your stressful bus ride this morning. I know it was difficult for you, but now that you've told me everything I need to know, you don't have to worry about it anymore. I'm taking this problem seriously, and by the end of the day, Mr. Sims and I will have taken proper steps."

I wanted to know what she meant by *proper steps*, but I knew I would be late for my class if I started to ask questions. So I thanked her, and asked where I needed to go for my second period class.

28. First Day at School

I TRIED TO DO as the counselor had directed, concentrate on what was happening here at school—today. I *wanted* to forget all about my morning on the bus, and the stressful meetings with Mr. Simms and Miss Greenly. Forgetting was not so easy, but I was able to calm down as time passed during the day. There were so many things to remember, and so much to learn with new teachers for every subject, and lots of homework assignments.

My second period class was English, and the teacher, Mrs. Whitaker, a small, white haired lady, took time to explain things to her new students. She told us what books would be required, the assignment schedule, and all about her grading system. Impressed by how well organized she was, I thought she would probably be strict, but fair, and that was okay with me. Two of the books on the required list were *Little Women* and *Tale of Two Cities*. That pleased me because I had already read *Little Women*, and *Tale of Two Cities* was already on my list of books to read. That meant that I had a head start for this class.

"Now then," Mrs. Whitaker concluded, "I want you to be prepared to answer questions every day about the assigned chapters in each book we read. Then, later on, everyone will be expected to memorize some important poems and short historical speeches. Learning to recite before a group is one of the objectives for this class."

Ouch, I thought. *Memorizing and reciting speeches might be a problem for me.*

I didn't like to do that kind of thing in front of a class. I remembered stumbling over words and being very nervous when I gave the oral reports required last year in sixth grade. Oh well, "later on" is a long way off, and by then it might not be so bad.

Biology was my third period class, and that seemed like it might be fun. Mr. Stevens said we would be taking field trips to Golden Gate Park. We would make notebooks with samples of leaves from trees and collect wildflowers, then memorize their names. I thought I would probably be good at this.

And so it went throughout the day, one class after another with a lunch hour in between. During lunch period, a pretty girl with short, curly hair came to sit beside me at a long table in the cafeteria.

"Hi there," she said. "My name is Katie, I saw you on the bus this morning. I sat two seats behind you."

"Hi . . . I'm Nadine," I answered hesitantly. "Where do you live?" I was hoping that she would not ask about Charlie being with me.

"Not far from you. I live off of Van Ness Avenue, in a little alley called Justin Court. Was that your dad who got on the bus with you?"

"No," I answered. Then, because she didn't say anything more, I supposed that she was waiting for me to explain.

"He's not my father, he's my mother's friend."

"Oh," Katie said, without seeming curious about any further explanation regarding Charlie. "What classes are you taking this semester?" she asked.

Katie and I exchanged information about our classes, and what our teachers were like. I found out that this was her first semester at Lowell High as well. She was so easy to talk to, and when she smiled the freckles on her nose seemed to stretch out in a cute way. It felt good to have made a friend on my first day in this new school. Then, when the bell rang for afternoon classes, we agreed to meet up after school.

"See you at the bus stop," Katie said, as she ran off to her afternoon P.E. class.

I had a sinking feeling in my stomach at the thought of getting back on that bus. I didn't want to be on the bus again if Charlie was going to get on it too. I needed to find Miss Greenly before the end of school today.

I didn't want to face Charlie again, and I didn't want to face Ma either.

29. A Long Ride Home

AFTER MY LAST CLASS, I ran to the counselor's office, hoping that she hadn't left. When I burst into the waiting room, she greeted me with a smile, as if she had been expecting me.

"Hi Nadine. Glad I didn't have to go looking for you at the bus stop. Ready for a ride home?"

I was surprised—to say the least, "What do you mean? Am I supposed to go with *you*?"

"Yes, Nadine. *You* are going with *me*. I called your mother, and she gave me permission to drive you home. I have several things to discuss with her, and a lot of things to talk to you about, so let's get going."

Miss Greenly did have a lot to tell me, and I hardly had a chance to say a word. So I listened—really listened.

"Okay," Miss Greenly said, as she started her car, "first things first. Mr. Sims and I talked about the events that occurred this morning, and formulated a plan."

I waited to hear what the plan was.

"Mr. Sims contacted security, and told me to make some phone calls, and this is how it all went: One—Security found that Charlie was still on school premises, and didn't have a good reason for being here, so he was escorted off the grounds."

I heaved a great sigh of relief. "Okay?"

"Two—Mr. Sims had security search the bus driver for the envelope that Charlie give him. There were drugs in it, so the bus driver was fired."

"You mean he can't drive the school bus anymore?"

"Right. And if he ever tries to drive another school bus, it won't happen," Miss Greenly said, firmly. "There are strict rules about drivers, drugs, and picking up anyone who is not a student on his route."

Wow! I didn't ask anything more about that, so Miss Greenly continued.

"Now then. Three—I called your mother, and found that she has a social worker assigned through the school district at Emily's school, and another social worker active through Family Services and Welfare. I didn't get to talk to all of them today, but I will follow up tomorrow."

"Which one did you talk to?" I wanted to know.

"I talked to Sandra Farnsworth, the social worker who said that *you* were the one mostly responsible for Emily's potty training. She told me that you were Emily's main caretaker during the summer."

Speeding up Portola Drive we passed the school bus taking the same route as we were. I looked up at the bus windows, searching for Katie, but I didn't see her. She was probably sitting on the other side, or maybe out of sight in the middle. But as we drew ahead, I did see the bus driver clearly, and sure enough it was *a different one* than had picked me up this morning. As I turned back to what Miss Greenly had said, I thought I should say something about Emily's social worker.

"Oh yes, Sandra. She came to potty train Emily. I guess she remembered me."

"She surely did, and it sounds like you were pretty busy during the summer. Didn't you have time to visit with your school friends, or other kids in the neighborhood?"

"Don't have friends near where I live. But I did visit Marina sometimes. Me and Emily like to go to her place. She has—or had—cookies and milk for us, sometimes . . . But now she's moved."

"Cookies and milk sound pretty good. Do you visit Marina when you're hungry?"

"No, usually I go there to ask questions—or just talk about things. She lived just across the hall, so it was easy to go there when I had time. She had a color TV set, and sometimes let us kids watch cartoons."

"So did Marina live there all by herself?"

"Yeah, most of the time, but then she got a boyfriend—his name is Ted—and he helps me with words too. But now they moved. It makes me sad."

Miss Greenly was asking a lot of questions, and I was getting tired of giving so many answers. But she wasn't done yet.

"So tell me about your mother, Nadine. You said that Charlie is her friend and father of your siblings. You told me about your mom losing the baby, and that after Charlie went to jail, she found a job. That's all I know about your mother, can you tell me more?"

I felt uncomfortable with that question, so I tried to find a way to avoid answering it. *(But I reminded myself to look up the word "siblings." I think I know what it means, but I'm not really sure, exactly.)* Now, about that question I didn't want to answer.

"Well . . . you said you talked to Ma on the phone . . . so did you ask her what you wanted to know then?"

Miss Greenly just smiled. "I guess that's what I should have done?" she asked.

"Yeah, maybe."

"Well, when we get there, I'll have time for any questions I have. I should have thought about that before, Nadine."

We were on Market Street now, and I wondered if there would be a place to park the car anywhere near where I lived.

Suddenly curious about why Miss Greenly was doing all this, I thought of a question I had wanted to ask when she mentioned social workers.

"What is the difference between a counselor and a social worker? Seems like they both make home visits and like to ask a lot of questions."

"Oh . . . Well, I guess they're pretty much the same when you think of it. But counselors work mostly work in high schools, and social workers go to different schools, and mostly do home visits. But then I'm doing a home visit too—aren't I? You really asked a hard question, Nadine. I'll have to think of a better answer to that one."

Just then I spotted a parking space, "Oh look, right there, you can park right there if you get to it quick."

We were lucky, and before another car came, we pulled up at the curb.

"Be sure you lock all the car doors," I warned, feeling protective of the person who had rescued me from Charlie. Now I wondered if she could protect me from Ma as well.

30. Ending the First Day

AS WE GOT OUT OF THE CAR and walked down Larkin Street, I saw Officer Phil coming towards us. I noticed that he was putting on weight, and wondered if he was spending more time at the police station than on his regular beat. I wasn't sure whether or not I should be glad to see him just then. Anyhow, it was too late to do anything about it.

"Hi there, Nadine," he said cheerfully, coming to a stop when he reached us.

"Hello Officer Phil, you're here late today. Did your time for this beat change?" I asked.

"No, not really, I just got tied up with a problem down the street. I'm off duty now."

He looked at Miss Greenly. She was standing there looking at him. I thought I should say something.

"This is my school counselor, Miss Greenly. She drove me home from school. It was my first day at Lowell High," I explained.

Miss Greenly extended her hand and said "Glad to meet you Officer Phil. I guess you and Nadine are friends?"

"Yes Ma'am, we've been friends a long time now. Was there some trouble at school today?" Officer Phil asked, pursing his lips.

"All taken care of Officer, I'm just making a home visit, to meet Mrs. Williams."

Officer Phil touched the brim of his cap, nodded his head, and said, "See you around, Nadine. Nice to meet you, Miss Greenly."

Waiting for Miss Greenly to ask questions about Officer Phil, I led the way to our building. No questions came, so we walked in silence, through the door and up the stairs to the third floor. Miss Greenly seemed a lot taller now than before, when we were at school. Her straight dark hair fell side to side as she looked around, taking it all in; the worn steps, dirty walls, the dim lighting—or maybe I just felt shorter as we got closer to where I lived. When we got to our apartment, I knocked on the door to give Ma a chance to know that we were there. Turning to Miss Greenly, I pointed to the door across the hall, "That's where Marina used to live," I said, stalling for a moment or two longer. "She moved last month. She got married too," I mumbled.

Ma finally opened the door, "Come on in. Don't just stand there," she said, abruptly.

I could tell that she'd been drinking, and knew that she was not exactly pleased to see me coming home with a school counselor.

"Sorry about this Mrs. Williams, I won't stay long. Just a few things we need to settle about bus rules and regulations."

Emily, who had been standing behind Ma, peeked around to inspect the stranger.

"This must be Emily," Miss Greenly said, smiling.

"Yes ma'm, this here's Emily. Her first day at school too, ya know."

"Yes, I do know, Mrs. Williams. It must be very stressful for you to have both your girls start a new school on the same day. Where are the boys? This is their first day back in school as well."

"They's gone ta play wid friends down the hall. Come an' sit down. I gotta git suppa started soon."

Ma was trying to get rid of Miss Greenly as fast as she could. But it was not going to be easy if Miss Greenly had a lot of questions. I knew that, for sure.

Miss Greenly turned to me then, "Nadine, why don't you and Emily go out for a while?

I wanted to stay around and hear what her questions for Ma would be. But a look on Ma's face told me I better get going.

"Then, you jes take Emily for a walk. She need a walk ta'day," Ma said, firmly.

With no further excuses, I took Emily by the hand, "Come on Emily."

At the door I hesitated, turned, and said, "Bye, Miss Greenly, thanks for the ride home."

"Goodbye Nadine. See you tomorrow."

Closing our door reluctantly, I wished I could go across the hall and see Marina. But those days were over, so as directed, Emily and I went down the stairs and out on the streets for a walk towards the library. All this time I was itching to know what was going on between Ma and Miss Greenly.

As we started on our walk, I talked to Emily, just as I usually do when she's with me. Knowing that she would not answer didn't make any difference. I kept thinking that maybe she might know what I was saying, or would remember some of my words. If nothing else, she'd remember the sound of my voice, and it would help her feel connected when she was with me.

When we arrived at the library, Emily and I spent half an hour leafing through a couple of picture books. When I figured we'd been away long enough, I put the books back on the shelf. Just as she got up to leave, Emily whimpered that familiar song that meant, *"I gotta go, right now!"*

We were too far from home to get there safely, so I decided to try the library restroom. After all, Emily had been at school all day and had used unfamiliar equipment there, so it should be okay. Well . . . it was almost okay. The floor did get a bit wet, and Emily wasn't completely dry, but considering where we were, she did pretty well.

Happy to be home at last, I changed Emily, then waited for the boys to settle down for dinner. They were really excited telling about their new teachers, making new friends, and complaining about the homework. Ma said not a word until the boys were in bed and Emily asleep. Then came the expected explosion.

31. Another Close Call

MA HAD NOT SAID ANYTHING when Emily and I got back home, nor did she mention anything during dinner when the boys were raving over new play equipment at school. I hoped that her silence meant that Ma was taking time to think things over, so I quietly washed and dried the plates and forks, then put things away. As I draped the dishcloth over the drawer and turned to walk toward the bedroom, my hopes vanished.

"Where you think you'se goin', Missy? You come set yourse'f down right hea," Ma said, nodding at the chair beside her.

Turning around reluctantly, I followed Ma's orders, sat down, and anticipated the worst. Pursed lips and clenched teeth told me it would be bad. Her eyes blazed while she jammed her cigarette into the ashtray with controlled fury.

"You's really done it good this time. You and your big mouth got us in a heap o' trouble. You got Charlie back in jail, you got a bus driver fired, you got them welfare workers all riled up, and you got a school counselor keepin' track o' everathin'. God dammit girl, your stupid bellyachin' gone too far."

Ma looked at me with such hate on her face, I knew she'd been holding something inside for a long time.

You's been nothin' but trouble since befoa' you was born. Evra'thing gone vera' bad since then. You is why I is leavin' home in Birmingham, you's why I's hookin' up wid Charlie, you is why we's livin' in this rat hole. Then you bring a damn copper hea'—and *now*—you is why Charlie's in jail and welfa'e's breathin' down mah neck!"

I began to panic at the long list of things Ma was blaming on me, and thought I better defend myself, before it was too late. "But, but it's not *my* fault Ma . . . *You* sent Charlie. If you hadn't sent him, none a' this would a' happened."

"*I* never sent Charlie, you stupid kid. You shoulda known betta'. How come *you* believe' him, you'se s'pose ta be so smart? Charlie never say a true word in all his life."

I was completely confused by Ma's denial. "But why? Why did he get on the bus if you didn't say so?" I asked.

"What Goddam use is bein' a gen'yus, you can' figga that out for youse'f?"

Ma waited for me to say something, but all I could say was "I don't know . . . I don't know . . . He said *you* sent him."

"So, not only is ya stupid, you'se really dumb! Charlie take care o' Charlie. He sell drugs now. Where you think is bes' place ta sell drugs? All them teenage kids wantin' ta try somethin' new?"

Ma waited for me to process what she said, but she wasn't finished.

"You know what else is waitin'? Them social workers an' school people? I can smell it comin'. They'se jus' waitin' for me ta beat the shit outa ya' so's they take me away too. An God knows nothin' make me feel betta than ta take a bat an break evra' bone in yo'a worthless hide. But I aint gonna lose no mo'a. I ain't gonna lose Emily, an' I ain't gonna lose mah welfa'e. Oh no, Missy, I aint gonna do that."

With those determined words, Ma got up from her chair, grabbed a handful of my hair and lifted me off my chair. Yowling in pain, I put my hands up to keep my scalp attached to my head.

"Stop it!" I yelled, "Stop it! Stop!" I didn't know what to do. My hands and arms were busy trying to hold my hair, while Ma was yanking on it.

"How that feel now, ya little piece o' crap? Now you know how it feel havin' somebody jerk ya round. Don' feel so good, right? And no marks either. One good thin' Charlie teach me—how ta hurt somebody an' no marks showin'."

I wanted to strike out, to push Ma away, to get loose, but I had to use my hands to fight her grip on my hair. She was gonna break my neck if she kept this up, I could feel it cracking. Then, in desperation, and because my legs were free, I kicked out as hard as I could. My shoe connected with Ma's shin.

That worked all right. Ma yowled, and let go of my hair to grab at her leg. I was instantly free and I rubbed my head to distribute the pain.

"Ya dare kick ME, you rotten kid, you gonna pay GOOD for that," Ma said, lunging at me. "Now I'm gonna KILL ya."

And this time I knew she meant it.

Lucky for me I was too fast for her, and jumped out of the way just in time. I felt the wall behind me, and turning quickly, found the doorknob, opened the door, and bolted.

I ran down the three flights of stairs and out into the street. I was free from Ma's rage for the moment, but I didn't know what to do next. It was really cold tonight. There'd been no time to snatch a jacket. I started to run towards my refuge at the library, but I realized that it was too late for it to be open. *So, where should I go this time?*

Nearing the library and running out of breath, I could see that Market Street was brightly lit and the warmth of all those lights seemed to be inviting me. A block away from Market, a stream of people were hurrying out of the Orpheum Theater, bundling themselves in warm coats and lined jackets. I really would have liked having one of those right now.

Watching theater goers leave by the side exit on Hyde Street, I got an idea. After racing down the street, I stood beside the exit door and waited for the next people to leave. It was easy to slide right in before the door closed.

An attendant spotted me. "Hey" he said, raising his right hand to stop me.

But I dashed by quickly using a panicky voice, "I . . . I forgot my jacket. I'll find it quick and be right back. It's really cold out there."

I raced down the middle aisle, considering whether I should just squat down in the middle of the center row. But I knew that there would probably be a cleanup crew after the last performance, and I'd get caught. Instead, I pushed myself up and climbed over the short wall in front of the stage and into the orchestra pit. I thought there might be a warm corner in there and sure enough, I found a carpeted area that suited me fine. Curling up with my back against the wall, I rubbed my sore head, and after a few minutes of feeling sorry for myself, fell fast asleep.

32. Where to Go?

WAKING UP EARLY the next morning, everything was dark, so I almost forgot where I was. My legs felt stiff, and I was terribly thirsty. Slowly, I felt my way out of the orchestra pit, and up the steps to the back stage area. There was a little light from some small windows high up on the wall, so I could see shapes vaguely. Feeling my way along a hallway, one of the doors opened into a restroom. Finding the light switch, I breathed a sigh of relief. It felt wonderful to wash up and drink my fill of cool, clear water.

Slowly, I tried to figure out exactly where I was, and where all those doors led. I needed to find the best way out of here. Peeking in at the huge curtained stage, I began to wonder what it must be like to perform there. Giggling, I started to imagine that, at this very moment, I could step out on that stage and pretend to be performing before an audience.

How should I entertain them, I pondered? Singing or dancing was out of the question—I had no ability in that direction. Perhaps I might act in a play, or maybe deliver a speech? But what would I talk about?

Ladies and gentlemen, lend me your ears . . . I will only borrow them for a minute or two.

That's just silly, and nobody would laugh. But I didn't want to tell a sad story either . . . *I'd better stop this nonsense*, I thought. It was time to find my way out of this theater, and get to Larkin Street where the bus would come to pick me up for school.

A door, at the back of the stage area, led out of the building and into the alley. As I raced away from the theater, I didn't worry about the alarm. By the time someone responded, I'd be long gone. Larkin Street was just around the corner and a few blocks up the street.

I was anxious about the time, and whether I'd missed my bus by taking too long backstage. Knowing that I had no intention of going back to the apartment, no matter what, there were some decisions I had to make. If I missed the school bus, should I go to the library, try to find Officer Phil, walk back to John Swett School and phone Miss Greenly, or what? I needed to make up my mind on how to get started.

Sure enough, as I turned the corner, I saw the rear end of the yellow school bus turning into Market Street. Speculating about whether I could possibly face Ma again, I shook my head. She might have calmed down enough since last night, but was that enough to make it safe now? Couldn't be sure. At any rate, I really didn't *want* to go back, even if she had calmed down. I'd only be waiting for bad things to happen again, sooner or later. Nope, not going back. *Wonder if there's a way to divorce mothers.*

But where should I go? I walked aimlessly toward my usual refuge. Knowing that it was too early for the library to be open, I sat on a bench in the square. After some time, I noticed that people were going in and out of City Hall. I'd never been in there, and wondered if there were some office to go to for help? Might they have an office for social workers?

Hey! A social worker! That's what I needed! Maybe I should go to Family Services where we went for testing? Mr. Lewis might help me find a social worker that can do something. Maybe a social worker could talk to Miss Greenly? Or maybe I could go to a shelter for kids, or a foster home? Lots of kids at school lived in foster homes, why not me?

Making a quick turn, I headed back towards the Orpheum Theater. Smiling all the way, I felt pleased that I had decided to go back there. I should of thought of it sooner, while I was leaving there from the stage door. All I'd had to do was turn the corner, go in the side door and up the stairs. That's where I headed now.

Using the elevator instead of the stairs this time, I walked straight into the office that had become so familiar during the summer. I hoped that the sour faced lady at the desk was on vacation, or something.

"I want to see Mr. Lewis," I said to the receptionist. (Unfortunately, it *was* the same lady at the desk that was there during the summer.) She dropped her chin, and looked at me over her skinny glasses.

"Do you have an appointment?" she asked, with no hint of a smile.

"No, I'm sorry," I said, trying to think of some excuse, "Uh . . . Our phone is out of order. But I do need to see Mr. Lewis urgently," I insisted, "Tell him that Nadine Williams needs to talk to him."

I thought that I might have sounded rude instead of urgent, so I changed my tone. "Please? It's *really* important."

The receptionist frowned, but turned around and went to the back offices. It seemed like I waited a long time for her to come back. When she did, it was with a look of disdain. She said, "Mr. Lewis is busy interviewing right now, but he said he would see you when he's finished."

She nodded toward the bench where we had waited for the interviews a few weeks ago, so I sat down and waited.

Mr. Lewis came to the reception area with his warm smile, and I felt suddenly relieved, thinking that things might possibly turn out well after all.

"Hello Nadine, come on into the office," he said, leading the way ahead of me.

Once we were seated, I was afraid that Mr. Lewis would began with questions I didn't want to answer.

"I'm surprised to see you here, Nadine. School opened yesterday, and I thought you were going to Lowell. Are you playing hooky already?"

The broad grin on his face told me that he was joking. But for some reason, when I heard his question, I burst into tears. I was disgusted with myself for being such a baby. It was two days in a row that I had not been able to start a conversation without bawling like a crybaby.

"Sorry, sorry," I apologized, when the sobbing stopped.

Mr. Lewis offered me the box of tissues from his desk, and waited for me to dry my tears. Then he leaned forward, with arms leaning on the edge of his desk.

"No Nadine, *you* don't need to be sorry. *I* should be the one to say 'sorry.' It was my fault for being insensitive when I knew perfectly well that it was something important that you wanted to talk about. *I'm* sorry—for making a joke of it."

33. One Solution, More Problems

WHEN I FINISHED TELLING Mr. Lewis about how this was the second time that I had run away from home, his face grew serious.

He frowned, "Well Nadine, I agree with your assessment. This seems to be a serious problem that you can't solve by yourself. I think it will probably take more than one person to help you. Also, it may take some time to get connected with the several agencies that should become involved." Then he raised his eyebrows. "By the way, your idea about divorcing your mother sounds like a good solution. But you're not quite old enough to apply for emancipation. You have to be at least fourteen."

"What is *emancipation* anyway?"

Mr. Lewis smiled, and patiently explained. "You used the word *divorce*, Nadine, but it is actually called *emancipation status* when separation from parents is found to be best for the child. However, kids younger than fourteen do not qualify, so you're not yet eligible for this."

Regretting that I was short of the required age for this *emancipation* thing, I said, "But I don't *want* to go back to Ma . . . I really don't think I *can*."

"I understand that you want to separate from your family, and I believe that you're perfectly justified."

Mr. Lewis paused for a moment, then went on, "Well then, let's find a solution to the first problem of where you might live. You need somewhere to stay temporarily. Do you have any ideas? Relatives you can live with for a while? Any aunts or uncles, cousins maybe? Any relative that can take you in for a few months?"

I thought about my conversation with Marina about where Ma came from, "No relatives here in California . . . If I have any aunts, uncles or cousins, they would all be in Alabama, I should think."

"That won't help. Whatever happens for you now, should happen in San Francisco, where we can keep track of you." Mr. Lewis pursed his lips as he nodded his head. He looked determined, but in a nice way.

That made me feel safe, but didn't solve my problem. I stared down at my shoes, then mumbled, "I did think about a foster home . . ."

Mr. Lewis nodded, "I think this is where we need that social worker that you mentioned. Any particular social services worker you were thinking of?"

"How about Sandra?" I asked.

"Oh, you mean the one who came to visit Emily during the summer?"

"Why not? She knows how Ma is. She knows Emily. She met the boys. She talks to other social workers, and she knows how to help people get what they need."

"Good idea, young lady . . . always thinking ahead, aren't you."

The compliment from Mr. Lewis made me smile. I waited for him to pick up the phone. Instead, he looked at me intently, and tilted his head to the side, "This is a really big decision. Are you *sure* about this Nadine? Once we start the process, it may be hard to stop. You're sure you won't change your mind in a day or two, and decide to go back home again?"

I understood what he was asking, and thought about all the familiar things I'd be giving up. There was Emily . . . how tight she held my hand . . . how she'd stand behind someone and peek out cautiously whenever there was a stranger around. Tom and Jimmy were a pain to take care of, but they were okay with having me boss them around—well, most of the time. Then there was my familiar corner in the bedroom . . .

"Oh! I need to get my books and my clothes," I said, remembering my notebook and backpack. "I do want to go to school, and I'd be lost without them."

"That's not a problem, Nadine. Whoever your case worker will be, that person will make sure to retrieve your personal belongings. My question is more about whether you would ever change your mind at any time in the near future."

Taking another minute or two to think about Emily and the boys, I said firmly, "No, I'm *not* going to change my mind."

"Okay then, here we go." Mr. Lewis reached for the phone decisively, and I felt a sudden surge of mixed-up feelings.

I wanted to think that whatever happened next would be better than staying with Ma. But I knew there was no guarantee. Where they sent me might be just as bad, or worse. Along with the *good* reports, I'd heard some horror stories about kids in foster homes. I wish there was someone to stay with that I already knew, like— "Marina!" I shouted. "Mr. Lewis, I could go live with Marina! I'll bet she would let me stay with her while this gets settled. She lives in the Mission now. I have her address and phone number in my book. I went to see her when she moved. I can get there on the bus."

34. What Now?

"WHOA THERE YOUNG LADY," Mr. Lewis said. "Who is Marina? If she's related, it sounds like a solution. If not, there's still a problem."

"But I know her . . . and she's a good person . . . and she likes me!" I insisted. "She was the one I went to see when Ma got really mad. Marina lived just across the hall and helped me whenever I needed it."

"I hear you, Nadine, but we'll need to follow the law on this matter. It is not easy to remove a child from her mother. Your Ma has legal rights too, and if we don't do this properly, she may insist that you return to take care of the laundry, and do the cooking, and all the other things that you did for her. She may say that you are necessary for the family to survive, and that she can't do without you. She can find a variety of reasons to force you to go back with her," Mr. Lewis paused here, probably to let that information sink in.

Then he went on, "It's wonderful that you know someone who is fond of you, and who might be willing to care for you, but the truth is that unless we take proper legal steps, your Ma is still in charge of your life, like it or not."

"I don't care what the law says, I'll *never* go back there! I kicked Ma in the shins! She's never gonna forget that! She said she wanted to kill me and I believe her. She nearly ripped my hair out of my head. I'm going to stay with Marina!"

"See here Nadine. Some kids do a lot worse than kick a parent, and are still sent back home. Unless we do exactly the right things here, you will have no choice in the matter. Running off to stay with a friend will not do what is needed." Mr. Lewis' expression had changed. Now he sounded seriously annoyed with me.

I didn't like the idea that having left Ma, I now had someone else telling me what I had to do. However, I thought it might be better not to argue with Mr. Lewis right now. Anything would be better than going back to

Larkin Street where I never knew what the rules were, but got punished anyhow.

"So—what are you gonna do now?" I said, resentfully.

"First things first, Nadine. We need to begin by getting you a case worker. I'll talk to the Department of Family Services. Just *be patient*, and let me get this set up for you, okay?" Mr. Lewis was really taking charge now, I could hear it in his voice. I didn't like it.

"It may be possible that this friend of yours could qualify as a foster parent," Mr. Lewis offered in a gentler tone. I think he said that to help me feel better, but it didn't work.

I took a deep breath and decided to keep my mouth shut. If Mr. Lewis said I should be patient, I decided to *show* him that I *knew* how to do that. But it really hurt, and I needed to get away from his office now.

Asking where the restroom was, I figured that I could be thinking about things alone, and not be corrected by Mr. Lewis. I was just slowing things down, and anyhow I did need to use the bathroom, so I left Mr. Lewis to his telephone calls.

When I got back from the restroom, I sat down and folded my hands in my lap. I decided to continue keeping silent, until I was asked to say something. In the meantime, I listened to Mr. Lewis' conversation on the phone. He was telling somebody about what had happened to me last night, and was asking about the possibility of having Sandra assigned to my case. When he smiled, I felt hopeful; and when he frowned, I imagined that there was a problem. Finally, Mr. Lewis hung up the phone.

He heaved a great sigh, "Well Nadine, there's good news and there's bad news. The good news is that Sandra's caseload would allow her to be your caseworker. The bad news is that she's on vacation right now, and won't be back until the end of the week. So they want me to take you to Juvenile Hall right now so the court can process things for you."

It was like being hit with a baseball bat. "Juvenile Hall! That's worse than going to jail! You can't take me there!" I said, and burst into tears.

Mr. Lewis let me cry and complain, and cry again, and just watched me until I got tired of yelling and crying. Then he pursed his lips and calmed me down with a soft voice, "I agree with you Nadine, Juvie is an awful place for kids. I wondered if you and I could work out something else?"

Grabbing a tissue from his desk, I blew my nose, wiped my eyes and nodded my head. "What else can I do?"

"If your friend will let you stay with her until Friday, Sandra can take over from there and do all the legal things the right way. It would be like "hiding out" for a few days. On my end, I can always plead ignorance because I never deal with the legal process anyhow."

While my eyes roved across his desk, the silence stretched between us.

"Do you have her number?" Mr. Lewis asked.

I recited it.

"Do I detect a tone of resentment in your voice, Nadine?"

Suddenly, I was ashamed of myself. Here was this nice man, trying to help me change my life, and here I was trying to show him who's boss. I should be on my knees thanking him, instead of creating problems.

"Sorry Mr. Lewis, guess I'm being snotty for no reason. It's just that I'm still feeling weird about everything that's happening."

Mr. Lewis hesitated for a minute, then shook his head sadly.

"I think most people would feel *weird* in your situation. You don't need to apologize for the way you feel, Nadine, it's simply how you feel right now. I wonder what my feelings would be if I woke up in a dark theater some morning, after taking abuse from a bully the night before?"

35. A Safe Place?

THOUGH I DISLIKED his ordering me around, Mr. Lewis was nice to include me in deciding which alternative would be best. He said I had the choice of accepting the social worker that could help right away, or waiting for Sandra, who I already knew and trusted. Those were my alternatives. *(That means to make one of two choices.)*

Mr. Lewis pointed out that if I decided to have someone other than Sandra, I would probably be placed in a shelter for a few days. If I decided to wait a couple of days for Sandra, I'd be taking a chance that Marina might not let me stay with her for some reason.

"Well, what do you think Nadine, try to hide out a couple of days and wait for Sandra to get back, or start the legal process right away and stay with other kids in Juvenile Hall?"

Beginning to feel uncertain about my own decisions, I asked, "What do you think, Mr. Lewis?"

"I think it would depend on how long it would take to find a proper foster home. It's a complicated process Nadine, and I'm not sure I understand all the details, but the court system is involved and that usually takes time."

"What does *that* mean?" I could feel my face scrunch up.

Mr. Lewis was shaking his head again. "It means that I don't know all of what's involved because I'm not a social worker."

He was turning his head right and left a lot today. "Basically, it would mean taking a chance either way," he said, "but you need to decide."

Should I go with starting the foster care process right away, and not know anybody at all at Juvie Hall? If I decided to ask Marina, I would be with someone familiar, but then I'd still have to go somewhere strange all over again. Here I was trying to make the most important decision of my life and I had to make up my mind right now! It was very clear that Mr.

Lewis was not going to tell me what to do, he was letting me make the decision.

Maybe, if Marina was willing to have me, I'd feel safe for a little while. It would be good to talk to her just like I did before she moved. I knew for sure that she would listen to me and be honest. So I stopped debating.

"Please—just see if she'll have me." I said, gulping back tears.

Mr. Lewis nodded and dialed the phone number I'd given him. I began to worry that Marina might be at work, but when he began talking, it meant she was home, and I heaved a sigh of relief.

"Hello, Mrs. Stevens? My name is Sam Lewis. I am calling from Family Services Center, and Nadine is with me at the moment . . . No, no, she's fine. But we have a situation in which you might be able to help."

Mr. Lewis then explained in detail, how Ma had hurt me bad when she lost her temper, and that I had run away from home, slept in the theater, and refused to go back home.

After a short pause for Marina to say something, he continued. "Yes, it is a shame . . . Yes, I agree with you . . . The situation now is that Nadine needs a safe place to stay until her social worker can find a foster home for her. She and I decided to ask if you could possibly provide her temporary shelter? . . . Oh . . . Well . . . If she can't stay with you . . . then we'll have to find something else."

Mr. Lewis turned to me and placed his hand over the telephone. "She's talking to her husband about it, but she sounds like she might be willing," he whispered. "She didn't say 'no' right away, and that's a good sign."

I smiled, and crossed my fingers on both hands. "Please, please," I whispered back.

Mr. Lewis went back to the phone, listened for a minute, and then said, "You're sure it will be okay if she comes right now?" He had a big smile, raised his eyebrows, and then nodded his head at me.

I jumped out of my chair and did a happy dance in a circle, right then and there, trying not to make too much noise.

After hanging up the phone, Mr. Lewis did something I didn't expect. He said that I should sit down for a minute, and listen to a plan he'd thought about while he waiting on the phone.

"Nadine, your mother knows me, and I know where you live. I would like to go and retrieve your books and your backpack. Maybe I can get your mother to give me some of your clothes too. Then you'll be able to go back to school right away. I can explain to your mom that you're going to stay with Marina for a few days. That way, she won't notify anyone that you're missing and start a search for you. I'll also have her permission that you can stay with Marina and Ted. What do you think of my plan?"

I was amazed that Mr. Lewis was willing to do all that for me, and so happy I almost hugged him—almost. Instead, I grinned. "That's a great plan, Mr. Lewis. Then we can call Lowell so the school bus can pick me up at Marina's address?"

"Right, and I'll leave that part up to you and Marina. After I pick up your things and drive you there, I'll have a lot of paperwork to do. So you'll be on your own until Sandra gets back."

Mr. Lewis was making sure that I'd get to Marina's safely, and I was grateful for his concern, but I couldn't help being impatient. "Okay, let's *go*," I said.

The rest of that day was like a dream. I thought that if it *were* a dream, I'd never want to wake up. Mr. Lewis took me to Larkin Street in his green Chevy and picked up my things from the apartment. He told me that Ma had yelled at him for "interferin' wid family bid'ness." He grinned when he imitated the way Ma talked, but I couldn't help but think he was a little worried.

Mr. Lewis didn't say much while he drove toward Market Street, but when he turned left on South Van Ness, I heard him say under his breath, "I may get into trouble for doing this—you should, you know, be in juvie hall, but I think it's the right thing."

I was so relieved that everything looked like it was working out. With a safe place to stay, I could go back to school, and in a few days Sandra would be back to find a good home for me. I even began thinking that if Marina could become a foster mother, I'd never need to move at all.

36. A Happy Place

MARINA AND TED welcomed me into their home. They found space for me in an empty room with a real bed. There was even a closet with some built-in drawers for my clothes. Everything was going well the rest of the week and during the weekend. But early Monday morning, the phone rang and Marina came to my bedroom with a worried look on her face.

"That was Sandra on the phone, Nadine. You won't be going to school today. She'll be here to pick you up around ten, and some legal matters need to be settled.

"Why can't I stay here until the legal things get done?" I asked.

"I don't think it can be done that way. I'm sorry Nadine, I wish you could stay, but the courts have strict rules about taking children away from their parents. Anyhow, we have to stick to the plan—remember? You were to stay here just a few days until Sandra got back?"

"Oh NO! They can't make me go back to Ma! I'll just run away again. I won't go back! I can't stay with Ma! She wants to kill me!" I yelled. Then I began to cry like a baby. Marina threw her arms around me and I think she cried a little too.

"Let's not give up yet Nadine, don't cry." She rubbed circles on my back and patted it. "You won't have to go back home. Sandra will explain it all as soon as she gets here. She said something about a place where other kids are waiting for a foster homes just like you. You don't have to be afraid that your ma will hurt you again."

"Why can't this be my foster home? I want to stay here with you and Ted! Why can't I stay here?"

The bell rang and I knew that it must be Sandra, so I dried my tears and tried to think of what to say to her so I wouldn't have to leave Marina and Ted.

Sandra came in with a look on her face that I'd never seen before. She was really upset, and though she hugged me and said how she remembered my helping her with Emily, her words came between clenched teeth.

"We have a problem, Nadine. Mr. Lewis took steps that were greatly beyond his authority. He should have known that he didn't have the right to leave you with Marina and Ted. Now we have to explain everything to a judge, and hope that it can all be straightened out," she said. The worried look on her face scared me.

"But he was trying to protect me. Isn't that what a person is supposed to do?"

"Well, you have a point there, Nadine, but we're talking about a legal system that requires specific steps to take to comply with the law. Marina and Ted were kind enough to take you in during this emergency, but you can't stay with them. You're going to need to stay with other children waiting for placement and we'll find a foster home for you as quickly as possible."

"Nadine was asking whether Ted and I might become foster parents, so she could stay with us legally," Marina said.

"That may take some time, but if you're serious I can bring the application papers to you tomorrow," Sandra said. "Now pack up your things Nadine, we need to get you processed into Juvenile Hall."

"But I want to stay with Marina, I know her and I know I can trust her. Why can't this be my foster home right now?"

"I'm sorry, that won't be possible, Nadine. We've already violated some important restrictions on what can happen here. The court is strict about how a minor is removed from parental custody. We'll just hope that your mother won't challenge this—the way it was done—or you may lose all your rights here Nadine. You understand this Marina? Can you explain to Nadine that she can't stay with you now?"

"Sandra's right, Nadine. It would be against the law for you to stay here. But I promise that Ted and I will fill out all the papers required to apply for foster parenting as soon as I get them, and in no time, I'm sure you can come back." Marina's smile was big and kind and I saw her wipe a tear from under one eye.

I couldn't decide whether to get mad or start crying about Sandra taking me away from Marina, or with joy because Marina was going to stand up for me. But right now, I didn't know where I'd be going or what kind of place I'd sleep in tonight. If there was something I could have done or said, I couldn't think of it. Running out the door and racing down the street to the church or the park would just mean more trouble, so I just cried as I packed my clothes in my backpack.

"It's not fair, it's just not fair," I blubbered. Then I gave Marina the biggest hug I could and followed Sandra down the stairs to her car.

37. Juvie

JUVENILE HALL was on Woodside Road, near where Twin Peaks and Market Street come together. It seemed like a long ride to Woodside Road. Sandra didn't say much along the way, and I didn't say anything at all.

When we arrived in the parking lot of the huge concrete building, I gasped. "This looks like a jail."

"You won't be here for too long," Sandra said, trying to sound reassuring. "You'll have plenty of company. There's a lot to do here with kids of your own age. You'll have a warm bed and hot food and high school classes during the day. The first thing they'll do is process your paperwork so that the application for foster care can get started the way it's supposed to."

It finally dawned on me to ask about Mr. Lewis. "Did he get in trouble for helping me hide out at Marina's?" I asked.

Sandra sat in silence, then she turned to me and squinted. "Yes," she said, softly. "But he didn't get fired or anything."

I wondered if she was waiting for me to say something. But after I learned that Mr. Lewis got in trouble over me, my breath had evaporated.

"I know all of this is hard for you Nadine, and I wish I could make it easier, but the law can't be ignored and even though it's a slow process, it will be better if we do it the right way."

She looked at me with that "let's be patient" attitude written across her face. I knew she was hoping I would go along.

"Sure," I mumbled.

"So let's get the show on the road," Sandra said, smiling.

"Sure," I said again, but a bitter taste rose in my mouth.

We opened our doors at the same time, got out of the car and walked up the ramp and into Juvie.

THE "INTAKE" PROCESS was a lot longer than I thought, and it was after lunch by the time I finished with answering questions and finishing up all the paperwork. Sandra stayed with me until the forms were filled out then she had to leave. "Goodbye Nadine, I'll see you soon," she said. And I was on my own.

Somebody helped me get a quick sandwich in the cafeteria, then I was sent to a classroom with six other girls around my age.

This was supposed to be my beginning week at Lowell High, when I'd meet all the new teachers, and have homework for every class. I had thought about being in a big school with lots of kids racing down hallways, trying to find the room for their next class. This was not what I had imagined at all. The six girls in this classroom were a sad looking bunch, all of them losers just like me.

The rest of the day was a blur. I hardly remembered anything from the classes I attended, but it didn't matter anyway 'cause I already knew everything that they were teaching. Dinnertime came and went and then it was bedtime. My bed was in a room with about eleven other girls between the ages of twelve and sixteen. The others had been here a while and were talking about a lot of things I didn't know anything about. I kept thinking last night when I was in a warm house with Marina and Ted—how safe it felt for me to fall asleep there. I was too upset to fall asleep here among strangers. So in my assigned bed at the far end of the room, I turned over to face the wall and cried myself to sleep.

THE FOLLOWING DAYS, I tried to pay attention to what was going on around me, but I had trouble concentrating. It felt like an eternity during those long hours of dressing, eating breakfast, going to classes, having lunch, more classes, time in the exercise room, having dinner, going to bed. Eating became a struggle, nothing tasted good, and I was never hungry so I left most of it on my plate. Unless somebody got into a fight, when everyone got excited, the routine was deadly. One day after another, over and over again, it seemed I'd never get out of there.

When the second week started, I tripped over a foot stuck out in the aisle during my social studies class. "What's your name and what's your game, sourpuss?" the owner of the foot asked.

I looked at a freckled face girl with a wide grin and decided not to make a fuss. Ignoring her, I took my seat and faced the teacher. It was another boring class about everything I'd already learned.

The freckle-face girl was waiting for me at the door. She was a lot taller than I thought, but really skinny. "Hi, my name is Heather, what do they call you?" she asked.

"Mickey Mouse," I said. "Leave me alone."

"Uh-oh, we got one of those prickly things, huh?"

I refused to answer and went off to the cafeteria. The annoying thing followed me and after getting a sandwich, sat at the bench across from me.

"What is it with you? Can't find a baby to pick on? Why not bother somebody your own size?" I was getting upset but didn't want to get in a lunchroom fight with freckle-face, or anybody else. "Just go away."

"Okay, okay, Grimface, I don't need to make friends with a Sadsack."

After she left, I felt kinda sorry. I told myself that she was probably just trying to make friends and I was being snotty just because I was stuck here instead of living with Marina and Ted.

The next time I saw Heather, she ignored me, doing just what I'd asked for. Now it was my turn to think about making friends. Maybe I could use a friend or two. It was bad enough to be in this place, but wouldn't it get worse if I didn't have anyone to talk to?

After a day or two of not talking with any of the other kids, I changed my mind about Heather and smiled as I passed her in the hallway. The next day I stuck my foot out to trip her in the classroom. The first thing you know we were exchanging stories about ending up there and what we were going to do when we got out. I thought that Juvie was not supposed to be a jail, but it sure felt like it. But then something good happened. Heather became my cellmate.

"So did you have a crazy Ma, like mine?" I asked.

"Naw, my Ma went off to jail last year. I was in a foster placement before I came here."

"So, did you do something to get kicked out? Or did you just run away like I did?"

Heather hesitated for a minute. "Just ran away," she said.

"For no reason at all? Just 'cause you felt like it?"

"Yeah, just 'cause," Heather said, with a smile.

I didn't learn until later that her answer was a legal term. "*Just cause*" meant that she had a good reason for leaving that home. The foster home she'd lived in was even worse than living with Ma. The man in the home insisted he had the right to have sex with her. And the other foster kids living there beat up on her because she got extra treats. She finally told the social worker on one of her surprise visits and all the kids were removed to Juvie. Heather had lied about running away, just so she didn't have to tell me about it at the time.

During the next two weeks, I began talking to other girls in my ward, and they had similar awful stories to tell about mothers and fathers and foster parents who made life miserable. I didn't like hearing these stories, but it didn't change my mind about running away from Ma. But I was still angry with the laws that made me leave Marina to come live in this horrible place. Heather and some of the other girls almost got to be friends with me, but I was super careful 'cause some of these kids were mean and would make trouble just to break up the boredom.

After my first ten days of misery, Sandra came for a visit.

"Everything is going well," she said cheerfully. "Marina and Ted have filed all the papers for foster care status, and the court is now in the process of making a decision on their qualifications."

"How long will that take?" I asked, cautiously.

"Another week maybe. I can't be sure. But I'll keep checking, and as soon as they're accepted, you'll be the first to know," she assured me.

Sandra waited a few minutes before asking how things were going for me. I think she already knew how things went here in Juvenile Hall, and really didn't want to know about it from me. I shrugged and didn't offer anything more.

Sandra continued then, "I told your mother that you were here, and that since this was the second time you ran away from home, you're now considered "ward of the court" waiting for placement in a foster home."

"What did she say when you told her where I was?" I asked.

Sandra pursed her lips as if she was not sure she should tell me. Then she seemed to relax. "Well then, your Ma said, 'Good! Da's jes' where she bee-long!'"

Sandra smiled after she imitated Ma's speech and I burst out laughing. It was the first good laugh I had in weeks, and I thanked Sandra for telling me.

After that, I waited and waited, hoping that the next day would bring news that all the legal stuff was finished, and I would be able to go back to Marina and Ted. I was allowed one phone call each day and I used it to talk to either Sandra or Marina, trying to understand why it was taking so long. I wanted to know if there was something I should do or say to make things move faster. But all I got was, "Patience, Nadine, patience. Everything that needs to be done is being done."

Being patient was not easy for me, I wanted to get out of there, and was feeling close to trying to break out. One afternoon I ran out of patience completely, when Donna, who sat behind me in science class, pulled the chair out from under me just as I was sitting down. My butt hit the floor, and the back of my head caught the edge of the chair. Stunned for a minute or two, I shook my head and turned around. Donna had her hand over her mouth, but I could see she was laughing. I got up slowly, afraid of getting dizzy, then turned around.

"Damn you!" I shouted, as I twisted my shoulders, drew my fist back and punched the hand over Donna's mouth.

"Owww!" she yelled, as her nose started to bleed all over the place.

That incident ended in detention for both of us for being "disruptive, aggressive, and combative."

Sandra appeared three days later and when I told her about the incident, she just shook her head and pressed her lips together, "I don't know if I would have done anything differently, Nadine. Controlling the impulse to retaliate after being injured is a really difficult thing to do, and I can't blame you for striking back." It made me feel better that Sandra understood, but I knew she was disappointed with my behavior too.

"So how are things going with the paperwork?" I asked, wondering about the definition of *retaliate.* I was pretty sure I knew the meaning, and was getting tired of making word lists.

Sandra explained that the department was still in the process of deciding on Marina's application for foster home eligibility,

"Just a few more days now and everything will be cleared for your placement," she said.

I tried to read Sandra's mood, but I couldn't tell if she was really sure everything was going well. I wondered if Ma had tried to stop the process. When that thought occurred to me, my heart nearly froze.

"D-d-did you talk to M-ma about this?" I whispered.

Sandra hesitated. "I guess you know your mother pretty well, Nadine. Yes, I talked to her, and she wants you to come home and take care of things again. She told the judge that she needed you, and promised that she'd stop drinking. She insisted that she'd never lay a hand on you again. I don't think the judge believed her, but most of the time parental rights are a pretty strong factor in deciding these cases. We'll just have to wait a few more days before there's a final decision."

I could feel the tears start, so I clenched my teeth, "No matter what the judge says, I'll *never* live with Ma again!"

38. Moving On

THE NEXT TWO DAYS, I was an emotional mess, but finally they called me to the office and told me to pack up my belongings.

"It's time for you to leave, Nadine," the counselor said, with a grin. "Sandra's on her way to pick you up this afternoon."

My throat closed, but I managed to squeak out, "Do you know where I'll be going?"

"Sorry, Sandra has all that information. I really don't know anything but the fact that she'll be here this afternoon. You need to be ready, so go pack up whatever you have to pack and be here in the waiting room by one o'clock, okay?"

When Sandra came in to sign me out, she smiled at me and said "Lucky kid! You hit the jackpot" and I knew it had all been worked out the right way. I didn't know whether to laugh or cry, so I did a little of both.

On our way to Marina's house, Sandra explained to me how the judge looked at all the evidence and weighed all the possibilities.

"He finally drew up an agreement with your Ma that allows her to reclaim parental rights when she meets all the terms of the contract," Sandra said.

A cold shiver snaked its way down my spine. "What kind of terms?" I croaked.

"Well, she has to attend AA meetings regularly, must provide evidence that she's stopped drinking, and needs to provide proof of successfully completing anger management therapy."

"You think she can do that?" I asked.

"I think it will be hard for her, and will probably take some time, but *maybe* she can."

By the time we ended that conversation, we arrived deep in the Mission District on Harrison Street and Marina's house. It was a great reunion with

Marina and Ted. They even prepared a welcome home cake, and Sandra stayed to celebrate with us.

BEING WITH MARINA AND TED was my Cinderella dream, and I wanted never to wake up. It took a couple of days before I got comfortable with the daily routine: up and dressed at seven—eat breakfast, make a sandwich for lunch, then catch the bus for school. Marina had already called Lowell High to make sure the bus would pick me up.

Marina drove me to school that first day so she could talk to Mr. Sims and Miss Greenly. After that, it was a matter of catching up with three weeks of homework. Every day I took the school bus home from school and had a snack of something with milk. Homework assignments were to be done first, then if Marina and Ted were still at work, I could walk around the neighborhood. Since I was going to help run errands, I needed to know where everything was located. It didn't take long for me to learn that this was an "ethnic" neighborhood. *(Ethnic means that most of the people living here have the same "cultural identity." In this case, most of them spoke Spanish.)*

Unlike the Tenderloin where many new families were Vietnamese (like Mr. Diem's), the Mission had mostly Latino families, people from Mexico, Central and South America. I thought that if I could take a class in Spanish, I would know what they were talking about.

Walking down 24th Street, toward Potrero Avenue, the wonderful smells of Mexican food floated around, making my mouth water. The grocery store on 24th and York Street had all kinds of things: fresh fruits and vegetables, a deli, frozen foods and shelves of canned food. It was called Ricci's Deli, and the guy at the register said that the owner was Italian, not Mexican.

"That's why there are so many different kinds of cheeses on display," he said. "And you won't find better salami, or mortadella, or prosciutto anywhere in the city, not even in North Beach."

Right across the street from Ricci's Deli was the *York Theater.* It advertised double features on Saturday, and though I didn't have spending money for movies, it was nice to know that it was nearby. I would wander in behind the ticket booth and stare at the pictures of movie stars, wondering how it would feel to have a big picture of me displayed like that.

On my way to 24th Street, I wandered to 23rd and York, where I saw the *Torino Bakery*. It was from here that every morning wonderful smells of fresh bread drifted into our windows. This neighborhood was a lot more interesting than the Tenderloin. People on these streets tended to business, going from one store to another, buying things, doing things, not sleeping on sidewalks, not wandering around looking for trouble like Charlie used to do.

After a few days of walking up and down the streets near Marina and Ted's house, I got the courage to walk all the way to Mission Street and that was really fun. Mission Street was much busier than 24th Street and had one block after another of interesting stores and restaurants. One day, after weeks of exploring in all directions, I thought I saw Charlie across the street at Mission and 28th. But it couldn't be Charlie, I thought. He was in jail and couldn't be lurking around here. When the man turned around I saw it was someone else who looked a little like Charlie. Heaving a sigh of relief, I proclaimed that the Mission District was a safe place to live and being with Marina and Ted was a good place to be.

When Ted and Marina were at home, I tried to be the kind of person they wanted to have around—not make a lot of noise and offering to help as much as I could. That was something I'd learned how to do well. After being there a few days, I decided to just keep out of the way. So I stayed in my room most of the time. It was lovely having a real bed and a place where I could sit and do my homework.

"You don't have to be by yourself, Nadine, you can come to the living room and talk to us if you want," Ted said, standing at the door of my room.

"Thanks. I'm just so happy to have a room of my own. I want to sit here on this real bed and think of how lucky I am. But if you want me to come and do something, I'll be glad to help out."

Marina joined Ted in the doorway, "No need for help right now, Nadine. We just want you to feel free to use the rest of the house. We don't want you to feel confined to your room—you're a part of the family now."

My throat kind of choked up and I almost cried. I never thought that being part of a family like this would ever happen to me. I wanted to say something nice to Marina, but the words wouldn't come out.

Most every day, we had breakfast and dinner together at the kitchen table. Marina was a good cook and I never had to eat oatmeal. Sometimes she cooked a whole chicken or sometimes enchiladas and beans. I ate a lot the first few weeks then began to slow down, cutting back on the huge helpings of everything.

"My goodness, Nadine, you would think that you had never had anything so good in your life," Ted teased.

"I never did, except when we went to Glide for holidays," I admitted, between forks full of spaghetti smothered in rich meat sauce.

Later on, I started thinking of what kind of food Ma was serving to Emily, Jimmy and Tom. Maybe, my not being there would mean they could each have a little more to eat. I wondered if they missed having me around. I thought about what Ma must have told them when they asked where I was. I was sure that they'd say *something* about why I wasn't living there anymore.

AFTER SCHOOL ONE DAY, I took the bus on Bryant Street to Van Ness, then walked over to John Swett school so I could check on Tom and Jimmy. Now that I was back in the neighborhood where Charlie used to hang out, I felt uneasy.

I found the boys on the playground for after school activities, and they were glad to see me. When I asked about Ma and Charlie, they seemed a bit reluctant to talk about them. "You guys afraid that Ma will get mad if she knew you were talking to me?" I asked.

Jimmy just smiled, but Tom didn't hesitate to speak his mind. "Yeah, how come you left us anyhow?" he asked.

"What did Ma tell you when I didn't come home?" I asked.

"She didn't say nothin' about *why*, she just say you wasn't comin' home no more," Jimmy said.

I took a deep breath and tried to explain as best I could. I wanted them to know it wasn't easy for me to leave them. "Well, you know how mad Ma gets sometimes, 'specially when I do something she doesn't like. So, after I came home from school that first day, she got so mad that I got real scared and kicked her, then ran away. I thought she wanted to kill me, so I couldn't come home again. See? I was too scared to come back."

I thought they might understand better if I didn't give them too many details. Jimmy just nodded, but Tom shook his head in disgust. "You know how mad she get. She been mad at you before, and you come back then." Maybe Tom thought I should have been braver than I was.

"How is Emily?" I asked, trying to change the subject. "And is Ma still working? I want to know what's happening," I persisted.

Jimmy started to explain that Emily was smiling more when they talked to her. Tom frowned and said that she was still a pest, but not so bad a pest lately.

Tom explained that Ma gave them permission to play in the schoolyard for an hour after school. He said that Charlie was out of jail on parole, but he came around less often, and that Ma had kept her job at the grocery store. She had decided it was okay to work for Mr. Diem, because he was a good Vietnamese man with a big family.

Hearing that Charlie was out of jail, made my heart skip a beat. Would he come after me for turning him in? He knew where my school was and how to get there. Would Ma send him to spy on me? Were they both so mad at me that they'd do something to get even? Now that I was older, what if they decided to do the worst thing? What if Charlie got me in his car, took me away and made me work on the street?

I was glad I'd gone to see my brothers. It had been a good visit and I was happy to hear that everything was okay with Emily, but now I knew Charlie was around, I felt a creeping dread.

I TOLD MARINA about my visit with the boys. "They seem to be doing okay. Ma still has a job at the grocery store and works during school hours, so she's there when Emily gets home."

"I'm glad that you went to see the boys. Maybe you can go to visit your mother one day?" Marina asked.

"I don't think so. Not now, anyhow." The information about Charlie's parole stuck in my throat like a chicken bone. I couldn't bring myself to tell her.

A FEW WEEKS LATER, I went to visit the boys again, but they shook their heads when I walked toward them, and said that Ma told them not to talk to me anymore. I didn't want to get them in any trouble, but did want to know what was happening to Emily. Actually, Sandra was really a better source for that information. I knew that she was keeping track of Emily's progress, so the next time we had an appointment, I asked her if I could visit Emily at Louise Lombard School.

"Let me check it out with the principal first, Nadine. Sometimes the children follow a strict schedule there, and I want to make sure you go at the right time," Sandra said. I think she was telling me that I shouldn't decide to go on my own, as I had with the boys. She told me that she would let me know if anything important was happening to Emily.

At our next appointment, Sandra reported as she had promised. "I want you to know that Family Services found a bigger apartment for your family, so they will soon move to another part of the city. Also Emily's school reported the good news that she was starting to talk."

I was happy about Emily, but I regretted not being there to hear her first words. Sandra asked me to wait a little longer when I asked if I could go to see Emily at school.

After my visit with Tom and Jimmy, I started having nightmares about Charlie. Sometimes, I'd wake up screaming, and Marina or Ted would come talk to me until I calmed down. I'd always have a hard time falling asleep again, afraid that the Charlie nightmare would come back.

One time, I dreamed that we were living in the old apartment and Charlie tied me up and pushed me down the stairs. I just kept rolling down and down those stairs and thought I would never reach the bottom. When I woke up, my arms were wrapped around my legs and it took a long time for me to stretch them out and make my muscles relax.

39. School Days

LOWELL HIGH SCHOOL was not as easy as I thought it would be. I had to make up homework for the weeks I'd missed at the beginning of the semester and it took me some time to catch up. I even thought that maybe my dream was also about too much homework. Those few weeks at Juvenile Hall did nothing to get me ready for the work at this school. I was glad to be taking Spanish though, because I was able to practice it in the stores on 24th Street and other places in the Mission.

Sometimes I couldn't finish all of my homework before bedtime, so I waited until I thought that Ted and Marina were asleep, then I closed my door , turned on the light and finished it all before going to sleep. I tried not to do that too often because I was really sleepy the next day.

Nearly every day during lunch periods at school, I saw my friend Katie. We talked about our classes and homework assignments even though we had very few classes together. She still lived near the Tenderloin on Justin Court and Katie said the neighborhood was getting worse every day with more homeless people around and old men sleeping in the streets. I asked her if she ever walked into the Tenderloin.

"Why do you want to know that?" she asked.

"I'm just curious if you ever saw anybody in my family, from when I lived there."

"Wouldn't know them if I saw them, would I? And if I did then what? Did you have a message for them?" she asked. Katie's smile was more a tease than a question.

"No, I wouldn't have any messages. But I've had dreams about my mother and her boyfriend, Charlie. I keep feeling like they're chasing me, or something."

"Who's Charlie?" Katie was serious now. So I told her all about Charlie and how he and Ma made us kids beg for money at Christmastime. I told her about how Charlie got on the school bus and followed me to school on my first day at Lowell. Katie listened but didn't ask a lot of questions, so I let it go at that, and tried to forget my bad dreams.

Katie and I only had gym class together, so we couldn't share homework ideas, but it was nice to have a friend I could talk to about schoolwork anyhow. Then things got more personal.

"What do you do about gym when you have your period?" Katie asked me one day.

I was surprised by how casual she was about "having periods" so I stalled before answering.

"Well, if we're using the pool, I just say *I need to be excused*," I said. "Otherwise, I do whatever activity is assigned."

Katie shook her head, "Oh, I can get out of the swimming with no trouble, but I wish I knew how to get out of playing basketball. Everything goes so fast in that game that I get out of breath all the time. I can never keep up. Besides, I'm too short to make baskets. If I ask to be excused, you think it might work with the basketball coach?"

"Always worth a try," I said.

Then we got to talking about boys. Katie had a steady boyfriend who lived on Geary Street. She told me that sometimes, when their parents were away, she and Jerry went to a movie together.

"I know you're younger than we are Nadine, but there are fun things to do in the City. Jerry said that his friend Anthony really likes you, and maybe we can do things together sometime?"

"I don't know Katie, I don't have much time to do anything more than I'm doing right now. Sounds like fun though."

"It's always worth a try, like you said?"

"I'll think about it."

And that's how our conversation ended. I did think about it, and was intrigued by knowing that some boy "liked" me. But right now there were too many other changes, for me to take on another one. I had so many things that were different for me now, I never thought about having a boyfriend . . .

Miss Greenly sent for me every now and then and asked how my new home was working out. And my homeroom teacher kept close watch on my grades and homework assignments. I was learning new words almost every day and always tried to ask my teachers for definitions, or I could always look them up in the school library.

I managed most of my homework on my own, but sometimes I asked Marina or Ted for help. Especially difficult for me were the problems in algebra, which were getting too complicated for me to solve easily. I usually turned to Ted for help in math. Marina was better with other homework, but Ted was better in math.

"How do I get this problem to work, Ted? The teacher was in a hurry when she explained it, and I kind'a got lost. Can you help me figure it out?"

"Sure Kiddo, let's see what the book says first."

And from there he took me step by step on how to convert and reverse, multiply, divide and solve. I was thankful for Ted's help, but always wished I could've done it by myself.

40. My Interesting Journey

TURNING FOURTEEN just after Christmas that year, I expected that I could apply for that "emancipation" that Mr. Lewis had talked about. I believed that having *emancipation,* I could never be forced to go back to live with Ma. It would be a terrible thing if that happened, but I remembered that Mr. Lewis said something about it being a *legal* issue. So since I didn't know how to do legal things on my own, the next time we met, I asked Sandra what I needed to do for emancipation.

Sandra smiled, chuckled, and then got serious, "Sorry for laughing Nadine, but I'll never get over how your mind plans ahead all the time. I admire your wanting to be as independent as possible, but in order to be eligible for emancipation the child must not only be at least fourteen years of age but also be *self-supporting,* and *living independently.*"

"Why do they make it so hard for kids to get protected?" I complained. "If I ever have to go back to Ma, she'll find a way to kill me. She hates me so much for being born, I know she'll do it when she gets mad again. Maybe I won't be able to get away next time!"

"I hear you Nadine, and I know how you must feel. But there's no way to get around the law. Those are the conditions that you must meet in order to have legal independence and live on your own.

Well, I was not supporting myself, nor was I living independently, so I needed to make other plans for the future, because Marina was going to have a baby. The baby would need my room, and there would be too much going on with Marina and Ted taking care of baby things. They didn't have any extra room, or any extra time to help me with my homework.

"I guess I'll have to go to another foster home?" I asked Sandra.

"I think you need to talk to Marina and Ted before we start looking for another foster home," Sandra said, firmly.

I began to wonder about how it would be to leave this house. Where else could I find such a great place to live? Marina and Ted were so good to me, and I think they really liked having me around. But with the baby coming, it felt like my luck was running out. For sure, another foster home would never be like this. The stories I heard from foster kids at juvie made me shudder. They told me that most foster homes had four and five kids living together, and it would be just like living with Ma all over again. I'm sure Sandra would do her best, but I'd probably land in a place where I'd have to do housework all the time and never have time for schoolwork. One of the girls said that her foster parents told her she had to work the streets for money because they were spending too much for her shoes and food. I thought she was making that up, but she insisted it was the truth.

I began to worry about what kind of foster home Sandra might find for me. I shuddered to think of what those girls at school described as their foster parents. It was even worse when I remembered from the kids at Juvenile Hall. I wondered if I would get a foster mother that might be worse than Ma, or a foster father like Charlie. My teeth clenched, and shoulders tensed so bad that it was hard to get to sleep sometimes.

When I finally got around to talking to Marina about my going to another foster home before the baby came, I could see that she was really surprised. Her jaw dropped and her eyes grew wide. She studied me for a few minutes before taking a deep breath, then took me by my shoulders and looked fierce.

"What are you talking about, Nadine! You just forget about such nonsense! You belong right here in this house, with me and Ted! And sure, the baby will be more work and a bit of adjusting for all of us. But it'll all work out just fine, believe me. I'll stay home for a few months, but I intend to go back to work sometime. So there will be days when Ted and I work the evening shifts at the same time, and we'll need a reliable baby sitter. Who better to babysit our baby than someone who lives right here with us!" she said, emphatically. "Besides, you're like my little sister now. Just like the sister I had in Brazil before my mother died. Did I ever tell you that story, Nadine?"

When I shook my head, Marina continued, "Well, before I came to San Francisco to live here with my aunt Gina, I lived with my mother and sister in South America. When Mama died, my sister went to Florida to live with one of my other aunts, and I came here to live with Aunt Gina." Marina paused and got a far-away look in her brown eyes, then spoke again, more slowly. "It's a long story Nadine, and someday I'll tell you all about it. But for now I want you to know that you belong with me and Ted, and that's final!" Marina smiled that warm smile of hers, tossed her curly dark hair, and hugged me.

I heaved a great sigh of relief, and I almost cried, but then we both started laughing. Ted came in to see what all the noise was about and I explained to him how worried I had been about finding a new home.

Ted grinned, "You are always full of surprises, Nadine. How could you think that we'd ever let you get away? Now that we have that settled, what's for dinner, Marina?"

Ted put his arm across my shoulder, and we all started laughing again. We had to tell Sandra that there was no need to look for a new placement, and we planned how the space could be arranged when the baby came.

41. Baby Melissa

BABY MELISSA decided to arrive one morning during breakfast. It was a Friday and I was sitting there spooning cornflakes, when I heard the worry in Marina's voice.

"Ah-h-h Ted? I think it's time. The contractions are awfully strong now. Get the hospital bag. I'm pretty sure the baby is coming soon. "

It was so exciting, I forgot all about breakfast, "What can I do? What can I do?" I shouted, jumping out of my chair.

"You do nothing young lady," Ted said firmly. "Finish your cornflakes and get ready for school."

"But the baby's coming, the baby's coming!" I insisted.

"Yes, Nadine, the baby's coming, but taking care of that is our job, Ted's and mine. You need to take care of *your* job and get ready for school," Marina said, agreeing with Ted.

Seeing that both of them were doing everything in a calm organized way, I stopped being frantic. The night that my baby sister died in the bathroom flashed through my mind, and I had to stop and think that this was different. Both Ted and Marina acted like they knew what to do and were doing it step by step. Blanket for the baby, toothbrush and comb for Marina, all ready to go in the bag they'd packed weeks ago.

Ted called the number on the notepad by the phone, got a warm coat for Marina, and put on his jacket. I left the house with them, watched Ted help Marina into the car, and waved goodbye as they left for the hospital. *It was going to turn out right this time*, I reassured myself.

THAT WAS THE LONGEST DAY I ever spent at Lowell High School. It was hard to concentrate on what the teachers were saying, but I wrote down the homework assignments and took a few notes, trying to keep up. I didn't tell anyone what I was concerned about, even though my friend Katie asked me why I was so quiet.

I could hardly wait to get home after school, but nobody was there. At first I was worried, but then remembered that not all babies came in a hurry, and maybe it was still being born. I wondered what that might be like, and whether Marina would hurt a lot during the delivery. It couldn't be easy to have a whole person come out of your body all at once. Maybe it would be quick for Marina, I hoped so.

Finally the phone rang. "Nadine, you have a beautiful baby sister!" he said. I could picture him smiling into the phone.

Baby Melissa had been born just before noon and was very healthy. Ted's voice was calm but he laughed when he said the baby had dark hair just like his. He said that Marina was fine and that he would bring her and the baby home in a day or two. He would stay at the hospital for another hour or so, then come home to have dinner with me.

42. Moving Ahead

AFTER TWO YEARS with Marina and Ted, and when baby Melissa started to walk, I began thinking about my past life as belonging to someone else. The old Nadine was someone who was scared all the time, always trying to guess what Ma's mood would be when I got home from school. It had been a long, hard journey for that Nadine. But right now I was a different girl and a very happy person. The bad dreams about Charlie and Mom had faded and I felt secure in this warm, loving family.

Ted wasn't sure whether or not I'd be interested in helping him with his chores, but he tried to include me whenever he could. When Ted and I worked in the garden he taught me how to plant string beans, tomatoes and zucchini. He explained everything carefully and only got annoyed when I made the same mistake more than once.

"Nadine, why do you keep *flooding* the plants with water? Didn't I tell you that with excess water roots will rot? Plants can't take too much water. Please try to remember when you're watering the garden—plants need some water every day— but not so much as to drown them. Okay?"

When Ted scolded me, I wanted to snap back at him. I wanted to say that he should do it himself, if he wanted everything done perfect. But thank goodness, I always stopped to think before saying the first thing on my mind. It was one useful habit that I'd picked up while living with Ma.

"Sorry Ted, I'll remember to be careful next time," I would answer.

Marina was usually more patient than Ted, but she wanted me to do things the right way also. When she first came home from the hospital with baby Melissa, she started lessons on "baby care" right away.

"Don't be afraid, Nadine. Babies don't break so easy. I know she's still weak and helpless, but you can pick her up without hurting her. Just start by putting your hand under her head, and slide your other hand under her back. Babies have weak neck and back muscles so she can't hold her head up by herself. In a couple of months she'll be stronger, and soon won't need for you to be so careful."

I couldn't remember picking up Tom or Jimmy or even Emily when they were babies. I did have a picture of baby Emily lying in the laundry basket, and know that I used to feed her with a bottle. My memories of what happened before Emily began walking were all fading away.

I learned to feed baby Melissa while holding her in my arms. That was a good feeling—holding her in one arm and feeding her with the other. It was getting easy to pick her up for a feeding or diaper change, while Marina stood by and smiled.

After a couple of weeks of watching while Marina gave Melissa her bath, Marina asked, "Are you ready for this job now?"

I had been watching carefully while Marina did this, but the way she was holding the baby seemed complicated.

"I can't do that!" I said, in a panic. "She's all wet and slippery and she'll slide off and drown! I can't do that." I whined. "It's okay for me to pick her up and feed her, 'cause I can hold her against me, but I can't hold her that way in the water."

"Nonsense, Nadine. I'm surprised to hear *you* say, 'I can't'. You've never been afraid of doing anything when you made up your mind to do it. Today you can watch one more time, then remember what to do at each step, and you can begin tomorrow. I'll be here to watch and help if you need me. I'll bet you'll be able to do it in no time," Marina said.

"It won't be long before Ted and I think about a double shift at work, so sooner or later you need to be ready for serious babysitting all by yourself. You'll have to know how to do everything for this baby sister, just like you did for Emily."

Remembering how I took charge of Emily's potty training made me feel more confident. Melissa was a lovely baby and had such a sweet way of smiling when I talked to her. With Marina's help, I learned to bathe the baby properly, keeping my left arm under her head and shoulders, gripping *her* left arm tight, and using my right hand to do the washing. It was not easy, but I was really careful, and never let the baby slide under my arm or turn herself over when I bathed her. While caring for Melissa, the best time was after her bath. Drying off her tiny body with a fluffy towel was so much easier than bathing her, it always seemed safer.

Then one day when she was sparkling clean and smelling like a fresh bar of soap, I picked Melissa up to kiss her nose before diapering her. At that exact minute she promptly peed on herself—and on me. Then she looked at me with a big smile and giggled. It was as if she knew she was playing a trick on her big sister. Cleanup had to be done all over again, beginning to end—Melissa's bath, clean clothes, another towel, and me. After that one time, it never happened again. Melissa had taught me a lesson that Marina didn't need to teach.

After a time of quiet contentment while learning to be part of a real family, I began to feel restless. Everything had become a kind of habit: breakfast at seven o'clock, on the bus for scheduled classes, school lunch with Katie, bus ride home, homework, dinner with Ted or Marina, in bed by nine.

Ted and Marina had been trying to work as many hours as possible since expenses kept piling up. Baby clothes, doctor visits, dental work (especially for me since Ma didn't believe in dentists), health insurance for the four of us, food, clothing—everything was so expensive. So while Ted and Marina were busy working overtime, I got stuck in routine things. There was nothing wrong with that, but it was not very exciting.

It wasn't long before Katie and I found ways of getting into trouble just to make things interesting. We considered ourselves outsiders in a way. We both came from poor families, and were a bit younger than most other kids at Lowell. As "out of district" students, with "special programs for gifted students" we didn't mix much with older kids.

After a long discussion about being left out of most social events because of being "too young," Katie and I still wanted to do fun things. In the middle of our senior year, Katie turned sixteen first. We began to talk incessantly *(That means all the time, never stopping.)* about learning to drive a car. I checked it out and I could get a learner's permit at fifteen and a half, so then I became obsessed *(That means preoccupied, fixated and passionate about something.)* with learning to drive.

When I mentioned the subject one night at dinner, Ted and Marina said I was not old enough, and should wait until I was at least seventeen, but eighteen would even be better.

"At your age it's not a good idea for young girls to be driving in the busy San Francisco traffic," Ted said.

"I just read about a horrible accident right near here on Potrero Avenue last week. It's a good thing that it happened near the hospital, or the kids in that car would never have lived through it," Marina added.

"But a lot of Lowell kids are already driving their *own cars* to school," I insisted.

"We're a long way from talking about that idea, Nadine. We don't even have enough money to consider getting a new car to replace our old clunker, let alone a car for you, young lady." Ted ended the discussion.

The first idea I had was one day when while we were having lunch. "Katie, what do you think would happen if we just walked in and signed up for the Driver Training Class? If we pass the course and prove we were really good drivers, maybe it would convince our parents to trust us with driving?"

Katie looked at me with admiration. "Great idea! Let's sign up next semester." Katie was really enthusiastic, and we planned our classes around the time that Driver Training was scheduled. I'd seen students from that class practice driving in the big parking lot across the boulevard by Lake Merced. I thought it would be a perfect place to demonstrate our driving skills when we passed the course.

Katie was such a wonderful friend. She liked my ideas, and I liked hers, so we got along really well. When she was thinking up something new she would tilt her head to the side as if trying to concentrate better, then toss her head to the other side making her hair bounce. Then she was ready to say what was on her mind.

When the new semester began and we walked into the driver training class, the instructor asked students for parental permission letters. I panicked as the others started handing the instructor their letters.

"I forgot to bring mine," I said when the teacher got to my desk.

"My father was out of town," Katie added a few minutes later.

"If you don't have your letter today, you may come back when you have it," the instructor said, dismissing us. We walked away trying to think of some way around the "parental permission" obstacle. *(That means something that gets in the way.)*

Katie and I put our heads together trying to think of how to get into the class.

Katie was first to come up with an idea, "Maybe we could write permission letters ourselves?" she speculated.

"Well . . . I know how Marina writes, I'm pretty sure I could copy her writing pretty well," I offered. I thought that if I practiced, I might do it well enough to fool the instructor.

"Yeah? Well, I'm not so sure I could copy my dad's handwriting," Katie said a bit worried. "He has a really funny scrawl that I can hardly read, let alone write it. You think we could type letters and then just sign them?"

Planning how to type and then sign the letters started to get complicated so we decided that it was too dangerous if both of us tried to forge permission letters. If we ever got caught, we'd be in real trouble at home as well as at school, and we would never be trusted again. All of our ideas about getting into the driving class without producing those letters fell apart quickly, and our frustration grew. Especially difficult for us was listening to the boys at the table next to us at lunch time laugh about how they convinced their parents to get the models they wanted.

"I just told my dad that I had researched the information on new cars and found out that the model I wanted was safer than the cheaper one they'd decided on," one of them boasted.

Another laughed and said, "My mom insisted that I get a brown car so it wouldn't need the carwash so often. But when I mentioned that the computer said that red was seen more clearly in heavy traffic, she decided to get the red one I wanted."

Katie frowned, "It isn't fair. Those kids aren't any smarter than we are, yet they have a license and get to drive, but we don't,"

"Yeah, and they go around bragging about how great it is to get the car they wanted for a birthday or something," I agreed.

With all this complaining about what a terrible injustice we suffered, deep down, we both knew that we were just being jealous, and should have left it at that. But instead of letting it go, we got more and more worked up. During one lunch period, we decided to run over to the parking lot and mark up some of those fancy cars. Using our lipsticks we drew cartoons on the biggest, newest cars we could find. We were so mad that those kids could do what we were not allowed to do. We just wanted to get even. It didn't make any sense really, but it made me feel better that we were getting away with something. Luckily we never got caught, but if we had it would have been awful.

The day after we marked up those cars, the principal made an announcement on the intercom, "It has come to my attention that some student possessions have been violated. Anyone caught vandalizing private property on our premises will be expelled or prosecuted immediately."

The whispering started immediately. *What had been done? Where did it happen? Who did it? When did it happen?* Everybody had questions and nobody had answers.

The following day when it was known that it was student cars that had been vandalized, there was some speculation that kids from rival schools were responsible. Others said that someone from the carwash in Stonestown needed to stimulate more business. Some even thought that jealous boys who didn't have cars had marked them. Very few suspected it was two girls who were expressing frustration.

Both Katie and I felt guilty and ashamed for being so foolish. We were dutifully studious and quiet the rest of that month. I decided that I wanted to spend more of my after school time exploring the Mission neighborhoods again, and cool off my relationship with Katie for a bit.

ONE AFTERNOON, after buying an ice cream cone at the corner of 24th and York, I crossed the street to check on what was playing at the York theater. So there I was behind the York Theater ticket booth, focused on a poster for Paper Moon. Tatum O'Neal looked like an orphan. I wanted to see this movie. When I felt a tap on my shoulder. I jumped, startled by the unexpected interruption of my own poor little girl fantasy. When I turned around, there was Charlie standing behind me, a big grin on his face.

He'd let his greasy hair grow long in a pony tail and had a scraggly, hippie mustache, but there was no question that it was Charlie. There he was right in front of me, strutting like a peacock and smiling.

"Hi there stranga'. Wad a surprise ta see ya. I hear you'se doin real good at tha fancy school ova' by Stonestown. Me and Helen is missin' havin' ya 'round."

I froze. "What're you doing here Charlie? Whadda ya want?" I was debating if I should run. Or maybe scream? How could I get away from him?? What was he going to do to me for getting him arrested?

"Not ta worry honey, jes' checkin' up on ya. Don' wanta lose track'a where you is and how ya doin. Tha's all." Charlie's voice was dripping honey, just the way he used to talk to Ma, when he wanted something from her.

"You leave me alone Charlie! Stop scarin' me or I'll call the cops!" I shouted, trying to act brave and tough.

I knew that Charlie didn't like cops, and hoped he would get scared and leave. But he didn't look like he was scared, nor did he leave. I felt the same panic as I did that day he got on the bus with me—on that awful bus ride to Lowell. I wondered how Charlie knew where to find me and how he planned to get even with me for turning him in that day. Is that why he came all the way to 24th Street? Did he come to scare me? To get even with me?

Charlie just tilted his head and grinned that awful grin he had when he's pleased with himself. "Aaw now" he said. "No need ta' make no fuss, honey, I 'jes do like yo' ma tole me. She wanna know whea' you is and how ya doin'. Now's I see you'se okay, I don' botha' ya no moa taday."

With that, Charlie turned around slowly and walked away. He turned right heading toward Potrero Avenue where the bus line runs downtown.

When my legs stopped shaking, I turned left, away from the theater, and ran home as fast as I could. When I raced up the stairs, and ran down the hall, I got to my room and hid my face in my pillow, trying to shut out the picture of Charlie's hideous grin.

When Marina got home from work, I told her all about Charlie finding me on 24th Street. I talked in a rush. I wanted to tell her everything, all at once. "I was scared, really scared Marina. I never thought I'd ever see Charlie again. I never thought he would look for me. But now I don't know what to think. If he can find me so easily, he can come after me any time he wants. He said he wouldn't bother me anymore *"today"!* Does that mean he plans to come back another day? What shall I do? What *can* I do?" I broke down in sobs.

Marina put her arms around me and tried to calm me down. "Hold on Nadine, let's think about this carefully. Maybe it was by chance that Charlie ran into you today."

I shook my head. "No. He said that Ma sent him to find me. Told me a story about her wanting to make sure I was okay. It's not by chance that he found me," I said, through hiccups and sniffs.

"But if he said that Helen sent him and he was just checking to see if you're okay, maybe he's telling the truth?"

I shook my head again, "No. Ma doesn't care whether I'm okay or not. He *always* says that Ma sent him when he does something wrong. That's just Charlie telling another lie about what he does for himself."

Marina gave that some thought. She had a way of pursing her lips and pressing a finger to her chin when she was thinking. "You may be right, but we don't know anything for sure. We're doing a lot of guessing about why Charlie ran into you on 24th Street. I think this is something for us to discuss with Sandra."

I agreed, "Maybe we should phone her right now and tell her that Charlie is stalking me."

Marina laughed, "Do you really think that's what he's doing? He only saw you once."

"What would *you* call it?" I challenged.

Marina frowned.

All I could think of was how that tap on the shoulder scared me. When I was calmer, I started thinking what to do about it. Burying my head in a pillow was not going to be the way to manage Charlie.

A FEW DAYS LATER, we talked to Sandra in person. She came for a home visit on her regular schedule. After Marina had called and informed her that Charlie was bothering me, Sandra had talked to Ma, who said she'd had nothing to do with it.

"I'm not sure what to make of Charlie's behavior," Sandra said. "I did believe Helen when she denied knowing what Charlie had done. I'm sure she was telling me the truth. In any case, I've contacted Charlie's probation officer and he's to follow up with a direct warning to Charlie that he's facing incarceration if he bothers you again. We agreed that this was not acceptable behavior, especially when probation was granted reluctantly."

Sandra tried to be reassuring, but the whole experience left me with an uneasy feeling. It was quite a few days before I worked up the courage to go for a walk by myself again. I decided to stay away from the busy traffic on 24th Street and began to explore the more open areas in the Mission.

Back at school, I told Katie all about my experience and she laughed when I told her I almost wet my pants when I turned around and saw Charlie standing there. She refused to be serious about the incident, and I began to see the humor in it too. Katie's laughter always made me feel better.

43. Testing the Waters

LATER THAT MONTH, Katie came up with another scheme, and this was really daring, since it involved leaving school premises without permission. But it was good fun while it lasted and I needed a distraction from the experience with Charlie. She suggested that since our last period of the school day was in Study Hall, we shouldn't waste our free time with things we already knew. Besides, homework assignments could be finished at home. This was especially appealing to me because Ted or Marina usually supervised my homework. I didn't know about Katie's dad—whether he checked her homework or not.

"So what are we gon'na do instead?" I asked.

"Hmm . . . Well, the Shopping Mall at Stonestown is near enough, and we can easily run over, walk through the mall, and get back before the school buses leave to take us home," Katie argued.

I was a little worried about breaking school rules again. What if we got caught this time? We were able to get away with marking up cars, but this was even more serious. Leaving the school grounds required a note from parents, and we didn't have that. Katie didn't seem to be worried at all, so I decided to go along. We left the school by the back door, ran south along Lake Merced Boulevard, then went left up to Stonestown. It wasn't far, but we needed to start back early enough to get back in time to catch the bus.

"I think we ought to try this one day next week just to make sure it works, okay?" I asked Katie.

We had no problem on the trial run, so decided that two or three days a week would be enough to keep us happy. After a couple of weeks of getting away with this routine, one Tuesday we stayed too long at Macy's trying on shoes, and I missed my bus to the Mission. When I got home I had to explain why I needed to take a streetcar instead of the school bus that day.

I had to lie. "Well . . . my math teacher asked me to stay after school . . . to go over one of the algebra problems that I missed on yesterday's test. That's why I missed my bus."

"Really? I thought we had all those algebra equations straightened out last week," Ted said. He sounded worried, like it was his fault.

"Oh, I got all those right," I said, quickly. "It was a surprise test, and the problem I missed came up after we did *tha*t homework," I lied, again.

"Guess we'll need to go carefully over algebra before you take your next math test?"

"Sure Ted, that would be great. Thanks," I said, heaving a sigh of relief that Ted didn't ask to look at the "problem" I stayed after school for.

After that, I was much more careful to watch the time when leaving Stonestown. I made sure I was back to school well before my bus left. I wondered why Katie never worried about the time. She had a school bus to catch, just like I did. Maybe her bus downtown left much later than mine?

A fast walk through the mall became boring and Katie agreed that it was not fun anymore. Since I dared not take any more chances with school schedules, we thought we might do something together on a Saturday or Sunday. We might take the streetcar to the zoo, or go window shopping in the Mission, or check out the Community Center on Potrero Avenue.

"Hey, how about going to a movie?" Katie exclaimed, during study hall one Friday afternoon.

That seemed like a good idea. "Sure, why not," I answered eagerly, "I can meet you at 24th and Potrero, and we can walk to the York Theater right down the street."

"Or . . . maybe we could go to the Orpheum or the Golden Gate on Market Street, downtown. Why don't you find out when Marina or Ted plan to be home on a Saturday, then we can plan for a *real* movie," Katie said.

"Okay," I said. "What movie do you want to see?" I asked.

Katie pondered, then looked at me with mischief in her eyes.

"Wasn't there a movie theater near where you used to live in the Tenderloin? Seems to me the paper said it was showing a movie about a *Green Door* or something like that?"

I knew full well what movie Katie was talking about. The boys at the lunch table next to ours had been whispering about that movie for weeks. Everyone had heard that it was full of kinky sex scenes.

"Gee Katie, that's one of those "adult only" shows isn't it? I don't think they'd let us in. Do you really want to see something like that ?"

"I've always been curious, haven't you?"

"I don't know," I giggled. "We'd have to pretend we were a lot older wouldn't we?"

"Betcha' we could do it! We could use makeup, and wear some older clothes. Besides, all they can do about it is say, 'Sorry we don't admit juniors.' Then we could go see something else on Market Street."

I asked Marina and Ted if I could go to a movie with my friend Katie the following weekend when Marina was home to care for Melissa. Asking where we would go and what we planned to see, I said we wanted to see a movie downtown, but hadn't decided which one yet.

Marina had met Katie when we went to the Mother Daughter Tea together. Marina had agreed to go as my mother and when I explained that Katie's mother had died several years ago, Marina offered to adopt her for the day. Katie and Marina seemed to like each other right away. So when I asked to go, Marina agreed. Since I'd been getting such good grades at school, Ted provided the cash for bus fare, lunch, and popcorn with the movie. He asked me if Katie's dad had agreed to this excursion, and I assured him that it was all approved by Katie's dad. This was true—according to what *Katie* had told me.

The following day when I reported that Ted and Marina had agreed, Katie was so excited she could hardly stop grinning.

"Wow Nadine, just the two of us? That's great!"

Then Katie got that funny look on her face. Pursing her lips and raising her eyebrows it seemed like a question was running through her mind. I waited and wondered what kind of new mischief she was planning.

"Bubble, bubble, cooking up trouble little witch?" I asked, smiling.

"I was just thinking. Do you suppose your folks might agree to a sleepover with me?"

I hesitated a minute, not understanding exactly what she meant, "You mean for *me* to spend all night at your place, and not go back home until Sunday?"

"Yeah, that's what I meant. Think you could ask about that? It would really be fun, Nadine. I really hate being alone all night when Dad's away on a business trip."

"You didn't tell me your dad was away this weekend. When did you find out he would be going on another trip?"

"I don't tell you *everything* Nadine. Besides why would you want to know about my father's trips?" Katie sounded annoyed.

"I'm just concerned. It means you're alone a lot if he's on so many trips. How often does he leave you by yourself?"

"Not often. Anyhow, it's no big deal. Now how about it? Can you ask about a sleepover, or do you *not* want to stay with me?"

44. Preparing the Deception

IT WAS ALL ARRANGED with Ted and Marina that Katie and I should meet early on Saturday, go to an afternoon movie, have lunch on Market Street then have a "sleepover" at her place.

"You know how to get from Katie's and the bus on Van Ness Avenue to take you home?" Marina asked.

"Oh sure, I know my way on those bus routes. I lived there for a long time, remember?"

"I know, but things are changing in that neighborhood, and I want to be sure you're aware about bus schedules that are different on weekends," Marina insisted. She was frowning and looked like she was worried about something.

"Sure, I know about that, I'll be fine. Be back tomorrow on the Bryant Street bus around noon, okay?"

"Sounds about right. See you then, and have a good time," Ted said.

I thought that Ted might want me out of the house before Marina had a chance to worry about something else. Remembering what Ma would say when I left our little apartment on Larkin, I knew how really lucky I was to have two parents who were concerned about my safety.

As we had planned, I met Katie at her place and we started to get ready for our big adventure. She had bought some makeup that I'd never seen before, and we started trying to make ourselves look older.

"Don't worry about your hair Nadine, we're going to wear bandanas that will hide part of our face and cover our neck too, so we won't look so girly."

Katie had thought of everything it seemed, so we wore big sweaters and slacks that covered everything that might give us away.

"Where did you get these baggy clothes?" I asked.

"There's a thrift store on Mission Street that I like to wander through," she said. "They have lots of these old clothes and sell them for practically nothing."

"Doesn't your dad ask about where you spend his money?" I asked.

"You are the most inquisitive person I've ever met, Nadine. Always asking questions about my dad. You want to marry him or something?"

I could tell that Katie was really annoyed, and I didn't know what to say, but I had to say something. "No, I don't want to *marry* him. I just want to *know* about him. Is there something wrong with that?"

"You ever hear the word '*butinski*'?"

I shook my head *no*, it was not one of the words I had on my list of words to learn. "How do you spell it?" I think I knew what the word meant, but if I was going to look it up, I had to know how to spell it. Besides, we needed a distraction from where this argument was going.

Katie laughed and she stopped being annoyed, which is what I wanted anyhow. "I'll write it down for you later," she said. "Now stop asking silly questions so I can help you put on these eyelashes."

I thought it was going a bit too far, putting on eyelashes, so I decided not to go along with that. I wasn't too happy about the dark red lipstick and rouge either, but I tolerated it.

"Really, they'll think we're "ladies of the night"—and it's only afternoon." I laughed, but Katie didn't.

"No they won't, they'll think we're grown up," she insisted.

"Well, then you can wear the eyelashes, I'll go without," I insisted.

"Please yourself," she said.

When we were finished with our transformation (*That means change from one thing to another.)* we looked more like clowns than grown-up women. But Katie was satisfied, and we left her place in time for the three o'clock show.

Katie said that the newspaper had all show times listed and I was sure she got the time right. However, I had become more and more doubtful about being able to get away with this adventure. I hoped that we would not run into anyone that I knew. Officer Phil might be on duty in that neighborhood, and I would have to explain to him what we were doing in these costumes. Maybe he wouldn't recognize me, I reassured myself.

We walked down Van Ness Avenue to Civic Center, and went over to the theatre. I was a bit uneasy, but Katie seemed so excited about seeing a film that all the older boys were talking about, I began to relax a little, but still had questions.

Stopping at one corner, I asked Katie, "Are you really sure that you want to do this? There's a good show at the Orpheum, we could go there instead."

Katie just laughed, "Come on Nadine, don't be so slow. We need to be there when it starts. It won't be the same if we get there in the middle."

In spite of my being anxious, I hurried to keep up with Katie. We had but a short walk, and before I knew it we were standing at the box office.

45. Echo from the Past

AS WE APPROACHED the ticket window, I could tell by her expression that Katie was not as brave as she pretended. She slowed down and tried to let me get ahead of her, hanging her head a bit. I wasn't going to let her put me out in front to ask for tickets, that was her job. She had our money, and it was her idea, so I got behind her and whispered, "This is what you wanted to do, go ahead and ask for tickets."

A flat voice came from the ticket window, "How many?"

I peeked over Katie's shoulder and saw that the guy had a blank look on his face, and was involved with something in his hands. A closer look and I could see the corner of a newspaper he was holding. He wasn't paying attention to either of us, and was probably reading the news or sports page. They were playing at Candlestick Park this weekend I seemed to remember. I poked Katie in the ribs, to make her hurry.

"Two please," she said.

The guy handed her two tickets without looking up, and took the four dollars she laid on the counter. She and I both heaved a sigh of relief and walked toward the theater entrance. This was not as hard as I thought it would be. No one challenged us, asked our age, or paid any attention to two kids sneaking into a "skin flick." At the door, there was no one waiting to collect tickets, so Katie put the tickets in her pocket and we simply walked into the lobby.

Heading toward where the sound was coming from, I wanted to hurry into the dark. Then I heard a voice behind us, "Well, well. Lookie here will ya? How is our li'le Nadine taday? An' who is yo' little friend, Nadine?"

My blood ran cold. I knew that voice!

"No need ta be shy girls, let's go in an' enjoy the show," Charlie said. Then he started laughing, and I needed to be as far away as I could get. I grabbed Katie's jacket and jerked her around toward the exit, "We're outa here," I shrieked, starting to run.

"What yo' ma gonna say 'bout this?" Charlie shouted as we raced out the door.

The two of us bolted from the theater, turned right, and ran the long block down to Market Street. Katie was out of breath at the corner. She grabbed my sleeve and stopped me from racing across the intersection.

"You wanna get killed, Nadine? What the heck is this all about?" she demanded. "Who was that guy?"

I took a minute to catch my breath, "That was Charlie. Remember? He's Emily's dad, and we're in trouble."

After our breathing slowed, we leaned against a wall. I reminded her how Charlie used to run things for Ma and us kids, and how he got in trouble with dealing drugs

I was frantic and could hardly keep my thoughts straight. If he tells Ma that he saw us, it will make real trouble for me! I should never have listened to you. This was a crazy idea. Why couldn't we have gone to a regular movie?"

Then I started to cry. I knew that going into a sleazy theater was just as much my fault as Katie's. I could have said 'No' at any time, but I didn't. I thought it would be fun.

Katie showed no sympathy for my tears, and shot right back, "Don't you dare blame me. You're the one that got all excited about seeing something that those boys were giggling about. I never held a gun to your head. You're really *nuts* if you think you can blame me for this."

"I know. I know. It's just that I'm scared about what'll happen now, I said, dancing around. "What'll I tell Marina and Ted when they find out?"

"Why should they find out anything? After all, we didn't stay to see the show. You think they'll be mad that we spent our money for nothing, is that it?" Katie shouted. There was a challenge I her voice, so I felt I had to explain my being upset.

"I lied to them, Katie. I told them we were going to an ordinary show on Market. They trusted me to be honest and truthful. When they find out what I did, they will never trust me again. Maybe I'll be grounded. Maybe they'll throw me out, send me to another home. What am I going to say to them?"

"Don't be such a baby. They won't send you away. It's not such a big deal, anyhow. You're making a big fuss before you even know if they find out about this. Do they know this Charlie guy? You think he's gonna tell them?" Katie was trying to make me feel better, but it wasn't working.

She continued talking as if it was all cleared up, "So shall we go see that movie at the Orpheum? It's too early to have lunch. You'll feel better if you do something else besides think about what might go wrong."

"Aren't you worried, Katie?" I asked. "What will your dad say if he finds out you were going to see one of these shows? Won't he be upset?"

"My dad is never going to hear about this, and even if he did he's not going to blow a fuse— I keep telling you— we didn't even *see* the show!"

"Well, I don't feel like going to any kind of movie now. Let's just forget the whole thing and go back to your place," I suggested.

"And do what? You'll just mope around and talk about all the awful things that might never happen at all. If you don't want to have some fun today then you might as well go home. I'm not wasting a perfectly good Saturday afternoon listening to you think of reasons to worry."

Katie was really hot under the collar now. I couldn't blame her for not wanting to waste her Saturday, but I began to wonder if she understood how serious this problem was. "What about our plans for the sleepover?" I asked.

45. Considering Alternatives

I WAS HOPING Katie would agree to going back to her place where I'd have time to think about what I should do about the problem of getting caught in a porno theater. But she was not going to agree that there *was* a problem. I figured it was not the same for her, since she didn't know about Charlie's connection with Ma. Maybe I should do what Katie suggested, and simply go back home. Maybe I could talk to Marina, tell her everything. I could explain how sorry I was about telling lies and planning secret things. Maybe if she were not too upset, Marina could help me figure out what to do about Charlie seeing us.

It seemed like a good idea, but I was reluctant. I didn't really want Marina to know what I'd done. I wanted her and Ted to be glad that they let me stay with them, not be sorry about it. I didn't want Marina to know that I had lied to her, that I knew I was planning to do something wrong and did it anyhow. But, how could I keep this from her, I wondered. Would she be angry, disappointed, disgusted with me?

I thought about when I ran away from Ma. It was without thinking that I got out the door and ran. It didn't take a minute to know the right thing to do then. But now, things were different. Marina and Ted never once raised a hand, or yelled at me, or said how stupid I was. Running away from them, or hiding things from them was not what I wanted. They had trusted me, and I wanted them to trust me again. I wanted to stay with them, not get away from them. I guess it was easier to know what to do, than to know what *not* to do.

"Can we just walk around a little? Could you just stay with me until I decide what to do? I won't worry you with any more complaining. I just need a little time," I said to Katie.

"Well, okay, but just for a few minutes. I want to have time to do something fun today," Katie agreed, reluctantly. "Sorry you feel so bad. I guess it's hard for you being in a foster home. You have to be so careful all the time."

I turned to look at Katie carefully, thinking how simple it must be to do whatever she wanted and not worry about it. I looked at her again, then burst out laughing. Katie turned to me with a puzzled look on her face. "What's so funny?" she asked, frowning.

"If you had a mirror, you'd be laughing too," I said, pointing at her face.

Since we left the theater, we hadn't changed our clothes or removed the makeup we had plastered on our faces. Katie looked awful. The running had made her sweat, and eye makeup ran down her cheek. Her lipstick was smeared all over her chin, and she looked like she was swimming in those big clothes. She was a little girl that was trying to look like an old lady, and it was really funny to see it all dissolve.

"You're a mess," I said.

Katie ran her finger down her cheek and started laughing too, "You're not exactly beautiful yourself," she said. We started removing our disguises, and tried to return to normal; taking off the headscarves, rubbing off the makeup with tissues, removing and folding the big jackets. We found a large trash barrel where we dumped everything.

"Didn't you want to keep some of the clothes?" I asked

"Nope. Don't plan on using those things ever again," Katie answered. "Nobody paid any attention to what we looked like anyhow."

Now that we had shared a good laugh, and were on friendly terms again, I figured it was a good time to go our separate ways. My problem was not Katie's problem, and it was time for me to take charge of myself again.

"I'm going home to Marina and Ted," I said. I was finally convinced that this was the right thing for me to do, and the only fair thing for Marina and Ted. Katie couldn't help me and I had no reason to think I would solve anything by walking around, or staying at her place overnight.

"You sure you want to do this?" Katie asked. For the first time, she seemed really concerned. "Do you want me to go with you?" she asked.

That offer warmed my heart and I felt we were friends again. I smiled and gave Katie a big hug. "Thanks, but no thanks," I said. "And, yeah, I'm sure it's what I want to do. I'm gonna tell them the whole story and ask if they can forgive me. You go on to your movie, and don't waste the rest of the weekend. Sooner or later, I'll have to explain things to Marina, and the longer I wait, the harder it will get. I'm walking back to Van Ness to catch the bus."

Katie grew serious, hesitated, then shook her head, "Okay then, if you think it's the best thing for you. Good luck with Marina, and see you at school on Monday morning."

I waved goodbye and we walked in opposite directions. The bus ride on Van Ness to 24th Street was the longest I ever had. I kept thinking of different ways that I could tell Marina my story. I couldn't decide on anything to say that I could remember for longer than it took to think up a better way. Finally I gave up planning, and figured it would be easiest to wait until asked why I'd returned home a day early.

46. Truth and Consequences

TED AND MARINA were working in the back garden when I got home. I got a drink of water in the kitchen, looked in on Melissa, then slowly walked downstairs. I watched them as they prepared a section of soil for planting vegetables. Ted was digging up weeds and Marina raked them together as fast as he could dig them out. They were laughing and teasing each other about who was winning the contest of working faster. I hesitated, thinking I might wait until they'd finished their work. Then I decided that I could not postpone *(That means to put something off until later.)* or I'd never get to it. Knowing that I had to face-up to their reaction sooner or later, I took a deep breath and said, "Hi!"

Still laughing over trying to keep up with Marina, Ted answered, "Hey there, I thought you were going to a movie. Did you ladies have a falling out over which show to see?" Ted's grin was casual and jolly.

"What happened, Nadine? Why are you home so early?" Marina asked in a more concerned tone. She probably sensed that something more serious had happened than what Ted had guessed.

I took a deep breath, "I think I'm in trouble. We ran into Charlie . . . and . . . and he said he would tell Ma . . ."

"Well, go ahead Nadine. Tell Ma what?" Marina insisted, dropping her rake. She faced me directly.

"Oh Marina, we did something awful. We tried to go see a porno movie," I wailed, bursting into tears. "I'm sorry . . . Really, really sorry."

"Okay young lady, let's go upstairs to talk about this. I want to hear the whole story, beginning to end. It sounds like you have some real explaining to do," Marina said. She put down her rake, walked over, and took me by the hand.

She led me upstairs to the kitchen, and we sat at the table near the window. Ted followed us, pausing to wash his hands at the sink. Marina waited for him to sit down at the table with us.

Ted spoke first, "Let's have it, Nadine—from the beginning please."

I blubbered out the whole story in a rush: about our decision to see the movie that kids were snickering over; about our trying to make ourselves look older; about walking through my old neighborhood in the Tenderloin; and about meeting Charlie in the theater lobby. When I finished telling them the story, I started crying all over again, let my head slump against my arms and used the table for support.

"Now, let's just stop that whimpering, Nadine. You know you've done something you knew we wouldn't like. You also lied about what you were planning to do. There will be consequences to pay for that," Marina said, firmly.

"I know, I know . . . ," I whimpered. "What should I do now?"

In a softer tone, Marina said, "I think what you should do now is wash up, settle down, and spend some time alone in your room. Ted and I will discuss this and decide what the next step should be."

I couldn't believe that Marina was so calm and cool. I thought she would be really mad at me. She had every right to be upset. I'd expected her to shout and swear and call me names, like Ma used to. Instead, it sounded like she just wanted time to figure something out—like it was some algebra problem that needed a solution. Maybe that was the best way to think of what had happened—a problem that needed to be solved.

I did as I was told and washed up in the bathroom, kissed sleeping Melissa's forehead, and lay down on my bed. I closed my eyes, but there was no way that I could fall asleep. There were too many things running through my mind about what we did and what we should have done.

After some time, Marina came in and sat at the foot of my bed. I sat up, waiting for the consequences. *(The penalty for doing something wrong.)*

Melissa's voice was solemn but calm, "Ted and I decided it would be best to talk to Sandra about this. She has charge of the legal work and can help us decide what we should do next."

"Sandra! Oh Marina, please, *please* don't send me away. I won't ever do anything like this again. I promise, I promise," I cried.

Marina put her arms around me, and trying to be soothing she said, "It's not about sending you away, silly. I made a commitment when you came to live here. I'm not giving up on you—not yet anyhow," she said, smiling a little and lifting her eyebrows. "You made a mistake, Nadine. Both of you girls made it together. But I don't know anyone who *didn't* make a mistake sometime or other. I'm more concerned about having Sandra help with what Charlie might do. I've known Charlie for a long time. Remember I lived across the hall from you, and every time I saw him, he made my skin crawl. Charlie will find a way to make trouble if it suits him. Calling Sandra will let her know that this might come up in the custody hearing with the juvenile court judge. Charlie could convince your mother to protest foster placement in some way. Sandra needs to be prepared."

"And you'll let me stay here with you and Ted?" I asked.

"Yes, you will stay with us as long as the courts allow. But it's time for us to discuss some ground rules while you're living here. There are things that Ted and I will *not* tolerate and telling lies is one of them." Marina frowned, looking into my eyes. "We need to be clear, Nadine, about what kind of behavior is okay and what is not. And you need to know what will happen when you violate the agreement. It's something we should have done long ago. But you seemed such a responsible girl that I didn't think it was necessary." She hesitated. "Now," she said, softly, "I think it is."

"Okay, okay Marina. Whatever you want me to do—as long as you don't send me away." I wiped a few tears from my face.

"It's not what *we want* you to do. It's what we agree between us that is reasonable and right. We'll do this together, and make a list to fall back on. Maybe Sandra can help with that too. Let's wait a few days and see what she has to say about what steps to take first, okay?"

BACK AT SCHOOL ON MONDAY, I told Katie what had happened when I confessed to Marina and Ted about our meeting Charlie at the porno theater. She pursed her lips, tilted her head and shrugged her shoulders.

"So, what does that mean?" she asked, seeming unconcerned.

"It means that when I decide to do something different, it needs to be discussed with Marina and Ted first. I can't lie to them anymore, or I take a chance on losing them as my foster parents," I said, leaning towards her to be clear about how serious this was.

"Oh? Bummer! Does that mean that we won't have fun anymore?"

"Well, it means I need to make sure I tell them before we take off on our own. That doesn't mean that we can't have any fun. But it does mean that there will probably be some rules about how far we can go."

"So what kind of rules are we talking about?" Katie wanted to know.

"It's not been decided yet. Marina and Ted are going to work that out with me. And Sandra is coming on Friday to help. She'll be there for a home visit, and we'll agree on what kind of behavior would be off-limits. Then Sandra will help figure out a solution to what might happen if Charlie decides to make trouble."

"Big deal, so you wait and see," Katie mumbled.

It sounded to me like Katie was not really concerned about our being in trouble, and I wondered if I might be losing a friend over this experience. Maybe her dad was less interested and not as troubled about it as Marina and Ted were. After all, Katie lived with her own dad, and didn't need to worry about placement in foster care.

"What did your dad say about our adventure on Saturday? He's home from his trip now isn't he? I guess you told him about it?" I prodded.

Katie frowned, shook her head and sounded annoyed. "I can't believe you're always asking about my dad! What difference does it make to you what he says about what I do?"

"Well, I tell you everything that Marina says, why are you so upset when I ask about what your dad says?" I asked, frowning.

Well, maybe we're different about these things," Katie answered, sharply. "What my dad says or thinks about me and what I do is my business, and I don't want to talk about it, okay?"

It was time for our next class to start, and I left Katie with a funny feeling that maybe we were more different than I thought. It seemed like having fun together was something to be kept between us, and she didn't want to involve her dad for some reason.

Did that mean that she was protecting herself from some kind of punishment? Fun loving Katie was becoming a puzzle.

47. Meeting With Sandra

THE BEGINNING of our family meeting with Sandra on Friday was not as I had imagined. I thought that she would be disappointed with my bad behavior and might scold me. Instead, she laughed about my conspiracy with Katie to appear older before we went to the porno theater.

"I wish I could have seen you two in makeup and old clothes riding on the bus and walking down the street," she said. She turned to Ted and Marina and asked, "Did you get to see her in that costume?"

"Not really, she was pretty much of a mess when she got home," Ted said, with a smile.

"She was even more of a mess when she started crying about it," Marina added.

"Why were you crying, Nadine?" Sandra asked, raising her eyebrows.

When I told her it was because we met Charlie there, she stopped smiling.

"Who is Charlie?" she asked, frowning.

"Well, when I lived on Larkin Street, Charlie came around to see Ma a lot," I began. "He went shopping with Ma's food stamps and money from the welfare check. He was *always* there when the check arrived in the mail."

"So this is someone who was around a lot? How did he treat you kids? Did he ever hit you like your mother did?" Sandra asked.

"No, Charlie never hit me, or any of the other kids. I didn't like him, but he tried to be nice to us, and sometimes bought special treats, like the day when Christmas vacation started."

"Was that to celebrate something special during the holidays?"

"No, I think it was to put us in a good mood for the lessons."

"Lessons for what?" Sandra asked. Her eyebrows rose.

"For how to beg for money from the Christmas shoppers," I answered.

When Sandra asked more questions about Charlie, I explained how he taught the three of us to ask money from people who were shopping during

Christmas holiday. "He showed us the best places to wait, and explained how to keep the money in a zippered pocket, so we wouldn't lose it," I said.

"What did you do with the money you collected?" Sandra asked.

"We brought it home and gave it to Ma ," I said. Then I remembered the time we *didn't* give it to Ma, so I kept talking. ". . . except once we used the ten dollars we got from a nice man at the Opera House . . . We were cold and hungry, so we had lunch at the Compton's Cafeteria that day."

I should have hung my head in shame, instead I clenched my jaw, lifted my chin, and looked straight into Sandra's eyes when I said that—as if I was sure that it wasn't wrong at all.

"But all the rest went to your mother and this Charlie person?" Sandra asked.

"Yes, it was only the one time that we spent the money we collected," I stated, firmly.

As I talked about Charlie, now and then Marina would add something to confirm what I reported. She told everything she knew, like I had.

"Did Charlie ever solicit you to do anything, or touch you in any way that made you uncomfortable?" Sandra asked. She turned to face me.

Even though I had a pretty good idea about it, I asked, "What does *solicit* mean?"

"That means did he ask you to do things with him or for other people for money," Sandra answered.

Deciding to act smart, I said, "Well, sure, he did solicit us to ask for money during Christmas vacation, didn't he?"

Sandra nodded, "Yes, I wrote that one down already. How about sex? Did he ever ask you to have sex for money?"

"No," I said quickly, ashamed that I had made Sandra say the word "sex" out loud.

She just smiled, as if she was not sorry that I was uncomfortable.

It was a long afternoon during which Sandra heard about Charlie's arrest on drug charges, and just about everything I could think of that happened when Charlie visited. Marina chimed in now and then and corroborated my story. (*That means agreed with what I said.)*

"Charlie had another party for his friends one time. That's when Ma had a miscarriage and lost the baby," I said, trying to include everything.

"And what was that party about?" she asked.

"Charlie got food and drinks and brought some records for music. Maybe Marina could tell you about that party," I said. "She went to that party, and all us kids were in *her* apartment watching TV."

"Yes, I remember that night very well," Marina said, ready to tell more about that evening's disaster.

"I'd like to hear about that, but I do have other appointments today, so we can talk about it another time," Sandra said. Then turning to me again, and frowning, she said, "I'm concerned that this Charlie person may convince your mother to request reinstatement of parental custody. If that happens, the court may terminate your placement here with Marina and Ted."

Preparing to leave, Sandra offered Marina and Ted some pamphlets about establishing behavioral expectations with children in foster care. She was in a hurry to go, but seemed worried.

"Give me a few days to review the records, then I'll be back to discuss what we need to do next," Sandra said. I watched her walk along the hall, down the stairs and out the door.

"What did Sandra mean about *terminate my placement*?" I asked, when Marina came back to the kitchen.

Ted answered thoughtfully, "I think she was concerned that when you attended a theater the Tenderloin without permission, it meant that you did not have proper supervision. And from what I read about the law, I believe that is one way a parent can claim that the foster placement should be terminated.

A cold chill rand down my spine.

48. Two Problems to Solve

IT WAS ALMOST THREE WEEKS before Sandra came back, and I could tell by the expression on her face that she was not happy. Marina made coffee for Sandra, and Ted, on his way to work, poured himself a cup of coffee and sat down. Marina poured me a glass of milk, but I didn't feel like drinking it. We all sat around the kitchen table and waited for Sandra to begin.

"Alright now, we have a couple of problems to discuss. Mrs. Williams has just filed to resume parental custody. Her argument is that moving to a larger apartment, and having held responsible employment for the past two years, she can provide a safe environment for Nadine. She also claims that since Nadine was seen at a porno theater in the Tenderloin, she demonstrates delinquent behavior under current conditions."

"No, no, no!" I whined. Feeling my body stiffen, I started to whimper. "I can't go back! I'm doing good at Lowell! Ted helps me with my homework when I need it! I'm taking care of Melissa—she'll be starting nursery school soon, she needs me! Marina is teaching me to cook!" I started to cry.

Marina put her hand across my shoulder. "This is ridiculous, Sandra," she said. "We know that Nadine can't be safe with her mother. Helen can't control her temper when it comes to this child. The abuse will start all over again. Living with Helen would *not* be safe—certainly not in Nadine's best interest."

"*We* may know that, but the court might be inclined to give Helen a chance to reunite her family," Sandra said. I could hear the regret in her voice, but I could also feel anger clutching at my throat.

"A chance? Ma already had lots of chances," I declared. "I know she wanted to kill me! If they make me go back, I'll just run away again. That's what I'll do!"

"Then, we'll need to do this all over?" Ted asked. "Everyone has already agreed that Nadine was badly abused, including a judge, right?"

"Yes, but that was true four years ago Ted, and things have changed," Sandra said. "With a steady job, and the family having a larger apartment, the judge may decide that the possibility of abuse is significantly reduced."

Ted stomped over to the coffee pot. "I can't believe this," he said. "After having nearly four successful years here with us, and filing all papers properly, why should Nadine be forced to move back? Surely going to a movie without permission can't be considered a violation of any kind for a teenage kid."

"I know this is a lot to absorb right now, but let's not get ahead of ourselves," Sandra reasoned. She seemed to understand Ted's frustration. "Helen's application for reinstatement has just been filed, and we'll have to wait for a date to be set for us to appear before a judge. In the meantime, I have more work to do."

Sandra turned to me with intense focus. "Nadine, do you remember, when Mr. Lewis called me after you ran away from home and spent the night in the Orpheum Theater?" Sandra asked.

"Sure I remember."

"Well, that's the day I was going away on vacation, and we decided to place you with Marina and Ted *temporarily*. When I came back to find a licensed foster home, you were already going to school and settled in with them. Then we filled out a lot of papers to get Ted and Marina licensed. We got all the approvals, and filed the proper records," Sandra said. "Now, that part of the procedure was completed, but with all the timing confusion, the files from the Welfare Office were removed and got lost."

Sandra paused a moment for a sip of coffee, "So that's where the second problem is. In the Family Services records, there was no mention of Charlie Johnson. And when I wanted to compare Family Services records with the Welfare Office files, I hit a dead end."

Marina got up to get the coffee pot. "Let me heat that up for you," she said to Sandra. After pouring coffee for Sandra, Marina filled her own cup before sitting down.

"Thanks Marina," Sandra said, and then turned to me. "Nadine, you need to tell me more about how Charlie was involved with the family. Marina, you can help too. When I visited Emily for potty training, this *Charlie* person was never around, and Mrs. Williams did not mention him. So let's see if we can clear up a few things about him."

Sandra sounded like she was frustrated with trying to sort things out. "Who is this man?" Sandra asked turning to me, with a frown.

She was so serious, I was afraid that I might say the wrong thing. Especially since I was really angry about the *first* problem, and I didn't really want to say anything about Charlie, because *he* was the one who told Ma about the porno theater. Charlie was the one who started all this trouble to begin with!

Instead of blurting out my anger, I took a deep breath and shaking my head side to side, answered slowly, "Like—I—told—you, Charlie came around when the welfare check arrived, made a list of things that Ma wanted, and brought in the groceries. Sometimes he stayed to fool around with Ma in the bedroom, and sometimes he left right away. He followed me to school one day, and got arrested for selling drugs . . . And that's *all* I know about him. I can't think of anything else!"

"So is he just your mother's boyfriend, or an uncle to one of you kids, or a cousin maybe?"

My jaw dropped, and I felt my mouth making a circle, "Oh . . . Didn't I tell you that Charlie is Emily's father? He's Tom and Jimmy's dad too. I'm sure I told you . . . didn't I?"

Sandra's hand flew up to her forehead. "No, Nadine, you did *not* tell me that."

"But he is not *my* father. I was born before Ma came to San Francisco," I said, relieved that I was putting distance between Charlie and me. But there was still a gnawing guilty feeling for having failed to tell Sandra about Charlie's relationship to the other children.

"So, where is *your* father," Sandra asked, with a sigh.

I shook my head and said, "I don't know the answer to that question. Ma never told me anything about my father. I only know what Marina told me."

Sandra turned to Marina, "What do *you* know about Nadine's other parent?" she asked.

Marina seemed uncomfortable with that question, but tried to fill in what Ma had told her—but without too many details. "Well, Helen told me that she grew up in Birmingham, Alabama. She got pregnant with Nadine when she was just fifteen, and when her mom and dad threw her out, her uncle provided money for train fare to Los Angeles. And she moved up here to San Francisco right after Nadine was born."

"Did she ever contact her family?" Sandra asked.

"She said that after coming out West, she never talked to them again. But she did mention that one day she ran into somebody from Birmingham who told her that Nadine's father had disappeared . . . and the grandfather had died? . . . or something like that." Marina sounded unsure.

Sandra heaved another sigh, and said, "Okay, if Nadine's father has died or can't be located, then Helen is still entitled to collect welfare for Nadine. In that case, she also continues to have legal rights over Nadine. But this information is *not* consistent with Family Services records. They state that Helen was widowed, that she lived on the streets several years, and she didn't know who fathered *any* of her children."

Sandra pressed her lips together. "If Charlie was father to any of her children then *he* is responsible for supporting them. It means that I'll need to track down the worker who filed the application with welfare—or start all over again. We have to get these records straight!" Sandra looked furious.

Then she turned to me and frowned. "This might take time to sort out, Nadine. Your mother could request reinstatement of custody, but if she lied on the Welfare Application, then she and Charlie are both liable. The Juvenile Justice System is slow and complicated, but the law is clear on welfare fraud."

Struggling with what Sandra said, I thought I understood most of it. My problem was that I imagined that all the offices were together, a part of one thing. Instead, it seems they're all separate. There was Family Services, where Mr. Lewis did the testing; Welfare Offices, where people apply for welfare; Juvenile Court, where the judge makes decisions; and maybe some others I haven't heard about yet. After considering all the work that Sandra had yet to do in these different offices, I hung my head, ashamed that I had made more problems for her by not mentioning that Charlie was father to Emily and my two brothers.

"How did it happen that Nadine's mother got away with collecting welfare for four children all this time?" Ted asked Sandra.

"There are lots of reasons for that to happen. The staff in these various departments are overworked and underpaid, and have to rush through things sometimes. That means that folders, files, and applications get misplaced or lost. Also, it is not unusual that welfare is sometimes granted without a complete investigation. With so many people applying, we usually believe what the applicant tells us. Most of the time people seek welfare out of real need, and factual information is obtained. However, now and then, false or incomplete applications slip through. I'm sorry this has happened, but I was not involved with Ms. Williams' case at the beginning, so I'll start by tracking down the intake worker at the Welfare Office."

"What should we do in the meantime?" Marina wanted to know.

"There's nothing to do now, but wait until after I contact the Welfare Office or find the original application. Things are more complicated now that Charlie is part of the picture."

It was time for Sandra to leave, and Marina walked with her down the hall until they reached the stairway. Ted and I stayed at the kitchen table, and I watched him sitting there with his elbow on the table, resting his chin in his hand. He was looking out the window and pursing his lips. I couldn't tell what he might be thinking with his face all scrunched up. Then he dropped his arm, turned and gave me a devious grin.

"Nadine, do you think your mom would be happy to face the judge when the question of Charlie's children comes up?"

49. My Friend Katie

AFTER OUR CONFERENCE with Sandra, Ted and Marina were quiet around the house. I could tell they were worried, and I thought they didn't want *me* to get upset with what they were thinking.

"I have an idea," said Ted with a pleased look, "We need extra help at the shop for busy week-ends. Why don't you try out for the job, Nadine?"

If he meant that for a distraction, it worked. "You think I could get hired? I've watched how the waitresses carry food from the kitchen to the tables, I think I could do it . . . Of course I could do it, Ted!"

"I'll bet you'd be good at it. I'm surprised I didn't think of it before this," Ted assured me, "What do you think Marina?"

Marina hesitated, then asked, "You're preparing for graduation Nadine, you think you could take this on too? Final exams are coming up and you need to do well if you want to continue with the program at San Francisco State."

"All my projects are finished and I'm sure that the tests won't take that much time to study for. I know I could work on the weekends. Please let me try it out." I pleaded. I was beginning to get excited about earning money on my own.

"Well, let's see what happens. If you train and start this weekend, we'll know better if it will take time away from schoolwork."

Everything eased up after that and discussions about my new job became a distraction from wondering what Sandra's news might be.

Even though excited about my first real job, I was still feeling miserable when I met Katie in the cafeteria. The noise was louder than the usual clatter, and I felt the wrinkle between my brows get worse. I guess Katie picked up my feeling of distress.

She put her elbows on the table and leaned forward. "What're you so grumpy about?"

"I keep thinking about our Friday meeting with Sandra. She said that Ma applied . . . for me to live . . . with her again."

Katie raised her eyebrows. "Well, that's not going to happen is it? What did Marina say about it?"

"She and Ted are worried, I can tell. But they don't talk about it when I'm around. I couldn't believe it when Ted seemed a little more cheerful this morning. He said he had to leave early 'cause he had some special errands to run. He was whistling as he went down the stairs to the car."

"What does that mean?"

"I don't know. But just because he was whistling, it didn't make *me* feel any better," I complained. "I do have some good news though. Ted is training me to work at the coffee shop, and this weekend I learned how to pick up and deliver orders at the counter. It was harder than I thought to keep up with it, but I learned fast. It was fun."

Katie paused. She seemed to be making a decision about something. "I have some good news too," she said.

"What's your good news?" I asked, surprised about Katie being in a good mood for a change.

"It's about my dad. You're always asking about him, so I'd like to tell you his story—just to cheer you up."

"I'm ready," I said.

"I guess I'll start by telling you that I lied about saying that my dad was away on business trips."

"If he wasn't on business trips, where then? And why'd you lie to me?"

"Okay. My dad was a soldier in Vietnam, and was injured pretty bad. So he's been in and out of the hospital for surgery."

"Oh, Katie. Why didn't you tell me?"

"Well, I don't like anybody to feel sorry for me, and Dad doesn't like anybody to feel sorry for him. So I decided it was easier to say that he was away on business trips instead of in the hospital."

"You had *me* convinced. So how is he doing?" I asked.

"That's the good news part. His surgery on Monday last week was the final one. As soon as he is well enough to walk on his own, he'll be coming home for good. No more hospitals, and no more waiting for the next surgery. Just for a while, after he gets home, he will need to use a walker—until everything heals perfectly."

Katie grinned from ear to ear and was so happy that I forgot my own problems. I wanted to know more about Katie's dad and asked lots of questions.

"What kind of injury was it, and how many operations?" I asked.

"I knew you'd want to ask questions about that," Katie laughed. "See, when my dad was in Vietnam, at the very beginning of his tour, he got injured. He got caught in what he calls a *crossfire*. A bullet hit his hip and shattered the bone. The doctors in Vietnam patched him up and sent him back here to Letterman. Then, it was one operation after another. He had short periods of time spent at home to recover, but this last operation a week ago, was the final one."

Katie said all of this in one great rush, as if she had rehearsed it. But the look of relief on her face told me that she was feeling good for the first time in a long time.

"Still, I don't know why you couldn't tell me about this before," I said, slightly annoyed.

"Like I told you—me and my dad don't like having anybody feel sorry for us. And that's the way it is."

I thought of all the times I had asked Katie about what kind of work kept him away from home so much, what did her dad think about this or that, and how did her dad feel about some of the things we were doing. Now I knew why she always avoided talking about him, and why she would get mad when I asked too many questions about her dad. I still didn't understand it, but at least I knew her reason for doing it.

"I can't wait to tell Ted and Marina your good news, Katie. It is okay for me to tell them, isn't it?" I asked.

"Sure, now that everything is settled, it's fine," she said. "Now, they won't need to feel sorry for me—or Dad."

50. Good News or Bad News?

IT WAS AFTER SCHOOL on Thursday, and Marina and I were sitting at the kitchen table with our afternoon snack. I had milk with two chocolate cookies, and she had coffee and Graham Crackers. I had told her about Katie's dad and she was surprised, but just as pleased as I expected her to be. We sat talking about how Katie's life would be more settled now, and maybe she wouldn't be so restless looking for different things to do with her spare time.

Then I started to ask questions about Sandra. It had been two weeks since Sandra's visit, and I wanted to know when she would get back to us.

"Sandra called this morning," Marina said, somewhat reluctantly.

"What did she say?" I asked, surprised that she had not mentioned it sooner.

"She said she had some news to share, and wanted to schedule a meeting with us."

"Well, what kind of news?" I asked, anxious to know all about it.

"That's the strange thing. Sandra wouldn't tell me on the phone. I even asked if it was good news or bad news, and she wouldn't say. I think she wants all of us together when we hear whatever it is she has to say."

"So is she going to come here to tell us? Do we have to meet her somewhere? What's the plan?" I insisted, getting more excited by the minute.

Marina kept the same puzzled frown on her face, and spoke patiently, "Sandra said she'd drop by here tomorrow afternoon after work."

Just then I heard the garage door open, and Ted was home from his afternoon shift at the coffee shop. I ran down the stairs and met him before he had a chance to get out of the car.

"Ted, Ted! Sandra is coming to tell us some news tomorrow. Marina doesn't know whether it's good or bad news. What d'you think?"

Ted laughed, "Whoa there, Nadine! How am I supposed to know what kind of news it is? I didn't take the call."

"Well what could it be?" I insisted.

Ted shook his head, put his hands on my shoulders, and turned me around. "Let's go talk to Marina, maybe she has a clue."

Back upstairs, we pulled chairs up to the table, as we always did for a family conference. Marina still had coffee, Ted had a beer, and I finished my glass of milk.

"Now let's talk about this," Ted said, turning to Marina. "What did Sandra say exactly?"

Marina raised her eyebrows and spoke slowly. "She said, 'I've got some news for you, but I want Nadine and Ted to hear it too.' Then I asked if it was good news or bad news."

"And her answer?" Ted prompted.

"She answered, 'I need to tell all of you at the same time, so right after work tomorrow, I'll drive your house. I can be there around five,' and then she hung up." Marina shrugged and raised her eyebrows as if asking a question.

"By the look on your face, you must think that it's not going to be *good* news, right?" Ted asked.

"No, not really, I just can't figure out why Sandra insisted that we all be together. Why couldn't she just tell me?"

"Well, maybe it's because she wants to be with us to see how happy we are to hear some good news?" Ted offered.

I watched the two of them looking at each other while they tried to figure this out. But it was my life they were thinking about and I was getting left out. "So does that mean I'll have to go back to Ma, or not?" I demanded, sliding forward on my chair.

They both laughed, and Ted teased, "*Bottom line Nadine.* No patience for speculation. Don't tell her—*maybe this or maybe that*—just the answer, please."

I didn't think it was funny at all. I really wanted to know what was going on, and I thought Sandra was mean not to tell us right away. I stood up, and hands on hips, began my tirade. "It's not fair! If Sandra knows something she should tell us! She was never so mean before, why is she being mean now?"

"We're just going to have to wait, Nadine," Marina said, calmly.

"I don't want to wait. I want to know!" I shouted, choking back tears. "What is Sandra's phone number? I'll call her right now! It's not right to make us wait. It's the rest of my life she's playing with." I stood up, ready to make the call.

Ted seemed to understand how I felt. He stood up and put his hand on my shoulder and began talking slowly, "If you promise to calm down, I think I might be able to give you a hint."

"What do you mean?" I asked, returning to my chair.

"I mean that if I tell you something about my visit with your mother, so will you stop acting hysterical?" He sat back down.

"You visited Ma? When? What did you say? What did she say?"

"I can tell you, but first you need to promise that you'll stop talking about calling Sandra—and by the way, we don't have her home phone, just her office number. So, can you promise to consider all possibilities calmly?"

"I'll promise anything, Ted. Just tell me something!"

"Alright then, I went to see your mother the day after Sandra was here. I explained to her that Sandra knows she lied to Welfare about Charlie. I told her that she'd need to pay back all the money she collected from Welfare for Charlie's children."

"What did she say?" I whispered, holding my breath.

"She looked very unhappy, but she didn't say what she'd do. She just told me to get out and leave her alone."

"Then what?"

"Then I left, just like she asked. I figured I'd given her enough to think about." I turned to Marina. "Did you know about this?"

"Yes I knew, but I wasn't sure if it was a good thing or a bad thing to do. Knowing Helen, she might feel scared and change her mind about wanting you back, or she might get mad enough to sue Ted for harassment. That's why I didn't tell you Nadine, because it could go either way."

51. Nothing Definite

AT FOUR-THIRTY on Friday, Ted, Marina and I were already waiting for Sandra to arrive. Dinner had been prepared and was in the oven. Marina had cooked my favorite casserole and was trying to be cheerful.

"I think that after we hear the good news, I'll invite Sandra to stay for dinner. She's been working so hard for us she deserves a little treat. There's plenty of salad and Tamale Pie for at least six people, and we've got a cake for dessert."

Ted interrupted. "Let's wait and see what kind of news she brings, Marina. Sandra may not want to stay if things are not going well," he warned. "How about it Nadine, shall we wait and see?"

"Sure Ted," I answered without enthusiasm. I had promised him that I wouldn't make a fuss no matter what the news might be, so I tried to be patient. But keeping that promise wasn't easy, as we sat around watching late afternoon TV, drinking juice and coffee.

Finally, the doorbell rang and I raced down the hall, ran down the stairs and flung open the door. Sandra was there with her usual briefcase. I'd never seen her without that thing, and it seemed attached to her left arm.

I tried being calm and polite, but it took every ounce of restraint. "Hi Sandra, please come in, we've been waiting for you," I said, as calmly as I could.

"Ted and Marina are both here?" she asked.

"Yes, neither one is working tonight. We're all here."

"Well then, let's go and get started."

Sandra's expression was impossible to read, I couldn't even get a clue. She was business-like climbing the stairs and heading for the kitchen. I decided to keep my promise to Ted and Marina about being patient, so without saying a word I walked behind her. That walk seemed endless from the stairway along the hall past all our rooms and through the living room and into the kitchen. Ted and Marina both got up from their chairs when Sandra appeared. They smiled and greeted her, saying "Hello Sandra" then set a chair for her at the table.

"How about a beer now the work day is over?" offered Ted.

"Or maybe coffee?" Marina suggested. Neither smiled.

"My, oh my, how serious everyone looks today," Sandra said. She finally smiled, and we all relaxed, but I was still anxious about what she had to say.

"No thanks on the drinks. Let's just get to work. To begin with, I need to ask some serious questions. Sorry about this Nadine, I know this has been really difficult for you, but the court requires that I do things a certain way; therefore, I have three problems now."

"Oh no!" I groaned.

Sandra smiled, placing her hand on my arm, "Oh yes, Nadine. First of all the Juvenile Court hires me to bring broken families back together again. So I'm your mother's social worker, and your social worker too. That means I have three problems to solve—what the court requires, what your mother wants, and what you need. Now I know you don't want to live with your mother. But, I need to be sure that you are truly afraid for your life if required to be reunited with her."

"I know that she'll kill me, isn't that enough?" I asked angrily, surprised that she needed to ask.

Marina followed up in a tired voice. "What are you asking, Sandra? Is Helen really insisting that Nadine live with her after all this time?"

"It's more of a legal question than Helen's preference at this point," Sandra answered.

"I think you need to explain," Ted said.

"I'll try," Sandra began. "The courts frown upon separating children from their biological parents—or parent in this case. The law insists that we make every effort possible to reunite families. I'm in the position of trying to determine if Helen is an unfit parent for Nadine. I don't know that I can say Helen is unfit when she is a caring parent for her other children. The boys are doing fine at school every day, and progressing nicely. Emily is blossoming at Louise Lombard as well. Helen is working several hours a day and keeps the house in order now that she has more room to move things around."

Beginning to panic, I interrupted. "So why does she need me then? She hates me! When she loses her temper again, she'll kill me, I know she will." I felt my legs begin to tremble.

"Not even if she's changed?" Sandra asked.

Ted took a deep breath and interrupted, "I think I better tell you what I did after our last meeting, Sandra."

"Helen told me about that Ted, and I don't blame you for trying to help. But sometimes trying to help makes things worse."

Marina clenched her teeth. "See Ted? I told you it might make things worse."

Sandra raised her hand, palm open toward Marina, "Well, it may not be exactly worse. It's just more complicated that's all."

52. Laying Blame

WHILE TED, MARINA, AND I LISTENED, Sandra continued to explain the legal complications, "The Juvenile Court judge has met with Helen and found her in compliance with all the criteria he set when Nadine was admitted to foster care. She's separated from Charlie, moved to a bigger apartment, is going to AA meetings, is gainfully employed, and attended therapy for anger management. He found no reason to reject Helen's application to return Nadine to her family."

Sandra's final words felt like lightning and thunderbolts . . . no . . . reason . . . to . . . reject . . . application!

"No! No! No! I don't care what that judge said, I'll never go back," I screamed. "I'll run away again. Only this time, I'll go so far away, she won't be able to find me. Maybe Katie can help me find a way to get out of the city. I know I can find somebody to help me. Besides, I'm nearly sixteen now, I can get a job somewhere and take care of myself."

Inside, I was falling apart. Is what I did with Katie that stupid afternoon so terrible? I tried to do everything else right—worked hard at school, helped Ted and Marina with the baby, followed rules working at the coffee shop—why had this happened? Since I'd really not done anything awful, I wanted to blame somebody. I couldn't blame Marina and Ted, so I thought of Katie again.

"It's all Katie's fault," I shouted. "I should never have listened to her. I knew I shouldn't have gone that show with her. That's why this happened. We went to a stupid porno theater and Charlie told Ma! I wish I had never met Katie!"

Sandra tried to calm me, "No need to blame anyone, Nadine. It wasn't your fault, Katie's fault, and not Charlie's fault either. It's all part of the legal process for foster care."

"I can't believe it! It's so unfair! Just because I lied one time?" I shouted.

Sandra interrupted again. "Didn't you hear me, Nadine? It's not because of what anyone did or didn't do. The Juvenile Justice System has a process and nothing that any of you says or does will change it."

Ted tried to calm me with less harsh words. "Nothing has happened yet Nadine. Let's try to calm down and hear from Sandra what needs to happen next."

I wasn't gonna tell Ted to be quiet, and I couldn't fold up and cry on Marina's shoulder. So I sat down, clenched my teeth, and waited for Sandra to continue.

"Alright then, the first step is for you, Nadine, to visit your mother. This first visit will only be for a few hours and under supervision. You'll not sleep over the first time, so you'll come back to be with Ted and Marina, and continue going to Lowell."

The word "visit" sounded much better than "live with" so I began to really listen. It was important for me to start thinking of a plan to get myself out of this. Sandra explained that the whole thing would be a gradual process to determine if things could go well over time. There would be increased amounts of time spent at Ma's place until I felt comfortable enough to sleep overnight.

"What if I never feel comfortable? What if Ma is only pretending to change?" I interrupted.

"Then we would want to find out why you weren't comfortable. If it was due to something in your mother's home, then we would try to change that. If it was because of your anger and your mistrust, maybe we could help you understand your feelings."

"You mean, she would go for therapy?" Ted asked.

"Something like that," Sandra answered shortly. Then everyone was quiet. I was trying to imagine what it would be like to come face to face with Ma again. I tried to think of something that might make her mad enough to hit me. That would show that it wasn't my feelings, but her bad temper that was the problem.

Sandra turned to me again. "So, how about it, Nadine. When would you like to try your first visit?"

It was clear in the way she said it, that she wasn't offering me a choice. If I still objected, then she would say that I had no choice. A few ideas began going through my mind. If I decided to go along with this "visiting" thing for a while, maybe I could make Ma show what she was really like, then Sandra could tell the judge how dangerous things could be staying with her.

Ted and Marina were looking at me, waiting for an answer. Resenting the absence of choices, I began to think that after all, the first visit would be short, and I *would* like to see Emily and the boys. I heaved a sigh of resignation, though I kept thinking I could find a way to solve this if I got smart enough. But right now, I had to say something and try to keep everyone else calm.

"So this is just a short visit, for a couple of hours?" I asked.

"That's right, and I will be with you the whole time, " Sandra said.

"And Emily and the boys will be there too?"

"If they're home from school, yes, they'll be there."

"Then why can't we wait a few weeks until summer vacation so all of us don't have to worry about school?" I offered hopefully.

Sandra hesitated, "I'll need to clear it with the judge, but maybe that can be worked out."

Marina sighed, looking relieved that I'd finally settled down, and was talking reasonably. "Now that's settled, how about staying for dinner, Sandra? We have a big casserole and plenty of food for an army, please stay?"

"Thanks Marina, but I'm committed for dinner tonight. Perhaps another time?"

53. First Encounter

IT WAS DURING the first week of summer when Sandra arrived to pick me up for my first visit with Ma. On the ride over, she tried to prepare me.

"I'm sure that you'll find things are a lot different now that your mother has a new place, some new furniture and less to worry about."

"What did she have to worry about before? I was doing all the work, and kept track of everything at school for the boys. She didn't have anything to worry about."

"Well, that could have been part of her problem. Leaving everything to you made her feel useless maybe?"

"You mean she resented my being in charge—even though she put me in charge?"

"Something like that."

I thought about it for a minute, and wondered if it was possible that Sandra was right. Ma would get mad when I didn't do things perfectly, but got even angrier when I did them well.

Sandra wanted me to be prepared with changes in my brothers and sister too. "You'll find that Tom and Jimmy are much more mature now that they're nearly four years older. And wait 'til you see Emily!"

"She's almost eight years old now," I said, smiling at the thought of seeing my little sister again.

That ride ended much too quickly. I could have used more time to talk to Sandra about what to expect. I had felt nauseous while anticipating this first visit. All I could think about was how she picked me up by my hair and started swinging me around. But now that I was nearly sixteen, she'd have a hard time doing that again.

AS SANDRA PREDICTED, Ma's new place was much nicer than the one on Larkin Street It had a separate kitchen, three bedrooms and a shower in the bathroom. The boys looked a bit unsure, but they just stood and waited for something to happen. That hasn't changed much, I thought, as I hugged them. Emily did not recognize me because it was so long since she'd seen me. She probably pictured me as much younger, if she remembered me at all.

She'd changed a lot, and after I said "Hello, Emily," I waited for her response. I guess I must have looked like a stranger to her, because she stepped behind Ma just like she used to whenever someone strange appeared. The boys were a lot taller, but I could still see the mischief in Tom's eyes and the little smile on Jimmy's face was heartwarming.

Ma was dressed in neat slacks and a clean beige blouse. Her hair was combed neatly, her nose powdered, and she was wearing lipstick. She'd lost some weight too, and had I met her on the street, I wouldn't have recognized her. She'd really changed, just like Sandra said.

At least her looks had changed.

Ma spoke first, "Long time—no see, Nadine," and I knew by her tone that she couldn't wait to get me alone. But with Sandra there, she acted very polite.

"Hi Ma, how are you?" I answered, with as much sincerity as I could fake.

I turned back to the boys and asked how they were doing at school. They told me that they both got promoted and were doing just fine. They had nice teachers and hadn't been in any trouble this last year.

Ma interrupted sweetly, "Did you think you were the only one that could look after them?"

"No Ma, I just wanted to know how they were doing now."

"Well, they're doin' jus' fine, thank you."

I was determined not to get into any arguments until I had a chance to figure things out, so I continued to be overly polite: "So how are things with you, Ma? Sandra said you got a steady job now?"

"Yeah, I got promoted ta stockroom boss. It's hard work, but the pay's good."

The boys excused themselves and went to their room. I knew they'd be huddled near their door listening to everything. They'd want to know if me and Ma would get into a fight. I didn't think that they'd lost that habit.

Sandra suggested that we sit at the table in the kitchen, and Ma offered her coffee.

"You wann'a coffee too, or juice maybe?" Ma asked turning to me. I knew that she was really trying to impress Sandra, so I answered just as politely.

"Juice would be very nice, thank you."

We seemed to hit a dead end at this point. I never was very good at talking to Ma. She usually just pointed at what she wanted me to do, or yelled orders. This was different. We were supposed to have a conversation, and we'd never had one before.

Sandra helped us along. "How are things going with your new job, Helen?"

"Like I said, bein' a stockroom boss's a lot tougher than stackin' shelves."

Thinking I'd better show some interest in her work, I asked, "So what does a stockroom boss do?"

"Well now, ya really wanna know, or ya jus lookin' fo' a turn ta talk?"

"I'm just interested, Ma, that's all. If you got a job you like and you got a promotion, that's something to talk about ain't it?" I hated using the word ain't, but being with Ma, it was easy to forget to speak properly.

"Sure, sure, Sandra 's right. With you'se comin' back afta foa year we gotta talk togetha' an' get along. So I hea' you'se got you'self a job too. What it's like to earn your way fo' a change?"

"Well, it's not really a full time job. I just learned to serve at the counter and Ted is teaching me to serve at the tables. It's just part time—on weekends when I'm in school, and if I'm good at it maybe during summer too."

"An' what do this par' time job pay?"

"It depends on how many hours I work. I'm paid by the hour," I answered. The gleam in Ma's eyes warned me that this was of interest to her, and I began to worry about what she was thinking.

54. Doing It Alone

ON THE WAY BACK, after my first visit with Ma, Sandra gave me time to think things over, then she asked, "Well, what did you think of your first visit?"

I heaved a great sigh, "I'm glad it's over . . . I was glad to see the boys, they haven't really changed that much, and it was nice that Emily got over her shyness. I think that when she heard me talking, she remembered who I was."

"I mean with your mother, how did you feel about that conversation? Did you feel threatened in any way? I was listening for her anger, and I didn't hear any."

"No, not with you there. She wouldn't dare get mad at me when you were around."

"Well then, if it's okay with you, let's try another visit next week. How does Tuesday sound to you?"

"Tuesday? Does it have to be so soon?"

"I think we better work on this as quickly as possible. I know you're signed up for classes at San Francisco State in September, so the sooner we complete this, the better."

"You mean, I'll be living with Ma when classes begin? Shouldn't it take longer, to see if it works out? I haven't really thought that far ahead, and I don't want to be living with Ma when I start college. It will make everything so much harder. Can't we wait a little longer than that, please?"

"I think we've waited long enough, Nadine. Remember, the judge wanted this started before you left high school. I was able to get a short postponement, but I won't be able to do that again."

"But if I got started with classes before I moved, I'd have a better chance of getting along with Ma. With lots of homework to do, I wouldn't have time to get in trouble with her. See . . . after I start college it would be much better, 'cause I won't be in her way if I'm taking classes."

"Sorry, Nadine you can't have it both ways. First you asked for a postponement so you'd have more time to work things out with your mother during summer. Now you want to delay so you can spend less time with your mother. I'm afraid, we've delayed as long as possible."

I tried to think of some reason more important than starting classes, but Sandra sounded like she had run out of favors from the judge. And I'd run out of excuses.

THE PAST WEEK, I'd been doing well at the diner, and Ted was pleased with my progress. Soon I'd be ready for a permanent schedule, he said. I was really happy, because I knew I'd need a part time job to earn money for books. There's no way Ma would help on that score. I decided to stop arguing.

"On Tuesday, I'll leave you and your mother to carry on your own conversations without me. I'll take Emily for a walk and be back to pick you up in a couple of hours. How does that sound?"

"If I tell you the truth and say that it sounds terrible, will it make a difference?" I asked.

Sandra laughed. "Afraid not, Nadine. You'll just have to make the best of it. Afterward, we can talk about how it went."

WHEN WE ARRIVED on the following Tuesday, things did seem less tense than the first time. The boys were ready to take off for a ball game with some guys on the block, so they said "Hi Nadine!" and then they left. Emily yielded to a hug without my need to reintroduce myself. Ma was as cool she was last time, well-groomed but ready to do what she had to do to get what she wanted. I was about to find out exactly what that might be.

As soon as Sandra left with Emily, Ma told me to sit down and watch television with her. She poured herself a beer and said I could get myself a coke if I wanted one. I thought Sandra said that Ma was attending AA meetings? While we watched the news, Ma asked a question now and then.

"So, how much does Ted pay you for working at the diner?"

I knew I had to be careful, "Uh . . . it's mostly for tips when I serve at the tables. A few dollars a day, maybe."

"And when you're serving at the counter?"

"Yeah, I get tips there too, but not so much."

"Ya putting' away some dough ta buy shoes? I see you's wearin' some ratty sneakers."

"Maybe," I answered, pretending to be watching TV.

"Don' Marina an' Ted got enuf ta buy clothes for ya?" Ma jeered, cracking a big smile. "And welfae' pay somethin' to foster parents. Don' ferget that, missy. Yous earnin' them money."

And stupid me fell right into her trap, "Marina and Ted been really good to me. They buy whatever clothes I need. The money I earn is for my school books."

"Oh, school books. Wadda you need'n school books foa? Thought ya's a'redy grad-u-ated from school?"

"But I'll be needin' books for my college classes."

"College! Well missy, ain't we getting up in this here world. An' when'd we decide we's goin' ta college, Miss Smarty Pants?"

"A long time ago Ma. I decided when I was a little kid that I was going to college. I never changed my mind."

"Always better 'n tha resta us? Ha! You ain't changed none. It jus' like Charlie say. You ain't change none a'tall. But ya kin fo'git tha' fool notion 'bout college, missy. You jus' fo'git all 'bout it."

I knew that this conversation was going very wrong, and very fast. I began to feel like running away—just as I'd felt so many times before. I could hear the way that Ma's angry words were building up on each other, working up more and more anger. I didn't know what to do next, so I held my breath. Keeping myself ready to jump up and run out of there the minute she raised a hand . . . I waited.

Then Sandra's voice was saying, "Well Emily, that was a nice little walk wasn't it? Sorry we had to hurry back. But when you gotta go, you gotta go."

God bless Emily's bladder, I whispered to myself, as I stood to leave.

On the way home from that second visit, I knew it would not be possible for me to live with Ma ever again. I told Sandra all about what had happened with her drinking beer and getting mad when I brought up that I was planning on going to college.

Sandra was thoughtful for some time, looking straight ahead as she was driving, then spoke seriously. "Well then, I'm truly happy that Emily had an urgent call of nature at the right time. I'm sorry that you were stressed out today, but before we do anything about it I need to talk to your mother. I really didn't know that she was drinking again. She admitted that she's unreasonable when she drinks, and she agreed to attend AA meetings. The anger management therapy and going to those meetings were two of the conditions for reuniting her family. Your mother assured me, and the judge too, that she had met all the conditions of that agreement. Will you give me a few days to investigate this violation?"

"Do I have a choice?" I asked, bluntly.

I guess Sandra found it amusing that I could be so blunt. She laughed and said, "Probably not."

WHEN I ARRIVED HOME, I told Marina and Ted all about my encounter with Ma. Both of them were interested in hearing all about it, and they seemed sympathetic. However, they encouraged me to wait for Sandra's evaluation of the situation before getting upset again.

"What would you have done if Sandra had not come back when she did?" Marina asked.

"I don't know," I answered, "try to get away, I suppose."

"How did Helen find out about your earning money at the diner?" Ted wanted to know.

"I don't know," I said, again.

Marina turned to Ted and asked, "What do you think Sandra will do now?"

"Ditto to what Nadine said," Ted grinned. Remembering what I'd said, we all laughed over the *'I don't know'* response being repeated so many times during our conversation. That laughter seemed to relieve some of the tension, and I eventually agreed to simply wait for Sandra's report.

IT WAS ONLY a few days later, that Sandra called to make another appointment. Again, she planned her visit on the last day of the week.

On Friday afternoon, we all waited impatiently for her to arrive. At last, the doorbell rang and I raced downstairs to open the door. This time Sandra's expression was not as serious as it was the last time she came. "Guess you've been waiting anxiously?" she inquired, as I opened the door.

"You guessed right. What did Ma say about my not going to college?"

"Whoa there Nelly, can I get to the kitchen first?" Sandra said. "Don't you think that Marina and Ted want to hear about this too?"

"Okay, okay, but hurry up!" I couldn't wait any longer.

Finally seated around the kitchen table, Sandra began by saying that she'd had a long talk with Ma, and wanted to get some things cleared up about the drinking. "Helen was glad to pour me a glass of her beer as soon as I mentioned it. She is drinking beer, but it's the non-alcoholic variety. She told me that at one of her AA meetings when she complained about being so accustomed to the flavor of beer that she couldn't give it up, someone suggested that she try beer without alcohol. So that's what she did. She got used to the non-alcoholic beer without any trouble at all. So when you were with her on Tuesday, she was not drinking regular beer, but the alcohol-free kind."

"Well, what about the 'not going to college' part?" I asked.

"Well, this is the really big problem. You see, when she regains custody, she actually can make some decisions about your education. As your mother, she has the legal responsibility to care for your needs, and keep you safe. But she's not required to do what you want to do, or agree to what makes you happy."

"So what does that mean?" I gasped. "Does it mean that if I'm living with her, I won't go to college at all?"

"It means that you'll have to abide by her rules as long as they don't harm you."

"But it will harm *me!*" I shouted. "It will harm *me* in the worst way!" Then I began to sob, and nothing anyone said could make me feel better.

"My life is over . . . If I have to live with Ma and do what she wants . . . I'll be a slave forever . . . and I'll never get back to school . . . and never be able to say anything, or do anything . . . ever! I *won't* go back to live with her . . . I'll just run away again . . . I'll live on the streets . . . I know how to do that!"

Sandra waited until my emotions were spent, and then spoke calmly, "As soon as you calm down, maybe we can consider how all those dire predictions might turn out differently."

55. Looking at Options

WHEN I SETTLED DOWN, Sandra began to talk very slowly, as if she wanted me to hear each word by itself.

Looking directly into my eyes she said, "I want you to try to recall something Nadine . . . something you told me a long time ago." She waited for me to respond.

I took a deep breath. "Okay," I said, waiting for what she'd say next.

"Do you remember talking to me about leaving Ted and Marina when you found out that Marina was pregnant?"

"Yeah . . . sort of."

"'Well, if I remember correctly, you said they wouldn't have room for both you and the baby, and you wanted to apply for something called emancipation?"

"Oh, yeah . . . and you laughed . . . and you said there were too many conditions . . . or I was too young? . . . or something like that? So-o-o, am I old enough now?" I asked. Slowly feeling a glimmer of hope begin inside me I almost started crying again. There was a sweet surge of possibility that something good was coming. I could hear it in Sandra's voice.

"Actually you were old enough then. That was not the problem," Sandra smiled as she started to explain. "There are really two problems. One is that in order to qualify for emancipation you have to be self-supporting, and the other thing is that you need to be living independently. Do you remember when we talked about that? It's not your age, Nadine, it's the other two conditions that kept you from applying even then."

Marina chimed in with a look of surprise, "Oh! I remember that day. I told Nadine to stop thinking about leaving us for a new foster home, but I don't remember anything about this emancipation thing."

I ignored Marina, and charged straight ahead talking to Sandra. I had no time to waste. “Okay, okay, so how do we do this, Sandra? How can I do those conditions now, and get free of having to live with Ma?”

Now Ted began getting excited too. “What needs to happen next? How can we help?”

“Let’s slow down here and think about one thing at a time,” Sandra warned. “Ted, how are things working out at the diner? Will there be a real job for Nadine in the near future, or is that something that will take a long time?”

Ted frowned. “I hadn’t thought of a full time position for Nadine because she planned to be taking college classes in September . . . But, sure, we can work that out in a week or two. But how about college, does Nadine just give that up?”

“Maybe we need to set some priorities at this point,” Sandra said. “What do we think is the most important thing to accomplish before the end of summer? Helen wants Nadine back home as soon as possible, and according to the law, she has that right. There is no time to waste. Nadine needs to make her first important decision fast. The choices are: continue home visits with Helen, then start college and hope for the best; or start earning a salary and work towards emancipation.”

“If I start working now, can I get emancipated before the end of summer?” I asked.

“If you start working now, and find a place to live on your own before the deadline, you can file for emancipation right away,” Sandra said.

I didn’t hesitate. “Let’s do that right away.”

“Alright then,” Ted said, “Patricia is going on her vacation next week. Maybe Nadine can take her place at the diner waiting tables at breakfast and lunch, then work into a full time position after that.”

“So, do we agree that working full time is most important right now?” Sandra asked, as she glanced from Marina to Ted.

“Agreed!” I shouted. “I’ll be self-supporting in two weeks!”

“And how about college, Nadine? What about your plans for college?” Marina asked, in a worried tone.

I only took a half a second to think this over and said quickly, “It can wait. I can do college anytime. There will always be next semester, or next year. I know I’ll get there sooner or later and besides, I’m like the youngest in the class. But getting away from Ma has to come first.”

Sandra waited for a moment then said, "Now that we've a plan for Nadine becoming self-supporting, there is one last condition to consider. Living independently may be a problem that's a bit more complicated. We've done a lot of work today, so let's take a few days before taking the next step. We'll all have time to think this over and come up with some ideas. How does everything sound so far?"

Marina jumped in, "What if Nadine used her salary to pay rent to us, wouldn't that meet the requirement of living independently? Then she won't have to leave here and can use her babysitting allowance to start saving for college."

At that point Sandra stood as if adding a period to Marina's question. She collected her coat, picked up her briefcase and indicated that she was ready to go. "It sounds good Marina, but if she continues to live with you, it's not independent living. This has been her permanent residence for four years, and you have been like parents to her, so by law, if she stayed here—even if she paid you, it would be the same as continuing to live at home. It's not considered independent living."

Ted, Marina and I looked at each other and frowned. I groaned.

"Sorry about that," Sandra said.

While trying to think of another way to solve my problem, I still felt a surge of hope. With all the help I was getting, I knew we could find a way. Then I grinned, and looked at Sandra as she was picking up her handbag. I stood up as if making an announcement.

"Sandra, you saved my life! I'm going to do this emancipation thing one way or another, even if it kills me," I declared with emphasis. With that, I stepped away from my chair and flung my arms around Sandra, almost knocking her off her feet with my hug. Ted and Marina started laughing, and for the first time in a long time there was a feeling of optimism.

Sandra regained her balance then stated, "Well! We wouldn't want it to kill you Nadine. That's the whole point. We want to work out a plan that will give you a chance at living."

56. Moving Ahead

WHEN SANDRA HAD GONE, we sat around the kitchen table and started to plan a work schedule for next week at the diner. Then Marina got up to heat water for our spaghetti dinner. She and I had prepared meatballs together earlier that afternoon and Marina mentioned that I was getting "very efficient" at chopping onions and garlic for the sauce. I suddenly got an idea and turned my attention away from Ted.

"Marina, do you think I'm good enough at chopping veggies to help in the kitchen at the diner?"

"What are you thinking, Nadine?" Ted asked, looking puzzled.

Marina came back to the table and sat down with us, "You're wondering if you'd make more money working with the cook," she said.

"I dunno? What d'you think, Ted?" I asked turning back to him.

"Are you considering working tables and helping in the kitchen too? That's a pretty heavy load, Nadine."

"Why not? If I can earn more, I'd have enough to live on that much sooner. That has to be better, doesn't it?"

"Something to think about," Ted said without making any commitment.

I got impatient, "I gotta do something fast, Ted. Didn't you hear what Sandra said?"

Ted frowned, "One step at a time Nadine. Let's not get carried away and do something that will make things worse."

Ted was being the cautious one, as usual. When he helped me with my math homework, I'd be wanting to finish as fast as I could. But Ted would always say "One step at a time will get you there faster the next time you run into this problem."

I knew he was right, but that didn't make things easier for me. I liked doing things fast. One step at a time didn't appeal to me at all.

"So is that a maybe?" I asked.

"It's something to think about," Ted repeated firmly. But he was smiling, and that was always a good sign.

I could hear the water bubbling on the stove, so I asked Marina if I should put the pasta in.

"Might as well if you're training to be a cook young lady," she said, with a big smile.

After dinner, I was so excited by what was happening in my life, that I had to call Katie and tell her all about it. She was delighted for me and we planned to get together at San Francisco State on Monday. I needed to get there to cancel my enrollment in the classes I'd signed up for. She and I had the same advisor and Katie wanted to add a class to her schedule. I was pretty sure that we could both work things out at the same time.

On Monday, I met Katie at the college cafeteria and she seemed more excited than I was. I found out that her excitement was not for me, but for something she had worked out for herself. She started talking right away.

"I was complaining to my dad about what a long trip it was from home to campus, and he suggested that since I was taking so many classes this semester, it would be a good idea to rent a place in Park Merced!" She practically jumped out of her skin while demanding me to respond, "Isn't that terrific? Isn't it?"

I felt stunned for a moment. I never imagined Katie living anywhere but in the apartment on that little street off Van Ness Avenue.

"You mean you'll be living near campus, by yourself, in a place of your own?"

"You betcha!" she said, gleefully.

When I recovered from the shock, I asked a thousand questions. So we spent all afternoon going over every detail about her living alone. Finally I asked, "How much will the rent be? And how far is it from campus?"

"Whoa, Nadine. I don't know the answer to those questions yet. We don't even know what's available. Dad is taking me tomorrow to interview for an apartment, and help me decide things with the manager . . . But don't you see what can happen here? Dad might find a place where you and I could live together! We'd be roommates! Share the rent!"

57. A New Beginning

AS SOON AS I ARRIVED HOME, I told Marina and Ted all about Katie's news. I was so excited that I had a hard time keeping things straight.

"And she's going to be right by San Francisco State! And she said I could live with her! Share the rent! Roommates!"

My jumping around and turning from one to the other while talking was making it impossible for them to understand what I was saying.

Ted grinned ear to ear, amused by my excitement. He said we should sit around the kitchen table to talk about it.

After we sat down, Marina asked the first question.

"Sounds like a wonderful plan for Katie, and I'm happy for her, but I'm not sure how you fit into this?"

"Well, she said I could live there. And right next to the college too! That would take care of the other condition for emancipation, right?"

Ted pursed his lips, "It would. But those Parkmerced rentals can be expensive Nadine, how do you plan to pay for your share of rent and food?"

"I'll be working. That's how I'll pay for my share," I said, confidently.

Marina persisted in her quiet, reasonable way, "I know how perfect it sounds, and I realize how excited you are, but you haven't even started working yet. We haven't heard anything from Sandra about the emancipation application, and Katie's dad might have something to say about someone living with his daughter."

I wasn't going to let Marina discourage me. Katie's plan was absolutely perfect and I wasn't going to let myself have any doubts.

"But I can do it. I know I can do it. I can start right away. When do I start full time at the diner, Ted? I can start this afternoon, can't I? Maybe do the night shift too? Please Ted, please!"

Ted was hesitant, "Look Nadine, I'm going to help as much as I can. And you can start working as soon as we do it the right way. You need to apply formally for a full time job. Up to now, you were working a few hours now and then, and I was okay with that. But there are different conditions for a full time job that we need to sort out. Remember, you've only just turned sixteen, and while you could work around the place part time, that was easy enough to arrange. But in San Francisco, labor laws are pretty strict when it comes to under age employment, and I need to be sure we follow them. If I break the law or get fired then we're both out of work. I don't think that's such a good idea, do you?"

"Okay, okay, what do we have to do?"

Marina got up to start dinner. "Can you take a deep breath first, and start thinking about what you've accomplished so far?" she asked.

"Sure, sure, okay," I agreed. And taking that deep breath, I sat back and felt a great weight lifting from my shoulders as I remembered the strange journey I'd been on for the past four years. Thinking back over that time, I began to appreciate what great good luck I'd had meeting all the good people along the way.

The night Ma was trying to kill me and I ran away, I felt I'd never be safe again. Then Mr. Lewis helped me find a place to live. Marina, Ted and Sandra kept me safe until I finished school. The teachers and counselor at Lowell kept Charlie from spoiling things on that first day. And Katie provided the first real friendship I'd ever had. I was really lucky to have had those people on my side exactly when I needed them. They all led me away from danger and kept me from making big mistakes.

Melissa picked the perfect time to wake up from her afternoon nap. "Can I have some juice too?" she asked, rubbing her eyes.

Marina, Ted and I burst out laughing.

"Why is everybody laughing at me?" Melissa asked, frowning.

I put her in my lap with a big hug. "We're not laughing at you Sweetie, we're laughing about how you came in at the right time."

"The right time for what?"

"The right time to cheer us up," Marina said. "We were talking about Nadine going to work and moving on with her life."

"What does 'moving on' mean?" Melissa wanted to know.

"That means Nadine is growing up and pretty soon, will go out on her own," Ted explained quickly, not taking time to think about how the four-year-old would react to that news.

Melissa's mouth puckered and I was afraid she might cry. I didn't want her to be sad, I wanted her to be happy for me.

"But I'll always be your big sister, no matter what," I assured her. "And I'll always be available to babysit for you. And I'll never be far away. And we can talk on the phone whenever you want. And I won't leave until the end of summer when you start school again. Then you'll be in kindergarten and learning to do all kinds of new, fun things."

That's when I lost it. In all my excitement, I hadn't thought about how much I loved my second family, and how much I would miss them. My tears came slowly at first then I excused myself to the bathroom to blow my nose. This feeling was not exactly new. It was the same sad feeling as when I saw Emily and the boys for the first time after four years. That day I'd had to choke back the tears so I could talk to them. Now I began to understand how hard it would be to leave this loving home where I'd first felt cared for and safe.

After a good cry over knowing and regretting that I had to separate from Marina, Ted, and Melissa, I decided to concentrate on plans for the future. There was only one thing bothering me now. *How was I ever going to get to college?*

58. Icing on the Cake

AS I WAS PACKING UP to move in with Katie, Ted came to my room to talk to me. He said we should have dinner at the diner tonight so that Marina wouldn't have to cook a last meal for me. It would be too sad for her to cook up some favorite dish, knowing that the following day would be moving day and I would not be around anymore.

Having dinner at the cafe sounded good to me, I was ready for a break from packing anyhow.

"Well, let's not forget that it'll mean good things will happen as well," Ted said, trying to put a good spin on things. "After all, Melissa will have a whole room to herself. And, just think, we can have oatmeal for breakfast whenever we want!" Both burst out laughing, and I gave Ted a big hug. "I'm going to miss all three of you so very much," I said, tears starting to form.

"I guess we'll kind'a miss you too. Now get busy and finish getting all your junk out'a here." Ted said.

"What are you calling junk!" I said, acting insulted.

Marina appeared at the door just then and said, "You get out of here Ted, there's a lot to do before dinner. Everything needs to be ready for us to load the car for Park Merced in the morning."

With some help from Marina, I folded coats and jackets and slacks into some big plastic bags. Shirts and underwear from the drawers all fit in one big suitcase. Shoes went in boxes we collected at the grocery store and by the time we were packed and ready to go, it was time to get in the car to go to the diner for dinner.

We started singing songs as we drove across The Mission to the restaurant. "*Dinner in the diner, Nothin' could be finer, la la lala la in Carolina*" we sang, trying to make a sad time into a happy one. Melissa laughed when the rest of us couldn't remember all the words. "La la la la la," she imitated.

We found a parking space around the corner from the diner and scrambled out of the car, careful not to open doors until the traffic cleared.

When Marina opened the door for us to enter the diner, I saw that everything was dark. I frowned, but Ted, who was behind me, gave me a little push—and—the lights went on and a bunch of people yelled "SURPRISE!"

For a minute I couldn't remember if there was a birthday party scheduled today, then I realized that the surprise was for me! Everyone was laughing and saying things to me and about me that made me feel wonderful. Sandra was there, and Katie and her dad, and even Mr. Lewis. The dinner was terrific and this was the best party anyone could think of.

After everyone had finished their dinner, and ate a big piece of the colorful cake that had balloons on it, Mr. Lewis gave a speech. He told the story about how I came to his office after sleeping in the Orpheum Theater, and how I talked and acted. He made everybody laugh when he said that I had been responsible for him breaking the law, and Sandra sat there nodding her head and shaking her finger at him.

"Now I'd like to propose a toast" Mr. Lewis said, with his lips pressed together seriously. When everybody got quiet, he looked at me, raised his glass and began, "Here's to a young lady who has *endured* numerous *complications* in her short *conspiracy* with the *vicissitudes* of life. During the time that she struggled to find a l*egitimate* method to achieve her goals, she faithfully *complied* with *regulations* and managed to avoid *deleterious consequences*."

Mr. Lewis was using *my* special words! With my hand over my mouth, and eyes wide, I looked at him, completely surprised. He winked at me and continued; "While investigating possible *solutions* to her problem, she was able to *deflect obstacles*, and *assume* responsibility for occasional *deceptions*. Congratulations on a successful journey to *emancipation*, Miss Nadine Williams!

When Mr. Lewis finished his speech, I laughed so hard my sides ached. He had spoken in such a formal manner, we could see that he was making fun. And I could hardly believe he had *integrated* so many words from my list. (He also added two more words for me to look up tomorrow—*vicissitudes* and *deleterious.)*

"How did you get my word list?" I demanded, when I could finally catch my breath.

Everyone was laughing now, but I was able to hear him explain. “Sandra got the list from Marina and we decided to make it a part of the celebration.”

It was a perfectly lovely party, and with all my best friends around me, a perfect way to begin my new life.

About the Author

JO CARPIGNANO writes fiction, poetry and memoirs. Born in San Francisco, she attended San Francisco State University and earned degrees in education, pupil services and psychology. After serving as an elementary school teacher for many years, she became a School Psychologist and specialist for children with special needs. At U.C. Berkeley Jo received a doctorate in Educational Psychology and practiced statewide. Upon retirement, Jo has produced a biography of her immigrant Italian mother, *Madeline's Story (2005)*, and a book of poetry, *Paper Wings and Other Things (2015)*. With wide experience in the field education and child development, Jo brings her experiences with children in public schools to weave the story of a gifted child with fierce determination who finds a way to escape abject poverty and parental abuse.

Acknowledegments

It has required intensive effort on the part of many in order to complete this book. First and foremost, thanks to my editing team at Crystal Springs Writers who read and re-read each chapter providing corrections and useful suggestions, Bardi Rossman Koodrin and Greg Erion in particular.

Many thanks also to Tory Hartman for undertaking the task of final editing as well as publishing Nadine in the Tenderloin.

A special thanks to Hertha Harrington for her invaluable assistance with technical advice.

www.ingramcontent.com/pod-product-compliance
Lightning Source LLC
Chambersburg PA
CBHW030412310726
48979CB00002B/377

* 9 7 8 1 9 3 7 8 1 8 9 1 3 *